Acclaim for the authors of
Hallowe'en Husbands

LISA PLUMLEY

"Witty, fun and just plain charming."
—*Fresh Fiction* on *The Scoundrel*

"Will remind you of your first kiss, plus melt your heart.
Lisa Plumley's style is the cure all for a bad day and I dare
you not to laugh, and maybe shed a tear as well."
—*Romance Junkies*

DENISE LYNN

"Nonstop action, a marvelous captive/captor plotline, a
hint of fantasy and more than a touch of passion converge,
making this book a memorable romance and a feast for
fans of medieval romance."
—*Romantic Times BOOKreviews* on *Falcon's Honor*

"High drama…a refreshing medieval."
—*Romantic Times BOOKreviews* on *Falcon's Love*

CHRISTINE MERRILL

"Mark Christine Merrill as an author to watch."
—*Rakehell*

"Merrill deftly delivers a well-crafted, potent
and passionate story."
—*Romantic Times BOOKreviews* on
The Inconvenient Duchess

LISA PLUMLEY

Lisa Plumley decided to take advantage of living in modern-day Arizona by immersing herself in the state's fascinating history—visiting ghost towns and finding inspiration in the desert and mountains surrounding her. Before long she got busy creating lighthearted romances like this one, featuring strong-willed women, ruggedly intelligent men and the unexpected situations that bring them together. When she's not writing, Lisa loves to spend time with her husband and two children, traveling, hiking, watching classic movies, reading and defending her trivia-game championship. She enjoys hearing from readers. You can contact her via e-mail at lisa@lisaplumley.com, or visit her Web site at www.lisaplumley.com.

DENISE LYNN

Award-winning author Denise Lynn is an avid reader of romance novels. Within them she has traveled to times filled with brave knights, courageous ladies and never-ending love. Now she can share with others her dream of telling tales of adventure and romance. Denise lives with her real-life hero, Tom, and a slew of four-legged "kids" in northwestern Ohio. Their two-legged son, Ken, serves in the USN, and comes home on occasion to visit and fix the computers, VCRs or any other electronic device Mom can confuse in his absence. You can write to her at P.O. Box 17, Monclova, OH 43542, or visit her Web site, www.denise-lynn.com.

CHRISTINE MERRILL

Christine Merrill lives on a farm in Wisconsin with her husband, two sons, and too many pets—all of whom would like her to get off the computer so they can check their e-mail. She has worked by turns in theater costuming, where she was paid to play with period ballgowns, and as a librarian, where she spent the day surrounded by books. Writing historical romance combines her love of good stories and fancy dress with her ability to stare out of the window and make stuff up. You can visit her Web site at www.christine-merrill.com.

Hallowe'en
Husbands

LISA PLUMLEY
DENISE LYNN
CHRISTINE MERRILL

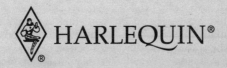

HARLEQUIN®

TORONTO • NEW YORK • LONDON
AMSTERDAM • PARIS • SYDNEY • HAMBURG
STOCKHOLM • ATHENS • TOKYO • MILAN • MADRID
PRAGUE • WARSAW • BUDAPEST • AUCKLAND

ISBN-13: 978-0-373-29517-3
ISBN-10:   0-373-29517-0

HALLOWE'EN HUSBANDS

The publisher acknowledges the copyright holders
of the individual works as follows:

MARRIAGE AT MORROW CREEK

WEDDING AT WAREHAVEN

MASTER OF PENLOWEN

This is a work of fiction. Names, characters, places and incidents are
either the product of the author's imagination or are used fictitiously,
and any resemblance to actual persons, living or dead, business
establishments, events or locales is entirely coincidental.

CONTENTS

MARRIAGE AT MORROW CREEK

Lisa Plumley

Dear Reader,

Thank you for reading *Marriage at Morrow Creek!*

Hallowe'en is the perfect time for a few spine-tingling thrills, and any time is the right time for a good romance. That's why I'm delighted to bring you Rose and Will's story! It's a special one to me, and I hope you enjoy it, too. If you spotted a few familiar faces, that's because this is my fourth visit to Morrow Creek. I hope you'll look for the other books in my Morrow Creek Matchmakers series, including *The Matchmaker, The Scoundrel* and *The Rascal.*

In the meantime, you're invited to drop by my Web site at www.lisaplumley.com, where you can sign up for new-book alerts or my reader newsletter, read sneak previews of upcoming books, request special reader freebies and more. I hope you'll visit today.

As always, I'd love to hear from you! You can visit me online at community.eharlequin.com/users/lisaplumley, send e-mail to lisa@lisaplumley.com, "friend" me on MySpace at www.myspace.com/lisaplumley, or write to me c/o P.O. Box 7105, Chandler, AZ 85246-7105.

Happy reading,

Lisa

> *To Linda Fildew, with heartfelt thanks.*
> *And to my husband John, with love.*

Chapter One

October 1884, near Morrow Creek, Arizona Territory

"Your sister has gone missing again."

At the sound of her father's gravelly voice, Rose Tillson jumped. Hastily she pressed her finger to the account book on her lap, trying to keep her place in the column of penciled figures she was supposed to be tallying.

"Hmm?" Trying to appear wholly innocent, Rose glanced up.

She felt immediately dismayed at the sight before her. Her father stood grumpily just outside the medicine show wagons that housed their belongings, his gray hair on end and his clothing askew. Typically, Dr. George Tillson prided himself on his dapper appearance. Today, though, Viola's latest escapade seemed to have upset him too much for him to bother.

"Oh, Papa! You haven't even buttoned your coat." Rose nodded at the fallen leaves swirling in the autumn breeze nearby. "It's cold! You'll catch your death outside. Here, let me help you."

Clambering down from the wagon—an enclosed affair, with the words "TILLSON & HEALY'S PATENTED MIRACLE ELIXIR & CELEBRATED PANACEA"'d painted in vibrant lettering on its sides—Rose buttoned her father's coat. Then she smoothed his hair and fixed his scarf.

"There." Satisfied that he'd be warm enough, she gave him an affectionate pat. "Now, then. You say Viola's not in camp?"

"Not since sunup, near as I can tell." Her father shook his head, peering into the ponderosa pine and oak-filled forest surrounding their campsite. A short distance from the doused fire their four horses nosed aside the frostbitten leaves, searching for breakfast. "She didn't feed or water the horses, either. I told her we were leaving straightaway this morning."

"I know you did. Don't worry. I'll go look for her."

"Probably off woolgathering again." He hunched his shoulders. "That girl doesn't have the sense God gave a goose. Or that mangy mouser that's been hanging around here lately."

He pointed. Rose looked, but caught only a glimpse as the small black cat raced into the trees. She had yet to get a good view of the creature. But with All Hallows' Eve only a few days away the appearance of a black cat *did* make her wonder…

"If I find out Viola's been mooning over some 'dashing' customer instead of doing her chores," her papa said, "I'll set her to shoveling horse patties for a week to make up for it!"

"Shh. Mind your temper, Papa." Sympathetically, Rose touched her father's shoulder. "Remember what Sheng Li says—staying calm promotes wellness. Whenever you feel agitated, you're supposed to breathe deeply and—"

"Don't you start on me. Sheng Li is smart as a whip with those celestial herbs of his, and his elixir has been a godsend to me, that's for certain. But if that Chinaman got close to the sun, he'd give it advice on how it could shine brighter."

"He *can* be a bit of a know-it-all." Rose pulled her wrap tighter. "No wonder the two of you get along so well."

"Indeed we do." A moment passed. "Now, hang on a minute—"

"Except *you'd* tell the sun to be both brighter *and* warmer."

"Cheeky girl." Her father's gaze softened as he placed his

palm to her cheek. "At least you'll never worry me the way Viola does with her shenanigans, Rose. You're as dependable as the day is long, and twice as prone to regularity."

"Papa, please." Rose made a face. "You make me sound like a dose of Lintel's castor oil!"

"That's not such a bad thing to a person who needs it." Her father stuck his hands in his pockets, visibly cheered. "Now, quit making that face at me. As your poor dear mother would have said, you don't want it to freeze that way. And when you find Viola, tell her there's no use her trying to sneak in under my nose. I won't be gulled by her tomfoolery. I'm old, not blind."

"I'll tell her. I promise."

"See that you do. And no lollygagging, either."

Rose agreed, watching fondly as her papa headed for their second wagon with his coat still crooked. An energetic man, Dr. George Tillson was also fiercely loving, famously intelligent and occasionally eccentric. He'd abandoned a lucrative medical practice in San Francisco to spread the word about Sheng Li's medicinal elixir, which had restored his own health years ago. Now Rose couldn't remember the days when they'd lived in the city. She only recalled trails and towns and days on the road.

Her sister, however, did remember their more sophisticated existence—and she yearned for it all the time. Even now Viola was probably gazing into Morrow Creek's general store windows, watching trains arriving at the depot or spending part of her savings on tea at the town's fanciest hotel, the Lorndorff.

Viola had a hunger for the bustle and flash of town life, and Morrow Creek—where yesterday they'd finished making elixir deliveries to accounts and conducting their popular medicine show—had captured her imagination more than most. It was one of Rose's favorite places on the medicine show's circuit, too, bordered by a protective mountain and filled with friendly townsfolk, charming houses and western-style shops.

But that friendliness couldn't compete with their father's rampaging protective streak. As far as Papa was concerned, all unknown men were potential degenerates, just itching to take advantage of a woman alone. Which was why Viola usually sneaked out to gain her freedom…and why Rose typically brought her back before their father realized anything was amiss. Today Rose had gotten distracted—disastrously so for Viola's sake. After all, nobody liked shoveling meadow muffins.

Resigned to her mission, Rose reached in the wagon for her gloves. Instead, her gaze fell on the bottle of Lintel's castor oil in a nearby basket. She glowered. *Everyone* she met thought of her in those castor oil terms—dependable, reliable and easy to digest. She'd had just about enough of it, too.

Although Rose had been traveling with her papa's show almost from the day she could toddle up to the wagons, she made it a point to stay out of the spotlight. She was the mousy assistant—the person who kept the accounts, mended the costumes, cooked meals and circulated among the crowd to sell bottles of Tillson & Healy's Patented Miracle Elixir & Celebrated Panacea.

She was not an exciting performer like Viola, eager to sing and dance with all eyes on her…or to skedaddle into town on a whim. But for one fleeting moment Rose dared to imagine herself in her sister's place, doing something brash and scandalous.

Her imagination stuttered at the very notion.

With a sigh, Rose plucked up her gloves, then hoisted her skirts and petticoats. Thirty seconds later she was on her way into the forest, searching for her wayward sister…and for her own path to undependable, unreliable, uncastor-oil-like living.

If only she had the first notion where to look.

The dried grass crunched beneath her feet. The scent of pine sap filled her nose. So engrossed was Rose in searching for Viola that she nearly missed the sight she savored the most every morning: Will Gavigan, their medicine show's driver, bagman and all-around Johnny helper, striding into the camp as he returned from wherever he'd made his bed for the night.

Riveted, Rose stopped in her tracks to stare shamelessly at him. Even tousle-haired, and focused on some other task, Will appeared magnificent. He'd outfitted himself in brown trousers, a white shirt, a brocade vest, a suit coat, an outer coat, a knit scarf and a flat-brimmed hat. He carried a bedroll beneath his arm as he strode with authority and purpose. He needed to shave, and a haircut wouldn't go amiss, either. But his features were perfect and his teeth were beautiful, and there was something intriguing about him. Something so masculine, so thrilling, so… So headed straight toward her this very minute.

Sakes alive. Will Gavigan had caught her ogling him.

"Rose. What are you looking at?" he asked.

His deep voice shook her, making her yearn for a way to keep him talking. Especially since he so rarely moved in the direction he did now…closer to *her.*

Startled, Rose blurted the truth. "I'm looking at you."

A baffled silence greeted her admission.

Rose scarcely noticed. She fancied she could feel the warmth emanating from Will's brawny, fascinating body, and she wanted to snuggle nearer to him—maybe touch his shadowed beard. Those bristly hairs looked as dark as those on his head…and on his eyebrows, which were currently raised in query.

I'm looking at you, she remembered herself saying. Oh, no.

Rose whipped her gaze upward, feeling her cheeks heat. "Your, er, walk is odd this morning," she prevaricated.

"Ah. That's the greenbacks in my boot." Appearing more easygoing now that she'd explained herself, Will dropped his bedroll. He slipped off one big boot, then withdrew the hidden currency from inside. "God bless fools and gamblers."

"Oh." *Brilliant.* Rose stifled a nervous titter. She'd loved Will Gavigan for days, months, *years* on end. For equally as long he'd been insensible to her infatuation. "You say that as though they're one and the same. Fools and—"

He smiled. "In my experience they usually are."

"But if *you're* wagering, aren't you a gambler, too? And therefore a bit of a foo—"

"Touché." Folding the bills, Will tucked them securely in his boot again. He replaced his footwear, then grinned at her. "As usual, you're my conscience, Rose. It's a good thing you can't play Faro, else I might never add a thing to my bankroll."

She wrinkled her nose. "First castor oil, now a conscience. At this rate I'll be downgraded to a pinworm by lunchtime."

He gave her a puzzled look. "A pinworm?"

"Never mind. It's not important. Especially not since—"

"Your sister is missing again. I know. I just saw your father a minute ago. He asked me to be on the lookout." Hoisting his bedroll, Will shook his head. "If it's not one thing it's another with Viola. That girl's a passel of trouble sometimes."

To Rose, his tone sounded approving—almost admiring. It galled her more than she cared to admit. As usual, Viola was audacious and attention-grabbing…while Rose was a walking, talking, helplessly smitten deterrent to Faro-playing.

"Especially not since I have such an important question to ask you," Rose barreled on, determined to change the subject. She crossed her arms and arched her brow, trying to appear an adventuress in her own right. "You've been traveling with the show for three years now, Will. When are you going to stop keeping to yourself so much? You sleep apart, take your meals apart—"

"Sometimes a man's better off alone."

"No one's better off alone. If only you'd try—"

His upraised hand stopped her. "Right now I've got to try to find that foolhardy sister of yours."

He touched his hat brim, then headed off in the opposite direction. Rose was left with only the sage and leather scent of him, the fleeting warmth of his nearness…and a desperate urge to bring him back.

"Will, wait!"

He turned. The sunshine highlighted his jaw, outlining its strength and stubbornness. My, he was splendid. If only he'd look at *her* with a little of the dedication and possessiveness he applied to his work for the medicine show. If only he'd see her for the independent woman she was, instead of the tagalong Tillson she'd been when he'd joined them on the road. If only…

"We could…search for Viola together?"

He shook his head. "Not this time."

"I could—" *hold your hand, gaze into your eyes, say something witty so you'd smile again* "—make you breakfast?"

Her offer earned her another of his delectable smiles. "Burned biscuits again?"

"They're well browned," Rose pointed out with a lift of her chin. "Just like the cookery book says."

"Thank you, but right now your sister is more important." Will lifted his hand in farewell. "Stay on the lookout, Rose."

Watching him leave, his broad shoulders marching against those shafts of sunlight as he moved between the trees, Rose sighed. *Your sister is more important.* Wasn't that the story of her entire life? What did she have to do to make Will see her?

To make him, if she were lucky, fall in *love* with her?

Before Rose could reason out a solution, a noisy splash sounded from nearby. The creek! Had Viola fallen while crossing the flat stones used as a footbridge? Had she sneaked back to their camp only to be waylaid by a freezing watery fall?

Holding her wrap tightly, Rose ran toward the water.

There was a woman at the creek, but it wasn't Viola.

The unknown lady flailed her arms, struggling to regain her balance at the edge of Morrow Creek. She'd been recently dunked. Her gown dripped like a parasol shedding rainwater, its sumptuous blend of deep brown silk, black lace and ribbon trim most likely ruined, and her hat perched cockeyed near her chignon.

"Oh!" Rose hurried toward her. "Are you all right?"

Upon finding herself in company, the woman glanced Rose's way with perfect composure. Her face appeared beautiful—a bit more wrinkled than Rose would have guessed from the distance she'd first glimpsed her, but subtly powdered and rouged to make up the difference. The woman's mouth curled in a smile.

"I'm just fine. Thank you very much for asking. That blasted fourth stone trips me up every single time."

"It's a very slippery pathway."

"So they say." The woman's smile widened in an enigmatic fashion. Even as she wrung out her reticule, dripping water on the creek bank, she emanated sophistication and elegant comportment—as though she spent most of her time not in such rustic surroundings but in lavish parlors and drawing rooms. "Well, thank you for your concern. I'd best be on my way."

"But your hat is crooked. And you're soaking wet!" Alarmed at the woman's sopping state—and still a bit astonished to have met her so unexpectedly—Rose tugged off her shawl. "Here. Take my wrap. It's quite warm." She tried to hand it over.

"Oh, no. I couldn't," the woman demurred. "But thank you."

"Are you sure? You'll catch your death of cold in those wet clothes." Concerned, Rose examined the woman, searching for signs of a shivering spell or chattering teeth. Fortunately—and to her bafflement—she found neither. Still… "Please. I'd feel much better if you'd take my wrap. I'll be fine without it."

She offered it again. The woman shook her head.

"Then would you like to come back to my family's campsite to warm up?" Rose suggested. "It's not fancy, but we could have a nice hot fire, lickety-split. And some good coffee to—"

"I'm sorry, but I'm afraid I'll have to decline. I'm late to meet someone as it is, you see." As though it were a warm summer day, and her accident a mere inconvenience, the woman reached up to adjust her hat. Rose noticed a matted spot in the woman's hair, a place weighed down with leaves and mud. Before she could point out the issue, the woman added, "I appreciate your offer all the same. It's unusually kind of you."

On the verge of disagreeing—because neighborliness was a natural attribute in her experience—Rose felt a strange warmth steal over her. On such a cool autumn day it felt beyond peculiar. So did the way it made goose bumps rise on her arms. In its wake she caught the fragrances of tobacco and…whiskey?

"Well, I'm off, then." Good-naturedly, the woman shook out her soggy skirts. She seemed not to have noticed anything amiss—but she did appear to have arrived at a decision. "I'm Maude Brown, late of Morrow Creek and currently—" she waved her hand "—from hereabouts. I'm very pleased to meet you."

"It's my pleasure, Mrs. Brown. I'm Rose Tillson."

Rose reached out, expecting to grasp Mrs. Brown's hand in a handshake. Instead, her new friend pointed downward.

"You appear to have dropped something, Miss Tillson."

Rose glanced at the mossy, leaf-strewn ground. To her surprise, she spied a folded, buff-colored card.

Mrs. Brown must have dropped it without realizing, Rose decided as she bent, then opened the paper. Because *she* did not lead the sort of life typically littered with invitations to…

"The Morrow Creek Hallowe'en Gala?" she read aloud.

"Oh! How *wonderful*! I adore fêtes." Mrs. Brown edged closer, reading over Rose's shoulder with keen feminine interest. "Who will be your 'and guest', I wonder?"

She glanced up, mouth pursed and eyes sparkling.

"Well, Will, of course," Rose said. Then she realized the foolishness of her declaration. She wouldn't be attending the Hallowe'en Gala with Will. She wouldn't be attending at all. "I mean, pardon me for prying." She offered the invitation to Mrs. Brown. "This must be yours."

Her new friend refused it with a shake of her head. "It's not mine. Perhaps you forgot about it until now?"

"Not likely." Rose pursed her lips. "My family's medicine show is always on the move. I've never even *been* to a proper party. I'm sure I would remember being invited to one."

"You *have* been invited—to *this* one! It's quite clear to me. After all, you're holding the invitation as we speak, my dear."

Intrigued despite herself, Rose followed Mrs. Brown's gaze to the invitation. She wished it *had* been meant for her.

"I'm sure there's more to it than mere possession. I couldn't simply…*appear* at a gala unexpectedly."

"Nonsense. Fortune rewards the bold." Mrs. Brown did not seem ready to call quits to her efforts. "That's my motto."

"Well, boldness certainly rewards my sister," Rose couldn't help mumbling. Boldness had earned Viola the boon of Will's attention again and again. Today was added proof of it.

"See? Then you know what I mean," Mrs. Brown insisted. "When it comes to living, the only way to get a leg-up is to take chances. Otherwise fate gallops right on past you."

"I never take chances." And she didn't behave impulsively, either, Rose reminded herself. She sighed. "There'll be other invitations. As long as a person works hard and does the right thing she's sure to be rewarded sooner or later."

"Pshaw. How do you know you'll have a 'later'?"

"Everyone has a 'later,'" Rose said, thinking her new friend was joking with her. But one glance told her that Mrs. Brown was not speaking in jest—she appeared deadly serious.

"Sometimes there's only now," Mrs. Brown said. "This day."

Silently, Rose gazed at her. She felt an unusual kinship with the woman—a warmth and connection she couldn't explain. She felt as if Mrs. Brown understood her. As if that invitation *was* destined for her…and she *could* be bold if she tried.

Rose lowered her gaze. "But we've finished in Morrow Creek. We're leaving first thing today. Just as soon as I find—"

"Rose?" The voice came from a distance. "Rose, are you out here?"

At the sound of that gruff voice, Rose started.

"That's my father!" She swung round, all thoughts of the Hallowe'en Gala vanishing. Had Viola returned at last?

Pine branches swooshed and swayed. Several twigs cracked. A rabbit darted from the undergrowth and raced sideways, making way for Dr. George Tillson to forge a path to the creekside.

"There you are!" When he spied Rose, relief softened his features. "Didn't you hear me? I've been calling for you."

"I'm sorry, Papa. I've just been speaking with—" Rose turned, intending to introduce her father to Mrs. Brown. "Er…"

The woman was nowhere to be seen. All that remained was that liquor and cheroots smell…and that odd lingering warmth.

"That's strange." Angling her head, Rose glanced toward a copse of trees. She glimpsed no movement—especially no movement highlighted by a fine gown, a patrician demeanor and a ladies' hat capped with a dyed ostrich feather. "She was beside me just a moment ago. You must have seen us standing here together. Me and a very nicely dressed woman with—"

"I've no time for your jibber-jabber, young lady." Clearly distressed, her father didn't so much as glance around for the missing Mrs. Brown. "I'm off to Morrow Creek to deal with *this!*"

He smacked a piece of paper in her palm. Startled, Rose unfolded it. Recognizing her sister's handwriting, she read rapidly.

"Viola has *eloped?* With the Morrow Creek pharmacist?"

"Not if I have anything to say about it, she hasn't." Tugging his hat, her father locked his gaze on hers. "This is the most fool thing Viola's done yet. I'm going to Morrow Creek to meet this *Henry Lundberg* and see what kind of man he is."

"Papa, you know perfectly well what sort of man he is. We've been delivering elixir to Mr. Lundberg for two years now."

"That's no excuse." Her father gnashed his teeth. "The rapscallion has seduced my Viola, and I won't stand for it!"

"All right. But let me go with you. I just need a few—"

"No. This is a father's job."

"Don't be silly," Rose urged. "If I could speak with V—"

"No. I'm leaving you here with Will, and that's that."

Like a clam she'd once seen at the oceanside in California, Rose shut her mouth instantly. *Will, Will, Will* swam in her head. *Leaving you here with Will.* As concerned as she was for Viola's well-being, she was equally certain her sister knew what she was doing…and would not be dissuaded from it, either.

Not that that minor detail would prevent her papa from trying. The Tillsons were legendarily obstinate. Everyone knew it.

"There might still be time to end this nonsense," her father forged on, waving his arm in a paternal fervor. "No matter how many stops we have to delay on the medicine-show circuit, I'm going to make sure my little girl is safe!"

"Of course." Rose couldn't resist testing her good fortune. "And I'm to stay with Will, all alone, while you're gone?"

"What do you think I just said? Clean your ears, girl!"

"So then…Will's already agreed to this?"

Dreamy visions filled Rose's head. Herself at Will's side, serving him perfect biscuits and beans. Will at her side, tenderly giving over the account books for reconciling. The two of them together, hand in hand, while they watched the sunset.

Her papa's blunt words snapped her to attention.

"'Course he's agreed. Now, you be good while I'm gone."

With a terse shake of his head, a fond pat on her arm and a great deal more blustering, her father headed toward town.

He did not slip on that tricky fourth stepping stone, the way Mrs. Brown had while crossing Morrow Creek. Nor did he glance backward to see his youngest castor-oil-reminiscent daughter watching him leave. But if he had, Dr. George Tillson would have seen something he'd never expected.

He would have seen innocent Rose with a decidedly devilish expression on her face…ready to grasp the opportunities that fate had delivered and eagerly planning to make the absolute most of them between now and All Hallows' Eve.

Chapter Two

In all his years of living on his own Will Gavigan had held many jobs. He'd been a ranch hand. A barkeep. An express rider, a saloon piano player, a medicine show strongman and more. But what he'd never been—what he'd staunchly avoided being until mere hours ago—was a chaperon.

He was none too pleased to find himself in that position now. Especially given the way his chirpy, fully-grown charge tailed him. It was as though Rose believed if she didn't stay within arm's reach at all times, she'd lose him.

Cheerfully she tracked him from the horses' posts to the nearest wagon, then back. "Will? What are you doing now?"

"Getting the camp ready for a longer stay."

"How long? A day? A week? Just until Hallowe'en?"

"That's for your father to decide. In the meantime, I made a promise to watch over things. I aim to do exactly that."

"You'll be very good at it, I'm sure." Rose sat on the steps of the nearest medicine show wagon, chin in hand, as she watched him work. "With those big muscles of yours, I mean."

With one hand on the wagon wheel he was mending—a task he'd delayed but now had time for—Will stopped. He glanced up.

Rose gazed back at him, her heart in her eyes and a spoony

expression on her face. He'd seen that look on her before. Most of the time he passed it off as Rose's usual dreaminess. But today, with *those big muscles of yours* ringing in his ears, Will suddenly discerned a different meaning behind her chatter.

Was Rose Tillson *flirting* with him?

At the thought, a peculiar heat started at his earlobes, then intensified—much to Will's incredulity.

"Why, Will Gavigan! I do believe you're blushing!"

Impossible. "Quit jabbering, Rose. I've got work to do."

"You're blushing because I said something nice about you, aren't you? I never knew you were so modest. Handsome and capable, yes. Loyal and strong, of course. But modest? I never—"

He gritted his teeth. "Don't you have something to do?"

"I'm doing it." From atop her perch Rose kicked her legs to and fro, sending her skirts swinging. She seemed plumb satisfied to stay there all day. "You carry on, though."

"I can't think straight when you're staring at me."

"Ooh! Well. I guess I'd better help you, then."

Before Will could reckon what she meant, Rose dropped from the wagon steps and skedaddled to his side, bringing with her the fragrances of rosewater and ironed cotton. Her cheeks looked pink with the chill in the air. Her long brown braid whacked him in the shoulder as she shoved her way onto the upturned barrel he'd been using as a stool. He didn't think he'd ever been this close to Rose before. He'd never had a reason to be.

Her hand landed atop his on the wheel…then squeezed.

The warmth of her touch made his whole body come alert. It started with a tingling in his fingertips, progressed with a whoosh of heat up his arm, then landed in his chest with a wholly unsettling feeling of comfort…and maybe more.

"There." Rose sounded breathless. She tipped her face toward his. "I've got hold now, too. What do we do next?"

Will could think of several things, none of them entirely chivalrous. Or pure. Or wise. For the space of a breath all he could do was stare at her, dumbfounded. He tightened his grasp. Unmistakably, Rose squeezed his hand again. At her touch, the truth smacked him hard. Rose Tillson *was* flirting with him!

Sweet, innocent, costume-mending Rose was snuggling closer, batting her eyes…even biting her lip suggestively.

At the gesture, Will's gaze lowered to her mouth. Without his approval his body leaned nearer. Rose was offering. He was a man not opposed to taking. What would be the harm?

But then, as a prelude to losing his head completely and sampling a taste of her, Will raised his gaze to Rose's eyes. What he saw there stopped him flat. Because to Rose this was not mere flirting. And to him that was all it could ever be.

Shocked, Will reared backward. "I'll fix this later."

"But…you were doing so well!"

"I've got other chores to take care of." He dropped the wheel and stood, feeling muddled. When had Rose Tillson become so brash, so seductive, so…tantalizing? "Leave me be, Rose."

"But you and I…we… Did I do something wrong?"

The disappointment in her voice made his chest hurt. Will didn't know what was wrong with him. An hour alone with Rose and suddenly he was noticing her eyes, her lips, her warm hands?

What was next? Would he find himself ogling her ankles? Or, God forbid, touching her? Even now, a lesser man might have been examining the fit of her gown, trying to gauge the state of her figure beneath all that bulky wool, yearning to undo some of the buttons that curved in and out on her bodice so temptingly…

Damnation. He was at it again. Scowling, Will jerked his gaze to the safe confines of the water barrel at the other side of the camp. He stomped toward it, determined to regain control.

He thrust the dipper in the water, then drank deeply.

There. That was better. He could think clearly now. He could remember that Rose was off-limits. No matter what. Even Dr. Tillson had reminded Will of that when he'd entrusted the medicine show—and his naive younger daughter—to Will's care.

After all, the old man had said with a chuckle, *it wouldn't do to lose* two *daughters to the local scoundrels this week!*

Remembering those words now, Will gave a rueful grin. If only Dr. Tillson had known that the greatest challenge to Rose's virtue would come not from Morrow Creek but from within his own retinue—from his own steadfast, upright bagman and driver.

Resolved to uphold his friend's trust, Will lowered the water dipper…to reveal Rose standing directly before him.

Her perky demeanor showed no signs of slackening. "If you like, we can simply hold hands again. That was nice."

"It was *not* nice. Rose, what's gotten into you? Have you been sampling the elixir? Are you tipsy?"

She scoffed. "You know Papa's remedy contains no spirits. It's nothing but safe, wholesome Chinese herbs and vitalizers."

"Then what are you up to?"

"I'm simply taking a chance for once. Today is all you have, you know. If you don't take a chance, fate gallops right on past you. That's why I—" Rose took away his dipper "—decided to tell you—" she trailed her hands down his coat on the pretense of making sure water hadn't dripped on him, seeming to delight in the contact "—how I feel about you. I'm…mad for you, Will."

Her voice caught on those final few words, but Rose got them out all the same, leaving Will stunned in their wake.

There was only one responsible thing to do.

"Rose, no." He frowned. Shook his head. "I don't— We can't—"

Her downhearted expression made that ache start up in his chest again. It pained him, almost as if he already cared for her and was loath to hurt her feelings. Which was outlandish. Will considered Rose a friend, to be sure. A solid, demure and trustworthy friend. But not a woman he wanted to kiss.

Until today. What in tarnation…?

"We can't let ourselves get carried away," he said. "Your father has put us in charge of things, remember?"

Aside from Toby, the local boy they'd hired to watch over the horses—feeding and exercising them as needed, earning a few coins for the job—it would be only Will and Rose at the medicine show campsite at least for another day or two.

"I see." At his gentler dismissal, Rose offered him a sage nod. "You want to be more deliberate about this?"

"Exactly."

"More…considering. More formal. More serious."

Relieved, Will nodded. "Now we understand each other."

"But Will…'serious' and 'formal' equate to marriage, and I don't think it's wise to get engaged without at least kissing first. Papa wouldn't approve of my being so forward, but—"

"No." Alarmed, Will backed up. "That's not what I meant."

"Oh, good!" With her face glowing, Rose pursued him to the medicine show wagon. She flung her arms around his shoulders, then closed her eyes and puckered. "Go ahead, then. I'm ready!"

With his back against the wagon's gaudily painted side, and his front nearly covered by an obviously willing Rose, Will was trapped. Contemplatively, he eyed her rosy lips. She'd need to be much more relaxed to enjoy a kiss, he mused. She'd need—she'd need *him* to stand firm, since she so obviously could not. Resolutely, Will steeled himself. "No, you're not ready."

"I'm not?" Rose opened one eye. Upon glimpsing his undoubtedly mulish expression, she loosened her grip. She sighed. "Admittedly I'm inexperienced in these matters, but the least you could do is perform your gentlemanly duty. Honestly."

He almost laughed. Rose's nearness had roused his entire body—as unlikely and unforgivable as that was—and she had the temerity to accuse him of being ungentlemanly? When he stood before her, yearning and confused, knowing that a kiss would only lead to more, and yet denied himself that very thing?

"I'm a rogue," he agreed, pulling a repentant face.

"Well, you're not being terribly cooperative."

"I'm not. I don't deserve your affection."

"But I'm not giving up!" Rose straightened and fixed him with the same look she wore while tackling biscuit making. "I will make you love me, Will. Just so you have fair warning."

Oh, hell. *Love?* It was worse than he'd thought.

"I can't do that, Rose. I have other plans."

"Your bankroll. I know. I'm aware you've been saving, but perhaps I can help with that. If I sell more elixir next time—"

"I'm leaving the medicine show."

Her mouth dropped open. Confusion filled her face—her pert, enchanting, surprisingly pretty face. Rose drew in a breath to speak…and Will hotfooted it to the other side of camp before she could say a word. He wasn't ready for her questions. Today he had no answers, only a hearty sense of confusion for himself.

"Leaving the show? Why? Are you going to stay in Morrow Creek like Viola?"

Stone-faced, Will refused to answer. He wanted his own medicine show. He wanted a chance to prove himself. He fully intended to get both. But, as shocked as Rose seemed by his plans to leave, he didn't have the heart to elaborate further.

Determined not to encourage her, Will shoved his hands in his pockets. "I never said I'd remain with the show forever."

Rose looked as though he'd slapped her.

But, as sorry as Will felt for hurting her, he knew the truth. With every passing day, being around the cozy, loving Tillsons grew more difficult for him. Their happiness knuckled into him somehow. It made him restless. He needed to claim his own future—and his future would not likely include Rose.

Letting her believe otherwise would be unkind. It would encourage her to become even more attached to him—and him more fond of her. So he took his meals apart from the family and slept away from their wagons. It was the only honorable way.

Rose jutted her chin upward, hands on her hips. "You'll never find a better show than ours. Never in a million years."

"I know." Will had been with other medicine shows. He'd seen sham doctors loading their remedies with laudanum, witnessed them selling colored bathwater and questionable powders, heard them promise the impossible. Dr. Tillson was a better man. The Chinese elixir he peddled for Sheng Li was a legitimate healing potion. "I believe in this show. I believe in your father. That's why I won't let him down."

"You won't! You never could."

"I would if I kissed you, Rose. I would if I loved you."

Her eyes shone with denial. "Love is always good."

"Not if you're living without it."

She narrowed her gaze. "Do you love someone else?"

Will took a step backward. "I have work to do."

"That's not an answer." Rose followed him. "What about the kissing?" Her cheeks pinkened. "I know you wanted to try it."

Of course he had. But he'd be a fool to admit as much.

Searching for a diversion, Will spotted the slinking black cat near the second medicine show wagon. He picked up a bowl. Without looking at Rose, he filled it with milk, courtesy of the Morrow Creek farmer who'd supplied them last, then hunkered down to set the bowl on the ground.

Still, Rose pursued him. "I want an answer, Will." She crossed her arms over her chest. "I know you wanted to kiss me."

He squinted beneath the wagon. "You can't know that."

"Viola told me that when a man wants to kiss you, he goes all cross-eyed on you. You *definitely* looked a little—"

"Viola reads too many novels."

"—cross-eyed. And your breath got faster, too. I—"

"Stop it." In a flash, Will levered upward. He grabbed Rose's shoulders. "You're playing with fire. You don't have the experience for this."

Rose's gaze searched his. Her eyes were wide, her mouth an

O of surprise…which quickly turned into a determined chin-jut. The Tillson obstinacy, so prevalent among the other members of the medicine show, was clearly coming to the fore.

Aww, hell. "Damnation, Rose. Don't you see? This—"

She rose on tiptoes and pressed her mouth to his. Her lips felt soft and warm, the contact between them brief and heady. Will's whole body tightened, even as Rose hastily lowered again.

"There. Now I've started gathering experience." She met his gaze bravely, then ducked her head and pulled her wrap tighter. "You're going to have to meet me halfway, Will. Time's wasting."

Transfixed by the memory of her mouth against his, Will couldn't speak. This thing between him and Rose was dangerous, he realized. It was dangerous, and it couldn't be trusted.

Just—as it had turned out—like him.

"I can't do that," Will said. But by then she was gone.

Sitting on a flat rock near the creek, Rose fashioned a wreath of rust-colored autumn leaves, her fingers working furiously at the task. *Stupid Will Gavigan.* She'd thrown herself at his head, and what had he done? Dished up a passel of excuses.

It was too much to be borne. Her cheeks burned with embarrassment, and her legs felt unsteady after her flight to the banks of Morrow Creek—or maybe that wobbliness was an effect of the kiss they'd shared. Rose didn't know. She did not—as Will had so roughly pointed out—have the experience to tell.

But, oh, it had been wonderful! Her heart had pounded. Her breath had run ragged. Rose had felt afire with the thrill of her brash behavior. And when her lips had touched Will's…

Bliss. For an instant he'd tightened his grasp on her shoulders, drawing her nearer. For a heartbeat he'd kissed her back. But then her courage had run out, her sham boldness had fled, and Rose had found herself utterly unable to carry on.

Not that Will had cared. Even now he was probably thinking up improbable new reasons why he couldn't love her.

"My, that's very pretty handiwork," someone said from nearby. "Why don't you offer your services to the decorating committee for the Morrow Creek Hallowe'en Gala? Then you'll feel right at home accepting that invitation, I'll wager."

Rose glanced up. Her new friend stood there, smiling.

"Mrs. Brown! Where did you disappear to? I wanted to introduce you to my father, but when I turned around—"

"I'd prefer we kept our acquaintance between ourselves, my dear. Especially given the soaked state I was in when we met."

She chuckled. Her joviality lightened Rose's mood, too. She wished *she* could accept setbacks as easily as Mrs. Brown did. Although the woman's gown still appeared a little damp at the hem, Rose noticed. And there was still a leaf in her hair….

"So, the decorating committee…will you consider it?"

Diverted, Rose transferred her gaze to Mrs. Brown's face. She shook her head. "I scarcely know anyone in Morrow Creek."

"All the more reason to join the committee, I'd say."

"Well…" Mrs. Brown had a point. Also, it occurred to Rose that if Will wanted a more sophisticated life, *she'd* need to be equipped to meet its demands. After all, she was well on her way to making him love her. "I suppose I could try."

"Excellent." Mrs. Brown arranged herself on a fallen log, looking as elegant as a lady on a fine settee. "Well done."

They sat in companionable conversation for some time, Rose finishing her wreath and Mrs. Brown offering helpful hints. She was, Rose discovered, an accomplished woman, with diverse interests—a woman much like Rose's mother might have been, had she survived illness to see Rose grow to womanhood.

Soon the sun dipped toward the tree line, casting long shadows over their meeting place and the trickling creek nearby.

With no further excuse for delaying her return—and with the sure knowledge that Will would grow worried over her absence—Rose stood. "Well, I'd best be going. It's been so nice talking with you, Mrs. Brown. I'm afraid I'm a bit deprived of female company today, with my sister off adventuring in town."

If Mrs. Brown wondered what kind of adventures those might be, she didn't let on. "I'm happy to be of service. Anytime."

"Thank you." Rose gathered her wreath, slipped it over her arm, then said her goodbyes. Just a few steps away, though, Rose turned again. "Mrs. Brown?"

"Yes, my dear?" her friend asked, curiously still in place.

"Do you have any suggestions for me…about men?"

"Men?" Mrs. Brown's eyes brightened. "I thought you'd never ask! Sit right down here." She patted her log. "We'll get started at once. *My,* do I have stories to tell…."

With new hopefulness, Rose tracked Will around the campsite the next morning. Her talk with Mrs. Brown had enlivened her, and today she felt downright intrepid—ready to enact a few of the strategies she and her advisor had concocted.

Will would not know what had hit him, Rose mused as she watched him haul elixir crates in his burly arms. He would not have the least defense, she decided as she admired his ability to untangle leather tracings, hammer together split joins and soothe restless horses. He would be *hers.* She knew it as she let her gaze roam freely over his broad shoulders and intent face. There was no question about it. As sure as Dr. George Tillson was not handing over his eldest daughter without a fight, Rose Tillson was not giving up on love without trying her best.

Her efforts appeared to have spooked Will a bit, though. While he worked, he glanced over his shoulder at her, a contemplative and somewhat perplexed expression on his face. Hoping to encourage him, Rose kept up the chitchat she'd begun.

"It was awfully kind of Mr. Lundberg's family to invite Papa to stay with them while Viola's and Henry's wedding plans are sorted out, don't you think so?"

Rose had learned this from her father, who'd returned to the campsite briefly last night. He'd told her about a certain "delightful" widow he'd met in town, then gathered a few belongings and left again.

Companionably, she followed Will to the woodpile, stooping to gather the smaller branches that had dropped from his latest load. "I mean, the Lundbergs didn't have to go to such lengths."

Will muttered something. She interpreted it as agreement.

"And they *must* be right-thinking people to have waylaid Henry and Viola on their way to the minister. Not just anyone could have convinced my sister to exercise patience."

More mumblings. Another meditative look—this time slipping toward Rose's ankles. Was Will actually admiring them?

Endeavoring to take advantage of his appreciation, Rose moved with more vigor as she snatched up the next twig. With a frisson of mischievousness she paused to examine her high-buttoned shoe. She hiked her skirt an entire inch, allowing Will a very long, very scandalous look at her ankle.

Breathlessly, Rose peeked upward. To her disappointment Will's back was to her. He hadn't seen a moment of her reckless display. Sighing, she straightened—and saw Will set down the chipped bowl, now refilled with milk, in the same place he'd left it yesterday, beside the nearest medicine show wagon.

"I knew it!" Rose said. "You've seen it, too. So has Papa."

He frowned. "I don't know what you mean."

"My ghost cat. You've seen it." Excitedly, she hastened to him. "A sleek black cat with glowing eyes—"

"Glowing eyes?"

"—and paw-prints that disappear *right* before your eyes!"

"Now I *know* you've been tippling on someone else's remedy."

But Rose refused to be put off, despite Will's amusement. "If not my ghost cat," she demanded, "who is the milk for, then?"

A pause. "It's for whatever…critters happen by."

"Critters?"

He nodded stiffly, then knelt and peered beneath the wagon.

"Aha! I saw you do that yesterday, too." Rose pointed. "If you're not looking for my ghost cat, then what are you—?"

Will emerged with a battered oilcan.

"What are you doing under…?" Rose stopped. It was quite evident what Will was doing. He was oiling the elliptical springs beneath the wagon. "I don't care. I still say you're up to something."

"The same could be said of you. Why are you so gussied up?"

Pleased, Rose pivoted while holding out her voluminous skirts. "This old thing? It's just a gown I added some lace to."

He frowned. "Looks like something Viola would wear."

Rose frowned, too. Why did her sister have to be the center of attention, even when she was nowhere near? "You mean, you think it's stunningly attractive? Go ahead and say it."

"On you…" Deep in thought, Will stroked his thumb over the oilcan. The movement mesmerized her. "It's garish."

"*Garish?* That's ridiculous." Rose crossed her arms. "You never said such a thing when Viola wore this dress."

"You, Rose, are *not* Viola. Not in any way, shape or form."

Wounded, Rose stared at him. "That's not fair. How—?"

With a charming grin, Will held up his palms. "Before you get yourself all in a pucker, you'd better let me explain."

"There aren't enough words in the world."

"Viola is talented, it's true. But you…you're real."

Slightly mollified by the complimentary way he'd said it, Rose allowed a grudging nod. "Go on."

"Viola is flashy, but you're kind, Rose."

Reluctantly, she unfolded her arms. "I'm listening."

"You're sweet and smart and funny." Will came closer to her, wearing an earnest expression. His warmth reached out to her, triggering an uptick in her heartbeat. With a conciliatory movement he caught her hand in his, rubbing his thumb over her glove the same way he'd rubbed that oilcan…only better. "And the way you tackle those account books just about beats all."

He *had* noticed her! Feverish with delight, Rose dared to

glance up into his face. He was cleanshaven today, rugged and familiar, and yet somehow new. She knew that if she stared long enough into Will's warm brown eyes, she'd lose herself entirely.

Forcing herself to be strong, Rose recalled the plan she'd devised yesterday with wise, worldly Mrs. Brown. *Leave your man wanting more,* her new friend had advised. *Leave him wondering.*

Well. That would be simple enough.

Just as soon as Rose…found the resolve…to nudge her hand…just far enough…to be out of Will's grasp. *Whew!*

The moment her hand came free, Will's gaze snapped to hers, surprise evident in his expression. Success! This plan, Rose realized, was going to be as simple as a cakewalk.

"I'm headed to Morrow Creek to volunteer for the Hallowe'en gala decorating committee." Cheerfully Rose hugged her wrap against the autumn chill, leaving a stupefied Will standing where she'd left him. "I'm finding myself quite drawn to town living these days." *Just like you.* "So don't bother to wait up for me tonight. I'm almost certain to be out late."

Chapter Three

It took Will three hours, one game of Faro and a generous slug of mescal to get what he needed. But by the time he stepped out of Jack Murphy's popular saloon and eyed Morrow Creek's bustling main street in the growing dusk, he felt more than ready for the task at hand.

Wagons and buggies jostled past. Some carried only drivers and passengers; others transported autumn apples, squash and Indian corn. Townspeople strolled by him on the sidewalk, passing the milliner's, the mercantile and Nickerson's Book Depot & News Emporium. Will had another destination in mind—and other news to give. Pulling down his hat against the woodsmoke-scented breeze, he headed out.

It was a short walk from the saloon to the tree-lined streets that housed Morrow Creek's residents, but moving between the two was like traversing from night to day. Away from the commotion of the business district the pathways were quiet. Lanterns glowed in nearby windows. Muted conversations reached toward Will, friendly and intimate in turn. The experience made a lie of the spooky days that supposedly lay between now and All Hallows' Eve—not that Will considered himself prone to ghostly imaginings or thoughts of hauntings. Those were for wide-eyed children. Or Rose and her "ghost cat."

Smiling in spite of himself—because the scrawny, mewling furball he'd been feeding for days had an appetite for food and petting unlike any apparition—Will reached the house he wanted.

The woman who answered the door was brown-haired and bosomy, with a baby on her hip and an inquisitive expression. Behind her Will heard feminine laughter, a persistent snickety-snick sound, and entirely more conversation than was natural.

"Sorry to disturb you, ma'am." He touched his hat brim, standing tall on the gingerbread-trimmed porch. "I'm looking for Miss Rose Tillson. I was told she might be here."

"I guess she might be. And you are…?"

"Will Gavigan. I've come to see her back home."

"Aww. Isn't that sweet?" The woman tilted her head, cooing the words to her infant. She turned her bright expression on Will. "I'm Molly. Well, Mrs. Copeland, to be particular about it. As you might imagine, we're an informal bunch around here."

She continued chattering at a pace that made Will wince. When he was onstage for the medicine show, he mostly moved props and accompanied Viola on the piano. Unlike some showmen, Will didn't run his mouth like an auctioneer or make audacious claims like a circus ringmaster. He was only himself—forthright and hardworking. Dr. Tillson's show didn't demand anything more.

"Anyway, why don't you come on in, Mr. Gavigan?" Mrs. Copeland stepped back, indicating a parlor just past her, and beyond that a kitchen packed with calico, lantern light and ladies in hats. "I'll see if I can rustle up Rose for you."

"No, thank you, Mrs. Copeland. I'll wait here."

"Don't be silly!" She tugged his arm. "Come on in."

"I only want to collect Rose." On the verge of protesting further, Will caught the fragrance of something freshly baked with sugar, butter and cinnamon. No wonder the women were so happy here. "But I guess coming in for a spell couldn't hurt."

He ducked beneath the doorframe. Inside, Will felt engulfed by feminine doodads, laughing chitchat and a homey aura he couldn't quite describe. It made longing rise up to choke him…which was ridiculous for a big, strong man like him. Obviously that cinnamon had him undone. He had to think about why he'd come here. Furrowing his brow, hat in his hands, Will spotted Rose at the table, laughing as she scissored orange and black crepe paper into the shapes of leaves and pumpkins.

He could not look away—because he'd never seen Rose look happier or prettier. Her blue eyes sparkled. Her hands flew over the fussy decorations. Her enthusiasm was palpable. If Will hadn't thought it preposterous, he'd have sworn that Rose adored the decorating committee in the same way she evidently adored the bustle of town life.

I'm finding myself quite drawn to town living these days.

As though pulled by his gaze, Rose looked up.

Although just yesterday she'd declared her love for him, now her hands stilled. Her smile dimmed. Will realized that her reaction was not because of him, but because she was sorry to see her sociable night in Morrow Creek come to an end.

And he was sorry to recognize the truth.

Because if Rose loved town life, and he loved the open road, he could not allow things to progress between them. It would be wrong to let Rose believe she could have a future with an itchy-footed rambler like him. Especially if she—like her sister Viola—wanted to stay here in Morrow Creek.

He saw evidence that she did.

To her credit, Rose tried to hide her disappointment behind a new, even more disarming smile as she rose to greet him. She made introductions around the table, presenting the various members of the Hallowe'en Gala decorating committee. But even as he made the acquaintance of each woman Will knew what had to be done. He had to make sure Rose didn't love him anymore. He had to make sure she wouldn't miss him when they parted.

To that end, he took Rose's arm. "It's time we left."

Oh, no. So soon? That was what he expected to hear.

But at his touch Rose beamed. "Fine. I'll get my things!"

Within moments he and Rose had stepped on that froufrou porch, she holding his arm and he wielding the box of cinnamon buns that Molly Copeland—a popular baker in town—had pushed on them.

"You'd better watch out," Mrs. Copeland warned as she bade them goodbye from the doorway. "Those cinnamon buns have been responsible for more than one love-match here in Morrow Creek."

"Thank you, ma'am." Will tipped his hat. "I'll be wary."

"I'll be back for more tomorrow!" Rose promised.

Will glanced at her, recognizing her eager expression. It was the same one she wore when embarking on any new venture—drawing up labels for their elixir bottles, learning to juggle, or writing stories for the *Tillson Family Gazette*—the popular almanac they gave to customers as part of the medicine show.

He needed to quash these romantic notions of hers—and quickly. Especially if, as Will suspected, Rose meant those extra matchmaking cinnamon buns to be exclusively for *him*.

They walked down the path to the street, Rose chattering nineteen to the dozen about the committee's plans for the Gala. Will found it difficult to listen. It required most of his attention just to ignore the way her body moved in rhythm with his. Easily. Lithely. As though they were meant to be one.

Smiling, Rose snuggled closer. "My, you can certainly tell autumn is here, can't you? It's quite chilly tonight."

Will nodded. Her hair smelled nice. Like flowers. Or maybe that delicate scent came from her skin. Curiously, he glanced at her profile, wondering if Rose smelled that good all over. Most likely she did. There was only one surefire way to find out….

"It was awfully kind of you to come collect me," she said.

"Mmm." He examined her plain wool coat and scarf. Rose had no business appearing so alluring in such utilitarian garb.

"All the ladies on the decorating committee were very welcoming. They absolutely *adore* Tillson & Healy's Patented Miracle Elixir & Celebrated Panacea—several of them are regular customers. And they didn't find it strange at all that I'd come along at the last minute. With only a few days until Hallowe'en I guess they need all the help they can get."

"I reckon so."

"Now I'll definitely feel at home at the Gala. I got an invitation, you see. All that's left is finding an escort."

"Mmm." Will couldn't manage to say more, especially since Rose's arm and hip rubbed convivially against his while they progressed from Morrow Creek's outer reaches to the road leading to their campsite. It wasn't a long walk, but he wasn't sure he'd survive it. Not chivalrously. Not when his entire right side felt aflame with heat, rigid with response to her softness.

"It's going to be quite a to-do. It's highly anticipated—"

"I've found a husband for you," Will blurted.

Rose stopped in her tracks. "A *what*?"

"He's a railroad man and a partner in the Morrow Creek bank. He's staying at the Lorndorff Hotel for now—"

"A *husband*, you said?" Appearing gobsmacked—doubtless thrilled that her dreams of hearth and home were so close at hand—Rose gawked at him. "A *husband*?"

"I'll introduce you. His name is Mr. Edmund Vance."

He was going to sweep Rose off her feet, make her fall instantly in love with him, and provide a good future for her. That way Will would know Rose was being properly cared for.

"I don't care what his name is." Rose pulled away from him. "I don't want a husband! At least not one who's—"

"The ladies at Miss Adelaide's say he's very generous."

"Will!" Her mouth fell open. "You went to a *brothel*?"

"Only to make inquiries. I had to be sure." Will didn't see what she objected to. His actions had been in her best interests, and perfectly reasonable, too. "The men at Jack Murphy's saloon say Mr. Vance's reputation is beyond reproach. He doesn't owe money, doesn't imbibe to excess and he never misses the spittoon."

"If that's your notion of sweetening the deal—"

"When you meet Mr. Vance tomorrow—"

"Tomorrow?"

"—you'll see what I mean." Determinedly, Will guided Rose past a dip in the road. "He's ideal for you."

Rose shook her head. "I won't do it."

"Yes, you will."

"No, I won't."

"You will."

"I won't."

"It's all arranged," Will said firmly. "You'll meet him."

"I will not," Rose said, equally firmly.

They reached the campsite, parted ways, then went about their evening chores. They did not discuss the matter any further. He, Will realized, with less liking than he'd expected, had properly won the battle. Rose was to have a husband.

A husband who was decidedly *not* him.

It was too late to meander to the creekside for another consultation with Mrs. Brown, Rose knew. She would have to tackle this latest development on her own. But she couldn't reason out why Will—especially after having learned of her affection for him—would shove her toward another man. The notion was daft.

Time was wasting, too. She'd seen her papa and met the Lundbergs while in town. Viola's and Henry's wedding plans were proceeding apace. When they were concluded, the medicine show would most probably move on, leaving behind her sister and Will alike.

If Rose hoped to avoid losing him forever, she'd have to secure his love, and quickly, too.

Hoping to do exactly that, she followed Will to the fire he'd laid. She held out her palms to the crackling heat, then chanced a quick look at him. He appeared as wonderful as ever.

The matchmaking chowderhead.

"So…how did you meet Mr. Vance?" she asked.

"I haven't yet." Will laid another log. "But I asked all over town to ensure his reputation. I'm not doing this lightly."

"No. I can see you're not." She also could see that his back and shoulders were magnificently broad, even covered in his coat and many warm layers. "That's what intrigues me so."

That and the maneuverings of his gloved hands as Will stoked the fire, which soon climbed high enough to illuminate his raw-boned face and his expression of resolve. Any minute now he'd retreat to his faraway camping place for the night. It was what Will did every evening.

Unless she found a creative way to waylay him….

"And that's why I've decided that I *will* meet Mr. Vance."

Plainly taken aback, Will glanced her way. Rose's gaze fell on his mouth. Dreamily remembering their kiss, she faltered.

"If," she made herself continue, "you agree to come, too."

"Of course I'll be there."

Startled by his acquiescence, Rose said, "That was easy."

"I'm not an ogre." Frowning, Will poked in another log. He sat beside her, resting his forearms on his thighs. "It's important to me that you're cared for, Rose."

She scoffed. "By another man? But I only care about—"

"Your father asked me to watch over everything, including you. This is an extension of that obligation."

Lovely. Now she was a mere duty to him. That would not do. Purposefully, Rose scooted closer. "I'll meet Mr. Vance if you agree to attend the Hallowe'en Gala with me."

"Rose," he began warningly, "you know I—"

"Fine." She stood, brushing off her skirts. "Good night."

She tromped all the way to the edge of the fire's glow before Will's husky voice followed her. "Wait," he said.

Rose paused, but did not turn around.

"You'll want someone else. Later. If so, I'll step aside."

"Is that a yes?" Rose fairly purred. "You'll go with me?"

A grudging assent, thrilling and deep, met her ears.

Goodness. This was working splendidly. Feeling elated, Rose turned. "*And* I'll meet Mr. Vance," she said experimentally, "if you agree to wear your blue necktie for the Hallowe'en Gala."

Will made a fearsome face. "You're enjoying this."

"Maybe a little. Well…?"

"Done. It's the one that matches your eyes anyway."

She raised her eyebrows at him.

He cleared his throat and pulled down his hat.

Very interesting. Will had noticed the color of her eyes. "*And* I'll meet Mr. Vance if you agree to forgo your campsite and sleep in the other medicine show wagon tonight."

With a rising sense of anticipation Rose held her breath. She darted a glance at the wagons, standing snugly side by side. When she looked his way again, Will only gazed back at her. The firelight and the moonglow lent a dangerous edge to his face.

Rose balked, feeling her new boldness waver. Who was she to make such demands? She was Castor Oil Rose—invisible to most, but reliable to all. "Er…just in case something needs repairs."

A moment passed. Will rose, a mysterious triumph evident in his smile. "I'll sleep wherever I like." He lifted his bedroll, then saluted her with his hat. "Good night, Rose. Mind the fire. It'll likely burn for some time to come."

He did not know the half of it, Rose thought as she watched Will stroll into the darkness. Because, given the fiery way he'd looked at her when she'd invited him to sleep nearby, the feelings between them were likely to smolder for some time longer…no matter how many denials or beaux he pushed her way.

Just past dawn, Rose awakened to the sound of meowing. Then, quite abruptly, it stopped.

Muzzy-headed and blinking, she stilled beneath her bed-clothes. The horses shifted nearby. A tree branch tapped on the wagon wall. But her ghost cat had stopped crying.

As quietly as she could, Rose dressed. She grabbed a hook, fastened all her myriad shoe buttons, then pulled on her shawl.

Outside, a low-lying mist hung above the ground like a fallen cloud, lending the campsite an ethereal air. A squirrel dashed past, gathering the puny acorns produced by the oak trees that grew here in the northern part of the territory. Rose's breath puffed white as she rounded the rear edge of the wagon, alert for another eerie meow. Will would think she was being silly, but she felt intrigued by the otherworldly feline. If it could be real, almost anything could happen…couldn't it?

After all, it was only two more days till Hallowe'en.

An orange dried leaf scuttled across her path. At the same time a new sound wafted toward her. Stealthily, Rose moved in its direction, intent on finding her ghost cat. If she found proof of the wraithlike thing, she could tell Will, and then—

Purring. The sound she'd heard was purring. And the reason she'd heard it, Rose saw as she padded closer, was because her ghost cat—a black ghost *kitten,* really—was curled up nearby, sleeping soundly atop the chest of an equally slumbering Will.

Astonished, Rose stared. Will lay sprawled in his bedroll, his dark hair tousled and his head free of his omnipresent hat. With his head naked, his eyes closed and his beautiful mouth open just slightly, he seemed unusually vulnerable. Rose wanted to kneel beside him, to hug him…to protect him.

But from what? The kitten? Even if it *was* a ghost cat—and Rose still believed it was—it seemed harmless enough. The poor creature had obviously come to haunt Will, armed with its phantom meowing and tiny vanishing paw prints, but had been lulled into curling up to sleep on his warm, brawny chest instead.

No wonder that cat was purring. Rose would have been, too.

And with Will *here,* only steps away from the wagon where Rose had dozed unaware all night…well, the implications were considerable. He'd clearly been loath to leave her. His pining was unexpected, but very sweet. Will might seem rugged and devil-may-care, Rose thought, but when it came down to true love—

He opened one eye, caught her gawking and swore.

"Oh! Wait," Rose said. "Careful not to scare the—"

The kitten jumped off his chest and fled.

Seeing it leap, Will gave a muffled squawk of surprise. He waved his arms, then glared after the creature with a baleful expression. He sat up, hat in hand. Awake, he appeared twice as formidable—and three times as likely to do just about anything.

"As I thought." Rose pointed with satisfaction, giving up her search as the kitten faded into the ghostly morning mist. "Did you see that? The paw prints *disappeared.*"

"That cat is not a ghost."

"Oh, no? Then how do you explain the lack of paw prints?"

Will only jammed on his hat, then swiveled to snatch his boots. Yawning, he dragged them on. Rose found it uniquely intriguing to glimpse his big feet in their gray knitted socks, toes wiggling to find an entryway into those boots. Usually Will slept too far from the family's campsite for her to see such intimacies.

"So…" Back to the matter at hand. Gleefully, she rose on tiptoes, feeling a smug grin alight on her cheeks. "You decided to sleep next to me all night after all? And I never even guessed a thing. That's terribly charming of you, Will."

He only grunted, standing to gather his bedroll.

"And in all your clothes, too. But that seems awfully uncomfortable to me. If you moved into Papa's wagon instead, you'd be more at ease. For a man who's so pragmatic, you're—"

"Enough." Will raised his palm. When he glanced at her, his frown deepened. "Quit looking at me that way, too."

"What way?"

"As if *I* made the sun rise this morning."

Rose considered him. He'd collected his toothbrush and straight razor, and if she didn't miss her guess, he was looking at *her* quite sappily himself. Glory be! It looked as if she'd never again be invisible to Will Gavigan.

"I'll make you a deal." Smiling, Rose wrapped her scarf more securely. "I'll quit looking at you 'that way—'"

"No more deals. I had all the deals I want last night."

"If you can resist sleeping next to me again."

Frowning mightily, Will glanced at the incriminating spot where he'd laid his bedroll last night. He pulled down his hat. "I only did that to protect you. I needed to stay nearby."

"Needed to…because you're secretly smitten. Admit it."

He grinned. "If I were smitten, darlin', you'd know it."

Will's rakish smile made Rose feel all aflutter. His use of that endearment didn't settle her heart palpitations any, either.

Darlin'. She wanted to hear him say it all day. All night. In between meals, during decorating committee meetings—which he'd promised to attend with her—and while holding her hand.

You'll know you're close when he denies his feelings, she remembered Mrs. Brown telling her. *Then you must back away.*

On the heels of such excellent advice Rose could do nothing except follow it—no matter how difficult it felt to leave the warm circle of Will's regard. But she did it.

"Good." Rose smiled back at him. "Then you won't mind watching me fall head over skirts for dear Mr. Vance today?"

Will's smile turned crystalline. "Not at all."

"Most women dream of meeting a well-to-do businessman like the wonderful Mr. Vance. You're a darling to arrange it, Will."

"My—" he gave a pained pause "—pleasure."

"Excellent." All of a sudden Rose's heart felt exceedingly light. "I'll just go get ready. It won't do to go to town in this old dress—everyone's quite fashionable, and I'll want to look my best for my future beloved. This is so exciting!"

"Yes. Exciting," Will echoed. He stood with his toothbrush and razor in his hardfisted grasp, his mouth pulled down as he contemplated Rose's meeting with her new beau. "Very exciting."

"Off I go!" Rose lifted her skirts and moved away.

Only a few moments passed before he said, "Rose—wait."

Her heart thundering, she stopped. She turned. Will's forlorn, perplexed expression almost made her resolve falter.

But she couldn't waver. This was far too important.

Instead she lifted her chin. "Yes, Will? What is it?"

From beneath his lowered brows he gave her a somber look. "If this Vance is not to your liking, tug on your ear. Like this." Roughly, he demonstrated. "I'll find a way to extricate you from your meeting with him."

"Ooh! A secret signal. How very clandestine of you."

"I'm serious. Rose, this is important."

It *was* important. Because loving Will meant the world to her. And Rose had no intention of letting herself get carried away with Mr. Vance—no matter how successful or well-thought-of he might be. The man for her was Will. Period.

But according to Mrs. Brown it was better that she not dwell on that fact with Will. So Rose silently thanked her friend for her wise counsel…then brazenly strode over to Will.

"Dearest Will." She patted his cheek, thrilling at the rough texture of his beard stubble beneath her palm. Unable to resist, she stroked her thumb over his cheekbone, then affected a sorrowful expression. "Would you promise me something?"

Squinting, Will nodded—doubtless expecting her to request another secret signal. He was considerate and intelligent. He planned for everything. But Rose had more than a signal in mind…especially after Will covered her hand with his.

The gesture was probably a prelude to making her release him. He'd been adamant about trying to keep his distance.

But now, with their hands cradled together, Will moved even closer. He'd obviously forgotten to be quite so straitlaced today.

He squeezed her fingers, and his warmth and strength touched her in a way it never had before.

"Er…" Feeling quivery, Rose breathed in deeply. She gazed into his lovely dark eyes, on the verge of getting lost in them. "This is actually more difficult than I'd expected…"

He rubbed her fingers. "Go on. What is it, Rose?"

Another deep breath. "Well…try not to miss me too much when I'm married and gone. I'd hate to have to worry about you."

He stared at her, flabbergasted. With great determination, Rose lowered her hand, just as she'd planned to do through Mrs. Brown's tutelage. Missing Will's touch was a powerful ache, but somehow she managed to stride away all the same…ready to meet her future, if not her intended husband.

Will had never before felt an interest—secretly or fleetingly—in a woman's earlobes. Today, though, seated in the Lorndorff Hotel dining room, with a windbag on one side and Rose on the other, he felt keenly absorbed in Rose's earlobes.

Go ahead. Tug, he instructed her silently. *Just one tiny pull.* But rather than offer the stealthy signal they'd agreed upon to end this shambles of an afternoon tea meeting, Rose simply sat with her hands folded in her lap. With big blue awed eyes, she gazed at Edmund Vance as he blustered on about a recent railway deal, not moving an inch toward her earlobe.

Most likely she was being balky just to provoke him, Will decided. He couldn't blame her. He had been forceful about finding her a suitable husband, and Rose was independent-minded enough to be bothered by that. He admired her grit, if not her enthusiasm for town living. But he could not believe she truly enjoyed listening to Edmund Vance prattle on about coal and cabooses and newfangled engines.

Still, Will could not quit. Even if it killed him.

This was for Rose's own good. For the sake of her future.

He had to admit she did seem perfectly at ease as she chattered on with Vance, her ladylike, attentive smile in place. Her hands were similarly delicate as they—

As they *moved*. Will froze, watching for the signal—the signal that would mean they could leave this charade behind.

With the merest glance at him, Rose raised her hand. While nodding at something Vance droned on about, she scratched her chin. Smiling vaguely, she folded her hands in her lap again.

Clenching his jaw, Will stared daggers at Vance. He couldn't see what Rose found so fascinating about the man. Yes, Edmund Vance was prominent, affluent and respectable. Certainly he was capable of providing a good home, reasonable affection and the place in Morrow Creek society that Rose so coveted.

But the man never quit jawing. He grinned like a loon, too. Will would have liked to leave him to his fancy imported tea and pull foot for someplace a touch less pretentious—where a man could feel the wind on his face and the soil beneath his feet.

Speaking of feet… Rose had kicked one of hers at Will.

Frowning, he ignored the sting in his shin in favor of imagining a scenario where the dining room's opulent rug came to life, picked up Vance and carried him away forever.

Another distinct kick. Will started, surprised to find his hand on his own earlobe. He smiled as his reverie ended.

"What's so funny?" Rose asked in a harsh whisper.

Will couldn't explain. Instead he glanced at Rose's hand, hoping for movement. It was nowhere near her ear. *Damnation.*

That was what he deserved, he knew. Because for the first time in all the years he'd known her he'd deceived Rose.

If I were smitten, darlin', you'd know it.

He'd said it, but it had been a lie.

Even as Rose cast her moony glances his way, Will found himself returning those spoony looks more every day…and he didn't know how to stop. He *was* smitten. Truth be told, his affection for Rose felt nigh unstoppable.

Firmly, Rose kicked him again. She cleared her throat.

"…splendid and varied pleasures of fashioning a glorious new community and watching it grow," Vance was saying in his highbrow tone. "Wouldn't you agree, Mr. Gavigan?"

In unison, Vance and Rose raised their eyebrows at him, waiting for his answer in perfectly well-mannered harmony.

That gesture, more than anything, made it clear to Will that he had vastly overestimated his capacities as a matchmaker.

"It's time we headed to the Lundbergs' to meet Dr. Tillson." He stood and tossed down his napkin. "Come on, Rose."

She looked up at him. "We're going to see my father? Now?"

It had just occurred to Will, but… "Yes. Yes, we are."

"Well. I can't argue with that, can I?" Rose turned her attention to Vance—her bright, blushing, overall maddening attention. She leaned nearer to the man, then gave a pretty, girlish pout. "I'm terribly sorry, Mr. Vance. I've had a wonderful time, but we simply must dash."

"Of course, Miss Tillson. Family does come first!"

Even the man's consideration was galling. Pushed to the limit by Vance and his citified ways, Will offered the man a bone-crushing handshake. He took Rose's elbow. "Let's hurry."

Upon her startled agreement, they left behind a perplexed-looking Vance. To Will's satisfaction they dashed through the tables of diners and travelers without looking back…until they reached the dining room's entryway. There, Rose paused.

She arrowed her gaze to the man Will had so unfortunately pinned as her future husband. "Goodbye! I'll see you soon!"

Vance waved. Rose simpered. Will rolled his eyes.

He could not remember how he'd gotten himself in such a fix. All he knew was that he was not at all himself these days…and that didn't seem likely to change anytime soon.

Chapter Four

That night Will moved into the second medicine show wagon. Strictly as a temporary measure, of course. He could not shake the feeling that he needed to stay at Rose's side—nor could he resist lingering near her while she prepared dinner, moving about the campfire with purpose and verve.

"Here." She shoved the evening meal at him. "Enjoy."

"The food is still in the skillet." Warily, Will eyed the steak and beans as they sizzled away. "How am I supposed to—?"

"I wrapped the cast-iron in a flannel cloth. Take it."

He lifted his gaze to her face. "Are you still upset?"

"Upset?" Rose slammed the skillet on its bed of firestones. "Why would I be upset? Tell me, Will. *Why?*"

Hands on hips, she glared at him. He'd thought they'd left this argument behind them already, on the road from Morrow Creek to their campsite. Clearly they had not. Evidently his earlier apology had not been enough. He would have to come up with more.

Lowering his brows in thought, Will opened the lid of the nearby Dutch oven. With speedy fingers he plucked out a hot biscuit. It was nearly blackened, but it would have to do.

"Don't bother trying to sweet-talk me, either," Rose went on. "You gulled me into leaving a perfectly sociable teatime with Mr.

Vance just so you could drag me to a farmer's cart. *Not*, as I might point out, straight to the Lundbergs', as you said, but to a farmer's cart in the middle of Morrow Creek Square."

Will glanced at the bag of items he'd bought at that farmer's cart, then went back to buttering the biscuit. He added jam, put the whole caboodle on a tin plate, then held it out to Rose. "Here. For you. It's blackberry jam—your favorite."

The treat didn't sweeten her disposition a whit.

Possibly because she didn't take it.

"Was my father visiting Viola at a *farmer's cart*, Will?"

He shrugged. He still didn't know what had gotten into him this afternoon. All he'd felt was an unswerving urge to get away from Edmund Vance—and especially from Rose's evident appreciation of the man. So he'd dragged them from the hotel, then detoured to the farmer's cart when an alternate plan had struck him.

That plan had yet to unfold, but it would soon.

He waggled the biscuit plate. "It's *well browned*. Mmm."

Huffily, Rose accepted the biscuit. She bit into it, then caught a dribble of jam at the corner of her mouth with her tongue…much to Will's fascination. Moodily, she chewed. "This does not mean that I forgive you. Not by a long shot."

"Of course not."

"Not for *pretending* we had a meeting with my father—"

"We *did* see him," Will pointed out. "And Viola, too. Eventually we did meet Henry and the Lundbergs at their home to discuss wedding plans."

"—and not for prematurely ending my tea with Mr. Vance—"

Will scowled. "The man has a face like a weasel."

"—and most *definitely* not for squashing that poor, dear man's hand when we said goodbye. You know you're bigger and stronger than Mr. Vance. You're a positive brute, Will."

Sorrowfully, Will nodded. "Sometimes."

"I'm glad you agree." Rose lifted her chin. She swallowed another bite of biscuit, then glanced shyly at him. "Did I—?"

She broke off. Concerned by her suddenly woeful tone, Will sat beside her. He ignored the skillet in the fire, the undoubtedly ruined steak, the sudden yen he felt to pull Rose in his arms and kiss her senseless.

Rose's gaze met his. "Did I behave all right today? At the tea with Mr. Vance? Because I'm not altogether accustomed to being in polite society." She rushed onward. "And sometimes I feel quite awkward in mixed company. I hope—"

"You were perfect."

Doubtfully, she set down her biscuit. "But I—"

"Perfect."

"Will, you're not listening to me. I felt very ill at ease today." Rose twisted a bit of her woolen skirt in her fingers, not looking at him. "It was *so* important to me that I handled things correctly today. I can't tell you why, but it was."

Will already knew why. He was sure of it.

He was sure that Rose wanted to leave the medicine show life…but was too stubborn to admit it.

He shook his head. "I know why it was important to you."

"You can't possibly know." Rose lifted her gaze to his, her expression predictably mulish but uncommonly vulnerable. "I've been so very clever about hiding it. That's why all I want to know now is…was I impressive today? Did I impress—?"

"Vance was fit to wed you on the spot. You saw it, too."

"Did I impress you?"

Surprised, Will stared at her. Then he nodded. "Yes."

"Good." She gave a relieved sigh. "Because I wanted—"

"Yes," he said again, and took her chin in his hand. He turned her face to his, marveling at the fineness of her features, the beauty of her skin…the trust in her eyes. "You were magnificent, Rose. You *are* magnificent. I don't know why it's taken me so long to realize it."

"Probably mere logistics," she piped up. "Because I—"

He couldn't help but grin. "No more talking now."

"But how else will I—?"

"Close your eyes," Will said, and kissed her.

The first touch of their lips was like steering the wagons over a hillside, unable to see what was coming next. The second was like realizing only green fields and smooth roads lay ahead. And the third…the third was insensible to Will.

Caught up in their deepening union, he could no longer think. All he could do was pull Rose nearer, nudge her lips apart, take possession of her mouth the way he'd yearned to do for so long. Maybe, he thought in dazzled confusion, he had always wanted Rose…had kept himself apart from her through strength of will alone. Looking at her now, as they finally parted, he could scarcely believe he'd managed it.

But what if, after having her, he could not let her go?

He would have to. Her happiness depended on it.

Eyes luminous, Rose lifted her fingertips to her mouth. "You," she said, "are *much* better at kissing than I am."

He looked away. "That's because you inspire me."

"Oh, Will!" She waved her hand. "You're joking with me."

"It's the truth. You're fine and good, Rose. And you look beyond pretty with your hair like that." He captured a stray tendril and let it curl around his thumb. "Whereas *I*—well, I truly am the scoundrel your father feared would sweep you away."

"My father?" Laughing, Rose shook her head. "If any man is good enough for me as far as Papa is concerned, it's you. He thinks the world of you, Will. You know that."

"You love me because you think your father would approve?" The notion made sense. "I'm usually the only man you see for miles, so I don't know who else you would choose, but—"

"Pish-posh. I adore you because you cut a fine figure in a suit coat. And now because you are marvelously romantic."

"I see." Gruffly, Will adjusted his hat. He swept it in his hands, then turned it by the brim. He examined his boots. He counted the buttons on his coat. But nothing he did could extinguish the growing warmth that sparked in his chest. It felt like hope. Or love. Or maybe just embarrassment. But, whatever it was, Will found it powerfully uncomfortable.

"Mostly I think you're wonderful," Rose continued. "You're kind and strong and brave, and impressively good at driving."

Taking full advantage of his nearness, she hugged his elbow as she chatted, probably unaware that the motion pressed her bosoms fully against Will's arm. He could think of little else.

"Nobody has to worry about a thing when you're around, Will. You're entirely capable, very loyal and—"

"And a scoundrel." Making an unhappy face, he set aside his hat. He clasped his hands at his knees. "Don't forget that."

Rose shook her head. "You're a good man."

"A good man would not be thinking of kissing you again."

"Perhaps." Rose's mouth turned up in an adorable and mischievous smile. "But a scoundrel would already be doing it."

Caught, Will stood. He fully intended to get away—to leave Rose behind for the night and see if a few hours spent alone on the cold, hard ground would restore his sense of reason.

Instead, she smiled up at him…and he fell to his knees before her. With a hoarse cry he wrapped his arms around her, engulfed in her nearness, swamped with affection, everything inside him demanding that he make her his—at least for now.

He flexed his arm and cradled the nape of her neck in his spread fingers—firmly, possessively, needfully. When he lowered his mouth to meet hers, Will couldn't help moaning with delight.

To his satisfaction, Rose moaned, too.

This was what he wanted, Will knew, as he lost himself in their kiss. This was what he needed. In a world without Rose his days would look dark, his nights lonely. More than ever he needed to stave off that lonesome future. For just a little while longer he needed to be with her.

"Oh, Will!" Gasping, Rose broke away. Her gaze met his, dark and radiant. "I dreamed, but I never knew you could be so—"

"Kiss me." He delved both hands in her hair to hold her to him. "Don't stop. I need you, Rose."

"I won't stop. I'm here. I'll never let you go."

She spoke the truth, but Will hated to admit it. Rose never would let him go. That was why he had to set her behind him. But with Rose warm in his arms, and the autumn sun slanting down on both of them, Will shut his mind to the truth. Instead he kissed her again, more deeply, and felt his heart truly expand.

"I so admire you, Will." Joyfully, Rose pressed a kiss to his head, his temple, his cheekbone. With more enthusiasm than skill she brought both hands to his face and cradled it in her palms. "I'm glad you've realized the truth about us."

Still aching with wanting, Will drew in a breath. He forced himself to stop touching her…before it was too late.

"I knew you would, too! I knew that if I persisted, I'd be rewarded with your love sooner or later. And now—"

Will gazed into Rose's lively face and saw the affection there, as plain as the flames in the fire beside them. Drawing in another breath, he set himself apart from her.

"Now you've finally come to realize what's truly between us." She smiled and kissed his nose, then laughed. "It's a Hallowe'en marvel, just for us. Maybe that's why your ghost cat—"

Roughly, Will stood. "It's not a ghost cat."

"I really believe it is…" Rose broke off, head canted to the side. "Do you smell that? Tobacco and whiskey in the breeze, as clear as your sizzling steak?"

"No." Already missing her, Will bundled his coat around himself. "I can't stay here. I'll be back late tonight."

"What?" Snapped to attention, as though just now realizing he'd stepped apart from her, Rose examined the distance between them. "Where are you going? You haven't even had your dinner."

"You take it." His hands felt empty. "I'm going to town."

She laughed. "You can't get a decent meal there!"

"I—" *I'm not hungry.* That was what Will meant to say. But

he'd never felt more starved in his life—desperate for a fullness he couldn't allow himself to have. "I have business to attend to. I've already delayed it for too long." He put on his hat, striving for a formality he didn't feel. "Good night. Sleep well."

"Wait." With confusion writ on her face, Rose stood. She gave an uncertain laugh. "At least let me kiss you goodbye."

Will nodded. He stood stoically as Rose came near, as she flattened her palms on his chest and brought her mouth to his. Her kiss was sweet and perfect. Far too good for the likes of him—a man who couldn't be with her but who had let her believe he might be. *Damnation.* He should go to hell for this.

But a traveling man needed freedom more than love, Will assured himself as Rose lowered to stand before him. He needed the open road. He couldn't allow Rose to fool herself into coming on that road with him. She'd only be miserable there. Especially now that she'd made so many friends among the decorating committee members in Morrow Creek.

"Don't worry." Mustering a grin for her sake, Will gave Rose a saucy squeeze. Despite everything, he took a manly delight in her squeal of pleasure. "I'll make sure everything comes right for you in the end, Rose. I promise I will."

Blushing, Rose buttoned his coat. "I can hardly wait."

Looking at her hopeful face, Will could postpone matters no longer. He pulled down his hat. Then, with no more promises to give, he headed toward Morrow Creek, set on making the arrangements that would determine their futures for certain.

Feeling buoyant, Rose hurried to the banks of Morrow Creek, a lantern swinging in her hand against the fading daylight. The fallen leaves seemed to have multiplied over the past few days. They piled on rocks and mossy ground with equal abandon, leaving the naked tree branches to reach toward the sky.

She shivered as she passed a gnarled oak, her thoughts turning to the upcoming Hallowe'en Gala. When she and Viola had been younger, their papa had always found a way to bring them to a nearby town for the festivities. Although he'd never allowed them to carve a jack-o'-lantern—deeming the practice a sinful waste of perfectly good turnips or squash—Papa had always done his best to make sure Rose and Viola could bob for apples or play Hallowe'en divination games to their hearts' content.

Maybe that was why Rose had a particular appreciation for the magic of All Hallows' Eve. Any day that could make Papa stop the medicine show for pure recreation was a singular day indeed. This year the special events had already begun—initiated by Will's new notice of her and sealed with his latest kiss.

"Mrs. Brown?" Bending to duck beneath a pine branch, Rose lifted her lantern. It was darker here near the creek, where the trees grew more thickly. "Are you here?"

To her disappointment, Rose heard nothing save the usual sounds of flowing creek water and animals scurrying through the underbrush. Even the breeze had stilled this evening.

"Mrs. Brown?" She peered again, and caught a glimmer of movement. For an instant uncertainty gripped her. Then Rose identified her friend's towering ostrich-feather hat. "Hello!"

The woman stepped into the circle of Rose's lantern light. Again her fancy hairstyle was askew. Her gown was spotted with mud. And tonight her face appeared downright pallid, too.

Rose hurried toward her. "Mrs. Brown! Are you all right?"

"I'm fine, my dear." Her friend mustered a wan smile. "Just tired. It feels as though I've been fighting with these stepping stones forever. They simply won't let me cross the creek."

"Not while staying dry, at least. That much is certain." With a commiserating smile, Rose patted the flat rock where they usually sat to visit. "You certainly have a colorful way of putting things. Do you have time for some company, or must you rush off again? I have some wondrous news."

"You have news? Please, share!" Elegantly, Mrs. Brown sat.

Rose sat, too—a tad less elegantly. Without preamble—because she was too excited to wait—she said, "Will has gone to town."

Her friend raised her brow. "And…?"

"I believe he's gone to ask my father for my hand."

Rose could scarcely breathe she was so ecstatic. Her corset didn't help matters, either. When Will had been kissing her, she'd wriggled so much she'd feared she might pop a lace.

"Miss Tillson! That's wonderful." Mrs. Brown seemed almost as pleased as Rose herself felt. Then, alarmingly, she sobered. She wrung her hands. "Unless…"

Unwillingly alert, Rose frowned. "Unless what?"

"Unless Mr. Gavigan has only gone to gamble or to visit Miss Adelaide's." Mrs. Brown said this last with particular distaste. "Did he *say* he was asking for your hand?"

"Well…" Rose refused to consider those alternatives. "A woman doesn't *require* an announcement, does she? Especially when Will was so romantic. So formal. He distinctly spoke about my father, too. I do believe we have an…*understanding.*"

"I hope you're right. You have no idea how much I wish for your happiness." Mrs. Brown glanced at the surrounding trees, her expression inscrutable. When she turned to Rose again, it was with curious intent. "But I must know. Did Mr. Gavigan *say* outright he was asking your father's permission?"

Rose pulled her mouth downward. "Well, not precisely—"

"Then you mustn't let up on your strategy, Miss Tillson. Only a fool depends on a man to stay true to his word."

With a laugh, Rose hugged her knees. "Honestly, Mrs. Brown. You sound as though a gentleman has done you violently wrong."

Her friend merely brushed a spot of mud from her bodice.

Spooked by Mrs. Brown's eerie silence, Rose shivered. A few leaves rattled nearby. The wind picked up. Overall, the ambience had grown distinctly chilling—not at all what she'd hoped for when coming here to share her exhilarating news about Will.

"Well, thank you again for your advice, Mrs. Brown." Rose

stood, gathering her coat closer. She offered the most cheerful wave she could muster. "You've been very helpful, as usual."

Without waiting to hear yet another quelling remark, Rose said goodbye. But before she'd even reached the higher ground at the creek's edge her friend called out.

"Godspeed, Miss Tillson! Good luck with your Mr. Gavigan!"

Rose glanced back. Alone on the rock, Mrs. Brown waved, looking small and bereft.

On the point of asking her friend back to the medicine show campsite for a reviving cup of coffee, Rose saw Mrs. Brown shake her head. It was almost as if she'd sensed Rose's invitation and regretfully could not accept it. It was most peculiar.

"However, Miss Tillson," her friend called with evident fondness, "if you can think of a way for me to cross these blasted rocks unassailed, I'll be most indebted to you!"

Over breakfast the following morning Rose eyed Will happily. He wolfed through eggs, bacon and a big stack of flapjacks, eyes shining like a boy's as he savored the drizzle of precious maple syrup she'd splurged on for the occasion.

There was something endearing about his appetite—and about the mission Rose felt certain he'd embarked upon last night. So far Will had not mentioned his meeting with her father, but she felt sure he would say something soon.

In the meantime… "It's a good idea to eat heartily." Rose flipped another flapjack onto Will's plate, then added one to hers, as well. "With the Hallowe'en Gala scheduled for tomorrow, we're likely to be very busy doing committee work today."

"That and a few other things, as well." Will forked up another bite. He gave a moan of appreciation, then hugged his flat belly. "Ah, Rose. Your cooking has improved. I reckon you'll make some lucky man a superb wife someday."

He winked. Her middle somersaulted in response. The rascal. He was going to pretend he *hadn't* asked her papa for permission last night. But what if he hadn't…? For a moment Rose faltered. If Will did not return her love, she didn't know how she'd cope.

But then she rallied. He must be teasing her.

"Yes, I *will* make someone a wonderful wife." Blithely, she reached for the coffeepot. "Perhaps…Mr. Vance?"

At the mention of her potential fiancé Will seemed strangely wistful. But then he forced a fresh smile to his face.

"Mr. Vance is of no consequence. Not right now. I aim to make this day special for you, Rose, and I will."

"Special…how?"

"It's a surprise." Balancing his plate on his knee, Will took her hand. He gazed at their twined fingers, his shoulders hunched protectively near hers. "You once told me that today is all you have—"

Reminded of Mrs. Brown's sage advice on that matter, Rose smiled. That dear lady had been correct. Without her new friend Rose would never have had the strength to pursue Will so boldly—or the incentive to vanquish her formerly castor-oil-like disposition. Now it was gone for good.

"You were right, Rose. That's why I aim to make today a time you'll remember. Long after…everything."

At his doleful tone, Rose realized Will would not be dropping to one knee and romantically proposing beside the uncut bacon. At least not yet. Perhaps he'd changed his mind?

Perhaps he didn't love her the way she loved him?

No. He was simply thinking of other things. That was all.

"Now, Will. Buck up!" She squeezed his hand reassuringly in hers. "It won't be that bad at the decorating committee today. Draping orange and black cheesecloth and fashioning *papier-mâché* spiders won't be too daunting. Besides, all you'll be doing is toting buckets of apples and Indian corn, because you're the strongest of the group." Laughing, she elbowed his muscular arm.

He gave her a somber look. "I only want you to be happy."

"I will be!" Rose sneaked a glance at their joined hands. They fit together perfectly, as though they were meant to be linked. "I am right now, just like this. If I could stay this way forever, I'd be plumb tickled." Gazing into his face, she drew a fortifying breath. "So…is there anything else?"

"Like what?"

"Anything…*else*…you wanted to ask me?"

Rose waited, gripping his hand with outlandish force.

Will frowned. "Nope." Then he stood and gathered the tinware and cutlery, seeming decidedly absorbed in the task.

Shaking her head, Rose watched as he marched off toward the creek, intent on doing her the favor of washing the dishes.

The man was a mystery, to be sure. And so were his feelings for her—at least for now. But not for long….

Chapter Five

Marching through Morrow Creek to the final Hallowe'en Gala decorating committee meeting, Rose reveled in the cosseted feeling of having Will as her escort. With one strong arm he guided her past potholes and muddy spots. With the other he carried a canvas sack bulging with…something.

She glanced at Will's sturdy profile. "What's in the sack?"

"Part of the surprise I mentioned." Smiling, he helped her navigate to the boardwalk, then cross the street. He tipped his hat at a pair of passing ladies. "It's for you."

"For me? Really?" Pleased, Rose inspected the sack with new interest. It was filled fit to bursting, but she still couldn't guess what lumpy secret it contained. "What is it, then?"

"I'm not so easy as all that." Will's smile broadened. "If you want to gull me, you'll have to be a much faster talker."

"Whatisitthen?" Rose asked breathlessly.

Chuckling, Will pulled her closer. He planted a kiss on her forehead, right there in front of the Morrow Creek residents and everyone. He gazed into her eyes. "I'm going to miss you, Rose. No one else can make me laugh the same way you do."

Galvanized, Rose stopped. *"Miss me?"*

"After I've left the medicine show."

He gave her another smile—somewhat forced, but charming all the same. Rose realized this must be more of his teasing.

"Ah, yes. You're leaving." She offered a wink, identical to the one he'd given her earlier. After all, he'd begun this game between them by pretending he hadn't visited her father last night. She could play along. "And I'm staying here. You'll have to promise not to belabor our goodbyes when they come, Will. I don't want any sadness between us, you know."

With a jerky nod, he walked silently onward.

Puzzled, Rose followed him. She sighed. "It will be nice to be settled down close to Viola. And dear Mr. Vance, too, of course. Perhaps a few other beaux, as well." With a sham innocent look, she adjusted her hat. "Which reminds me—do you suppose you could rustle up a respectable lawyer for me? Or a newspaperman? I find I have a weakness for the professional type. Since you performed so splendidly in finding Mr. Vance, I thought—"

"I will not help you meet other men." A muscle in Will's cheek flexed. "One suitor at a time is enough."

"But a lady likes to have a choice in these matters." Holding back a grin, Rose batted her eyelashes. "Please, Will."

He stopped, his face unexpectedly stormy beneath his hat brim. He looked away. "Who were you meeting with last night?"

Startled, Rose stopped, too. "Last night?"

"At the creekside. I circled back to pay Toby for watching the horses and heard you talking. I saw someone with you, but only for a minute. The next they were gone. Who was it?"

"Why, Will." She studied him. "You're positively *glowering!*"

"The hell I am." With evident difficulty, he turned his gaze to her face. He scrubbed his palm over his beard stubble, as though trying to regain his composure. "It's not the first time I've seen you talking with someone at dusk. Was it Vance?"

"Will—" Perhaps this game of theirs had gone too far. Sympathetically, Rose touched his arm. "It's not—"

"Because if you'd *prefer* a weasely windbag for a husband, I'm not likely to track down a better candidate for you."

She couldn't stifle a smile. "But, Will, the weasely windbag is the last word in husbandly candidates this year. *Godey's* said so. And if *Godey's* says it, ladies everywhere believe it."

"Humph." He took her hand and tugged her past the offices of the *Pioneer Press* newspaper. "We'd better hurry. Come on."

Never before had Rose glimpsed a man so eager for the company of ladies doing handicrafts and chitchatting about the relative size of bustles in the Paris fashion books. All the same, she permitted herself to be towed toward the meeting.

It was just as well she allowed Will this one minor indulgence. Because once she made him love her forever, there would be no turning back. True love was love for all time.

After all, Mrs. Brown had assured her it was so.

"Mr. Gavigan! I'm so glad you're back with us again today."

At the sound of that feminine voice, Will turned.

Sarah McCabe stood before him, dressed in a modest but feminine frock, looking every inch the schoolteacher-turned-organizer of this Hallowe'en Gala shenanigans.

Will tipped his hat. "It's my pleasure, Mrs. McCabe."

Her warm smile touched him. Despite her reputation as an adept planner, she seemed about as commanding as a baby duck. "Are you ready for the special duty you volunteered for?"

"Yes, ma'am." He felt oddly prompted to stand straight.

"Oh, good." She gestured. "May I take your bag?"

He surveyed his sack. Seeing it reminded him of how cavalier Rose had been about their impending separation. He'd never cursed her desire to stay in Morrow Creek more. At least she might have shown a little unhappiness. Instead she'd all but wallowed in her admiration of Edmund Vance. The weasel.

"No, thank you. I'm on my way to take this to Miss Tillson."

"All right." With a nod, Mrs. McCabe glanced at the table of handicrafters. "Rose has been a wonderful addition to our group. You'd never guess she's only just joined the community."

"Yes. She seems downright at home here."

"Morrow Creek affects some people that way." Mrs. McCabe aimed a speculative glance at him. "The new residents themselves often don't see it coming. This town's a wily suitor."

"I've never known a schoolmarm to be so fanciful."

She laughed. "My husband Daniel says the same thing. Perhaps I *am* a bit caught up in the Hallowe'en spirit. But when I see the effect this holiday is having on people like Rose—"

At that moment Rose unfurled a showy crepe-paper banner.

"It does my heart good."

Will wished he could say the same. But right now his heart felt bound in a thousand knots, all of them keeping him from Rose.

A young boy approached Mrs. McCabe and tugged her sleeve. After a quick consultation, she straightened to face Will again.

"I'm sorry. I have to sort out an emergency with the children's craft table. Good luck with Rose, Mr. Gavigan!"

With her mysterious smile broadening, Mrs. McCabe bade him goodbye, then headed for another task. Left alone, Will caught snatches of conversation, gales of feminine laughter…and a curious glance from Rose. Instantly he veered toward her.

All the ladies she was with—Mrs. Copeland and Mrs. Murphy, plus Fiona Crabtree and another woman Will didn't recognize— fell silent as he neared. The quintet offered him perceptive grins— almost as though they expected something *specific* of him.

Awkwardly, Will swept off his hat. "It's time, Rose."

"Time for what, Mr. Gavigan?"

"For this." Reaching in his sack, Will withdrew a tremendous orange pumpkin. He set it on the table in front of Rose. "I volunteered us both for the jack-o'-lantern carving. I know no better person than you to do it with me."

"Oh." Rose touched the pumpkin, disappointment plain on her face. "I see. *That's* what you wanted."

At her disheartened reaction, Will felt gutted. "Unless you'd rather not," he amended roughly. "I could do it myself."

"No. No! I'm surprised, that's all." Visibly rallying, Rose gave his arm a gentle squeeze. "I wasn't expecting this."

Before Will could ask what she *had* expected, she rambled on with as much fluency as she'd displayed with Mr. Vance. "I've never carved a jack-o'-lantern, you see, so I—"

"There's always a first time. *You* should have a first time, Rose. I know you have a special fondness for Hallowe'en. I remember you and Viola pestering your father to let you carve jack-o'-lanterns every year. You always seemed sad when Dr. Tillson said no."

"So now *you're* going to say yes?" For a moment Rose seemed downright teary-eyed. "You're going to make sure I can carve a jack-o'-lantern at last? Oh, Will. That's so sweet. Truly it is."

She rose from her seat, on the verge of hugging him. Hoping to avoid a spectacle, Will reached for his bag again.

"I wasn't sure what would be best." He pulled out an apple, a butternut squash, a turnip and an acorn squash. "Opinions varied—" He broke off, ill at ease under the enthralled gazes of the female decorating committee members. "So I got you one of everything. Including this."

He extracted the final item, a gourd of indeterminate origin and impressive girth. Its weight made the table shudder. With one hand to her ruffled bodice, Rose thumped to her seat.

"My goodness!" Her gaze swept the array of harvest vegetables. "Will, I hardly know what to say."

"Say you'll make a jack-o'-lantern with me."

Her surprised gaze met his. "I never knew you were paying so much attention. You always kept apart from the family."

Will shrugged. "I guess you Tillsons got to me somehow." *Especially you,* he wanted to say—but not with an audience. He unwrapped the pair of stubby knives he'd stashed at the bottom of his sack, then held one out to Rose, handle first. "Here."

Rose smiled in wonder—but she did not accept the knife. As her indecision persisted Will became increasingly fearful that she would refuse to carve a jack-o'-lantern with him. He would be left standing there like a fool, with vegetables enough for six stews and a…a thing of possibly inedible nature.

He pointed to it. "The squaw who sold me that one says it's got magical powers if you carve it right." It couldn't hurt to ladle a little honey on the deal. Again he offered her the knife. "If anybody can make Hallowe'en magic, Rose, it's you."

"Awww," cooed the ladies gathered round the circle.

Ignoring them, Will only had eyes for Rose. To his chagrin, though, he felt his cheeks heat. It was damnably hot inside.

Rose tilted her face to his. "I could *never* say no to you."

Her statement seemed fraught with meaning, but Will couldn't reason out why. The moment Rose accepted the knife he searched for a chair. Three ladies leaped from theirs, offering him places near Rose. With husky thanks, Will accepted the closest seat, then grabbed the pumpkin. He buffed its vibrant surface with his sleeve. "Shall we start?"

"Oh, yes." Rose smiled. "But with this one, please."

Blushing, she pointed to the enormous gourd.

Will raised his eyebrows.

"I can use all the magic I can get," Rose explained.

Will nodded. He could use all the magic he could get, as well. Because he loved Rose…and he could no longer deny it.

If only he could believe they were meant to be. If only he could still his roving feet. If only Rose could quiet her yen to sleep amid falsefront buildings and train depots. If only none of those things mattered and love won out in the end.

But that kind of magic was harder to come by than *papier-mâché* spiders or knitting-yarn cobwebs. Will recognized that truth more than most. Whether Hallowe'en was approaching or not, he wasn't sure there was magic enough in the world to keep him and Rose together…but that didn't stop a man from wishing.

* * *

That night Rose persuaded Will to come even closer—all the way to the medicine show wagon she usually shared with Viola.

Of course she had to pretend a screeching fear of the tiny, meowing ghost kitten to do so. But, as Mrs. Brown herself might have said, all was fair in love—even a bit of subterfuge. So when Will appeared at the door of Rose's wagon—able-bodied and concerned about her shrieking—she didn't feel the least bit of worry over her minor deception.

"I just *know* that ghost cat is haunting our campsite!" Acting her role to the hilt, she hastened Will's entry into the enclosed wagon. "And tomorrow is All Hallows' Eve—the night its bewitching powers will be strongest!"

"Now, Rose." Will ducked his head and crossed the threshold, his greater weight making the vehicle sway, then settle. He frowned, placing his hat atop a crate of Tillson & Healy's Patented Miracle Elixir & Celebrated Panacea. "Exactly what do you think that little kitten is going to do to you?"

"I don't know." Rose widened her eyes. "That's the scary part, isn't it?" She dragged him closer. "Hold me, Will!"

She flung herself into his arms. Naturally he embraced her.

"That's better." Wearing an unabashedly content smile, Rose relaxed. Filled with affection, she laid her head on Will's shoulder. "I guess you'll just have to sleep here tonight."

Will stiffened. "I'd be tarred and feathered first."

"Don't worry. There's Viola's bunk right there." Rose nodded toward it. "Everything will be perfectly respectable."

"No. I promised your father—"

"To protect me. And that's exactly what you'll be doing. Protecting me from that terrifying apparition of a cat."

"No, Rose." He eyed the bunk and shook his head. "No."

"Yes, Will." Dreamily Rose lowered her gaze to his mouth. She recalled their first kiss…and envisioned the next. "Yes."

Without meaning to, she swayed. But she was safe in Will's

arms. In a gesture as romantic as any she'd experienced, he swept his fingers along her jaw and tilted her face upward.

Whatever he saw in her eyes, it made him groan. As though helpless against her, Will nodded. "I'll stay awhile." His eyes looked dark and intent. "I'll stay long enough to—"

If he meant to say anything more, it was lost beneath a glorious kiss. With both hands in her hair, Will held her to him. His mouth descended on hers again, making Rose cry out with everything that remained unsaid between them. *I love you,* she thought as she kissed him back. *I'll love you forever.*

Then with her next embrace, *Please love me, too. Please.*

Squeezing her eyes shut, Rose forgot everything except this moment…this man. Will was the only one she cared for. If he could not love her back—if he could not see, at the Hallowe'en Gala or before, how perfect they were for one another—well, she didn't know what she would do.

But she did know one thing for certain: no quantity of All Hallows' Eve magic would be enough to mend her broken heart.

Chapter Six

With butterflies in her stomach, and an elaborate hairstyle on her head, Rose waited on the front porch of the largest and fanciest two-story brick house in Morrow Creek. This was the site of the Hallowe'en Gala, and already the festivities appeared to be in full frolic. Chattering partygoers streamed past Rose to join those inside, and pumpkins and Hallowe'en decorations abounded on every inch of the pillared porch.

Behind her in the autumn night mist curled around the nearby trees, wrapping them in a ghostly fog. The moon soared overhead, bright enough to illuminate her very best gown, her gloves and her borrowed brocade wrap. Rose patted her skirts, hoping she looked nice. She'd slipped away from the medicine show campsite shortly after the noontime meal, hoping to get ready for the Gala in comfort, away from Will's curious gaze.

In the end she'd successfully bartered a bottle of Tillson & Healy's Patented Miracle Elixir & Celebrated Panacea for the additional fripperies she wore tonight, giving the remedy to a garrulously grateful Mrs. Lundberg—Henry's mother—who was one of the kindest ladies Rose had ever met. It was no wonder Viola felt keen to join the Lundberg family.

"Well, don't just stand there with your mouth hanging open

like a flounder, Rose." Viola skipped up the steps and good-naturedly poked her shoulder. "I'm missing all the fun. Henry's promised to play divination games with me all night!"

The man beside her—gangly, earnest and bespectacled—gave a nod. "That's right. Would you like me to escort you inside, too?"

Stymied, Rose looked around the lamplit porch. She had not envisioned this problem, having never attended a gala before.

"It's all right, you know," Henry urged. "I don't mind. I'll have the two loveliest ladies in all of Morrow Creek to—"

"That won't be necessary," Will said.

He stepped from the mist like a phantom gentleman, tall and handsome in his finest suit. His coat fell open as he strode to meet Rose, taking the porch steps two at a time.

His lips met her cheek, warming her. At the same time his bracing scent reached her—the fragrances of castile soap and leather. Swamped with excitement, Rose touched his arm.

"Will!" Her gaze swept over him, greedily taking in the details of his best boots, his trim midsection, his masculine shoulders. She stopped and smiled. "You wore your blue necktie."

"I promised I would. Whatever else, I'm a man of my word."

"I think you look very handsome."

They gazed at each other, their breath faintly visible in the cool evening. Invigorated from the tips of her shoes to the top of her head, Rose could not get enough.

Neither, it seemed, could Will. "I'll do. So long as I match up to you." He held her hand. "You look so beautiful."

His eyes, dark and intent, told the truth of his words. Rose felt her heart pound wildly. Tonight would be the night Will proposed. She just knew it. She could scarcely wait.

With trembling fingers, Will pinned a corsage of yellow Hallowe'en chrysanthemums to her collar. Rose touched them, feeling wholly smitten. She could not stop smiling.

"Thank you, Will. They're absolutely lovely."

"No lovelier than you."

"And no kinder or more thoughtful than you."

"Only because you encourage me."

An exasperated sigh came from behind them. Rose had told her sister about her new closeness with Will, but apparently their romance could not hold a candle to the impending party.

"Come on, Henry." Skirts swaying, Viola edged her way to the door. "These two could be here spooning all night."

Will's grin looked seductive. "Only if we're lucky."

He offered Rose his arm. With an equally besotted smile, she accepted his offer of an escort, then stepped into what she felt sure was to be the most wondrous night of all her life.

"Go boat, go!" Rose cheered.

With interest, she watched the walnut races—a Hallowe'en game in which partygoers fashioned boats of walnut shells with candle stubs in their centers. Once the boats were ready, players affixed their names on a slip of paper, then set them in a tub of water. If two boats glided together, their owners' futures would be linked; if they parted, disaster loomed.

"Veer left. Left!" Will shouted, his face alight in the glow of the tiny candles. "Damnation." He sagged. "Mine sank."

"Aww, don't fret." Taking his arm, Rose cheerfully moved them onward. "It's just a silly game. Let's try peeling a fortune-telling apple instead. That's bound to be better."

Squeezing past toe-tapping partygoers—a few of them in costume—she and Will passed Indian corn and orange cheese-cloth draperies. Jack-o'-lanterns glowed in the dim lighting, and spooky gray, spun-yarn cobwebs hung overhead. Rose didn't know whose house this was, but it was a fine place for a party. By all accounts the Hallowe'en Gala was a rousing success.

"I know you'll excel at this one. The committee ladies described it to me at length." Eagerly, Rose handed a small knife and an apple to Will. "There. Go ahead."

He stared at her quizzically.

"Just peel it," she instructed. "All in one strip."

He did, ending with an impressively long bit of peel.

"Now, twirl it overhead—" she grinned as Will did so, very enthusiastically "—then let it drop over your shoulder."

Frowning with concentration, Will let the apple peel fall.

"Now look." Rose steered him toward the dropped peel. "Its shape should form the first initial of your beloved's name."

They both peered downward.

Rose beamed. "It's definitely an R!"

A man stepped between them. "I beg to differ, young lady. That's an H, by any measure. And that's *my* peel, too."

"Papa!" Happy to see him there, Rose rushed to hug him.

He stepped from her embrace, flushed and dapperly dressed, then gestured to a nearby lady. "Rose and Mr. Gavigan, I'd like you to meet the charming Helen—the Widow McKenzie."

"I'm so pleased to meet you both." The lady in question had a gentle manner, a lively smile and a distinct interest in the apple peeling on the floor. "You say that's an H, George?"

"Indeed I do. I won't hear any different."

"Then that settles it. I suppose you're stuck with me."

"Happy to be so, and that's for certain."

Watching the two of them, Rose realized the truth. She should have guessed! Her father's interest in the Widow McKenzie went beyond good neighborliness—all the way to romance.

There was no reason it shouldn't. After all, love was in the air tonight in Morrow Creek. Romance had enlivened everyone it touched, from Viola and Henry, to Molly Copeland and her husband Marcus, to Sarah McCabe and her husband Daniel.

Jubilant, Rose allowed Will to sweep her into a dance. She knew she would remember this night forever. And as she glimpsed her papa and Mrs. McKenzie dancing nearby, she felt almost giddy with hopefulness. Perhaps now was the moment. Now, with all their family and friends nearby. *Now,* with her in Will's arms and he gazing down at her with naked affection.

"Rose," Will said in a husky tone. "I—"

This was it! Will was about to propose! Rose could scarcely keep dancing she was so thrilled. Her entire being tingled with the importance of his next words. She strived to sound calm. Instead she feared she sounded squeaky. "Yes, Will?"

Solemnly, he gazed at her. All the other partygoers seemed to blur beside them, inconsequential next to the love and wonder and determination in his eyes. He lifted his hand to her cheek and caressed her, with a curious savoring to his touch.

"Rose, I spoke with your father."

"I knew it!" Rose crowed, poking him. "You didn't fool me."

"I told him I couldn't stay with the medicine show. I told him I planned to move on, to find another show." Appearing pained, Will continued, "I didn't say it was because of you—"

Confused, Rose stumbled over the next dance step.

"But he probably guessed." Will righted her, safe in his strong arms. His gaze struck a mark just over her shoulder, his face impassive. "He offered to sell me the medicine show."

Relieved, Rose smiled. "You mean, as an engagement gift?"

"No." Will's frown stopped her cold. "As a financial transaction, plain and simple. I paid cash, with more to come later. He gave me a fair price and exclusive rights to distribute Mr. Li's formula. It was mighty good of him."

"But I thought…" Perplexed, Rose stared at him. She wished he would meet her gaze. "I thought you were staying here in town. Like Viola! That's why I've been so—"

"No. I'll leave Morrow Creek to you." Will tightened his jaw, still not looking at her. "To you and your 'dear' Mr. Vance."

"But—" Rose's dancing feet turned to lead. "But I was only joking! I never wanted Mr. Vance. Truly. I only wanted—"

You, she meant to say. But Will spoke again before she could.

"I'm the last person to keep you from the life you love, Rose." Roughly, he brought them to a halt, then maneuvered her to a more private position. "You told me you didn't want any sadness. Nor a belabored goodbye between us. But before I go—"

"Before you go? Before you go *where?*"

"—you need to know this: someday you'll find a man who can give you what you need. Who knows? Maybe Vance is that man."

A rueful smile quirked Will's mouth. Still baffled, Rose stood motionless as he came nearer. Very gently, Will brought his mouth to hers. But his touch lingered for far less time than she needed…and his kiss had the taste of a goodbye.

"Whatever happens, I hope you'll be happy." Will fisted his hat, then nodded at her. His voice sounded hoarse as he finished, "That's all I ever wanted for you, I swear it."

"Will, stop this." Plaintively, Rose touched his arm. "I said once that I'd never let you go, and I meant it. Please—"

"One of us has to do the right thing. You know that."

"Maybe." Stubbornly, Rose stared him down. She didn't know what had put these ideas in Will's head, but she did not intend to let him break her heart this way. "But this is the *wrong* thing to do. Don't you see that? I—"

"I'm leaving tonight." Grim faced, Will dragged on his hat. "Goodbye, Rose. I won't forget you."

Unbelievably, he managed a wink. Then he turned to stride through the partygoers. In disbelief, Rose stared as Will shouldered past the decorations they'd made, past the crepe paper they'd hung, the jack-o'-lanterns they'd carved only yesterday.

Tonight everything was different.

"Will!" Rose called, standing on tiptoes. "Wait!"

Shoulders rigid, Will stopped. He turned, incongruously flanked by Hallowe'en revelers. His gaze met hers…then drilled straight through, as though she weren't there at all.

In that instant Rose realized the truth.

She hadn't really changed. Despite her bravado, despite her clever tactics and Mrs. Brown's savvy advising, she was still plain old Castor Oil Rose—dependable, reliable and utterly invisible. At least to Will Gavigan she was. It looked now as though she always would be. No matter what she did.

Bravely, Rose lifted her chin, determined not to let Will see her cry. She held up her palm in a final salute, desperate not to crumble in front of him and everyone else. She nodded.

"Goodbye," she whispered…and then let Will go.

Blackly, Will stepped into the unforgiving cold of All Hallows' Eve, still haunted by the look in Rose's eyes as she'd said goodbye to him. Behind him, the towering house rocked with music and revelry. Ahead of him, darkness lay thick and bleak.

Almost as bleak as his future without Rose.

Hoping for guidance, Will glanced up. But the full moon had slipped behind a cloud, and although there were other houses nearby the feeble lamplight in their windows seemed too far away to be real. All that existed now was the ironclad control he'd needed to look at Rose…to look right through her, giving him just enough detachment to leave her behind.

There was no point lingering now. Forcing himself to move, Will wrapped his coat more tightly. Its thick fabric didn't warm him, but he started walking anyway. At first he didn't consider where he was going. Eventually he found himself, by rote, on the rocky path to the medicine show campsite.

Before long he'd crossed the creek. Its waters babbled under the bridge he'd traveled so often, mocking Will with their jollity. Tonight there was no happiness, only the fierce force of will. But no matter how far he walked, it wasn't far enough.

He thought of Rose, happy among her family and friends, enchanted by the Hallowe'en Gala and all it entailed.

He thought of her enthusiasm for the homespun divination games and the merry dances. Seeing her happiness had pierced his heart in a way he'd wanted to deny but hadn't been able to. In the end he'd had to set her free.

Frowning mightily, Will strode onward. It had been all he

could do to say goodbye. It had been all he could do to put his hand to Rose's cheek, to kiss her, to offer that final false wink of assurance, knowing that it was the last time he'd allow himself her softness, her warmth…her love.

Because it was no secret that Rose loved him. If he'd been a different kind of man Will would have claimed that love and never let go. He'd wanted to. But that would have hurt Rose. More than anything else, he placed her happiness above his own.

That was why he had to keep moving. Even when his feet, stubborn cusses that they were, wanted to carry him back to her.

Determinedly, Will topped the rise. Thanks to Dr. Tillson he could hitch two horses to the single medicine show wagon he'd bought and leave tonight. With Morrow Creek at his back and Rose behind him he would have no chance to change his mind. Without him to muck up her future Rose would be happy. Eventually.

This is the wrong thing to do. Don't you see that?

Remembering her woeful question, Will steeled himself anew. He'd always known Rose was stubborn. He could not let her obstinacy keep him from doing what was right. Soon enough she would forget him, swept away by Vance or another citified beau. Soon enough he would be on the road to untold adventures.

All that was left, Will saw with dour perception, was to set the medicine show campsite to rights. Because somehow, sometime between his leaving to accompany Rose to the Hallowe'en Gala and his returning now, the whole place had been torn to pieces.

Disbelieving, he stepped into the center of the campsite. One of the wagons was askew, as though it had been dragged. The other's drop-leaf was open, grinning into the darkness as though ready for another of Viola's popular performances. Corked elixir bottles and issues of the *Tillson Family Gazette* lay scattered on the leafy ground, highlighted by the hide-and-seek moon.

Tack and tracings trailed past the fire pit and beyond, leading to empty posts where the horses should have been. Clothing hung from nearby tree branches. Wooden crates lay emptied of their contents and forlornly cast aside. Cooking pots perched upside down on boulders like absurd cast-iron hats.

Everything appeared to be here. But nothing was in its proper place. Whoever had accomplished this ransacking had not had ordinary thievery in mind, but Hallowe'en mischief.

Frowning, Will pushed aside a clump of medicine show flyers. Bending, he snatched a lamp from the ground. Once lit, it illuminated further curious sights—from a bottle of Lintel's castor oil in the wagon's driver's seat to a pile of accounting ledgers atop Will's piano sheet music. At that reminder of Rose and her damnably adorable fondness for figures, he scowled.

Whatever tomfoolery had struck the campsite tonight, Will wanted no part of it. What he needed was to pack and leave. What he'd gotten was an unalterable delay. Unhappily, he stooped to collect the flyers—just as the wind kicked up, sending the papers scurrying before him like so many autumn leaves.

Swearing, Will followed. He grabbed one. Another. But the wind swirled and strengthened, forcing many more flyers just beyond his grasp. With an intent expression he chased them.

Still they eluded him. With another curse, Will stopped where he stood and looked around. He'd be damned if some of the scattered belongings hadn't *moved* in the past twenty seconds.

Impossible. Drawing his brows together, Will reached for the nearest item. His fingers touched softness, then a spooling length of knit. One of Rose's scarves. Foolishly, he brought the thing to his nose. Before he could stop himself, he'd inhaled.

Her fragrance made his belly clench. His heart stabbed at him, making him grip the scarf more tightly. Glancing around the campsite, his eyes stinging, Will realized that—improbable as it was—everything within his reach belonged to Rose.

Surrounded by reminders of her, Will ruthlessly made himself stuff the scarf in his coat pocket. Doggedly he stomped to the left, then reached for a crate. Just before his fingers touched it the wooden slats fell apart, nails pinging outward. Before his eyes one of the slats crept slowly across the mossy ground, then thudded to a stop near his boot.

Spooked, Will took a step back. He had to be imagining things. But even as he grabbed for shirts from the low-hanging tree branches, or bent to retrieve elixir bottles wedged between tree roots, he knew the items *moved* before he could touch them. As though a ghostly hand were playing tricks on him, Will's every effort to put the campsite to rights failed miserably.

With a determined lunge, he picked up a familiar ceramic bowl. As its slick surface met his palm ridiculous triumph sparked inside him. *There.* He'd finally made progress. At this rate he'd be on the road not long after midnight.

But then he peered at the bowl—the same one he'd used to leave milk for that pitiful kitten—and a fanciful thought struck him. Could the creature really be a ghost, as Rose had insisted? Could it somehow be at fault for the camp's condition?

Feeling beyond foolish, Will looked for feline paw prints. He searched for ghostly glowing eyes. He spied neither.

But the very fact that he'd seriously considered the existence of a ghost cat left him feeling unhinged. Clearly leaving Rose behind had done him in. Just as clearly he had to get away from Morrow Creek, before anything worse happened.

Setting his jaw, he turned…

…and spied an ethereal figure moving among the trees.

Damnation. It had to be the same person who'd wrecked the campsite. Closing his fingers unthinkingly on another of Rose's belongings—*those* he found it perfectly easy to collect, despite the bizarre circumstances—Will aimed his gaze toward that otherworldly figure. Then he set his boots in motion.

"Please, *please* don't cry." Looking concerned, Viola pushed a handkerchief at Rose. "I didn't know you cared for Will this much. Perhaps he didn't, either, and you simply misunderstood."

"I didn't misunderstand anything." Miserably, Rose accepted the handkerchief. "Will is leaving, and he wants me to stay here in Morrow Creek. Here! With you and Papa."

"Well, Papa *is* quite taken with Mrs. McKenzie—"

"And undoubtedly with that weasel of a man Mr. Vance."

"Who?" Viola blinked. "I can't keep up, Rose."

"But I don't know why! Why would Will believe I want to stay here *without* him? *He's* the one who hinted he might leave the medicine show to settle in Morrow Creek."

"Will? Leave the medicine show?" Viola frowned. "I'm not sure I can reconcile that, Rose. He's always loved traveling."

"Yes. And apparently that's *all* he's ever loved!" Rose dabbed her eyes, then gave her sister a probing look. "Why can't Will love me back, Viola? *Why?*"

"I don't know. You're very lovable."

"Not to Will." Rose sniffled loudly. She stared balefully at the secluded upstairs alcove she'd found herself in after her teary flight away from the Hallowe'en Gala. "I thought he was going to *propose* tonight. Instead he barely looked at me."

"Well, he *was* saying goodbye," her sister suggested in a soothing tone. "Maybe it was difficult for him."

"Ha!" Angrily, Rose crumpled the handkerchief. "Nothing is difficult for Will. He's good at everything."

Viola patted her. "He's just a man. He can't be good at—"

"He *is!*" Tearfully, Rose stared at her sister. Her chin wobbled. "He is good at everything. He's kind and strong and good and brave and brilliant and handsome, and I—"

"If he's *that* wonderful," someone said in a brisk tone as they clumped upstairs, "then you oughtn't let him go."

Startled, Rose glanced to the side. Grace Murphy had joined them in their secluded spot. Without an ounce of timidity the suffragist of Morrow Creek inserted herself between Rose and her sister, then offered them both an invigorating smile.

"Men are exasperating. I'll be the first to admit that," she said without preamble. "But when you find the correct one, he's worth hanging on to. Besides—" widening her smile, Grace took Rose's hands and rubbed the chills from them "—what woman ever succeeded by letting a man tell her what to do? If Mr. Gavigan says your love is over and you know it's barely begun, then fight for what you believe in! Fight for *your* future!"

"Yes!" Viola cried, obviously moved by Grace's stirring tone. "You must fight. You must find Will and bring him back."

"Bring him back?" Rose blinked. She tugged on her handkerchief. "Back here to Morrow Creek? But I don't even—"

"We women owe it to ourselves to be masters of our own destinies," Grace Murphy interrupted. "Onward, I say!"

"Yes!" Viola shook her fist in the air. "Onward!"

"You've both taken leave of your senses. This is not a suffragist rally." Rose sniffled. "It's my life. My future!"

Only slightly chagrined, Grace and Viola exchanged eager glances. They were going to be fast friends, Rose could tell.

"Sometimes men need to be brought to heel," Grace said.

"Ooh!" Viola perked up. "Could you tell *me* how to do that?"

Rose had had enough. Loudly, she blew her nose.

They both stared at her as she pocketed her handkerchief.

"Could we concentrate on *my* troubles just for a moment?"

"I'm sorry, Rose." Grace hugged her. "Let's do."

"Yes, I'm sorry, too." With a somber look, Viola took Rose by the shoulders. "I knew this was coming. You're a grown woman now, with a grown woman's practical needs. Papa believes the same thing. That's partly why he's decided to stay in Morrow Creek—to give you an opportunity to meet potential suitors."

"I've already done that," Rose said. "I don't want them. And as far as Morrow Creek is concerned, I don't want—"

"I know a fine man at the *Pioneer Press* offices."

"I do believe Henry has a suitable friend."

"Stop." Feeling despondent, Rose held up her hands. Neither

of them understood her—just like Will. Just like everyone. "I know you both mean well. But this is…too much. The important thing is Will Gavigan is not part of my destiny—on Hallowe'en night or any other. I'll simply have to get used to that."

"Rose, no. You're giving up? That's not like you at all."

Mulishly, Rose set her jaw. "Maybe tonight it is."

"But I've seen you and Mr. Gavigan together at the committee meetings," Grace urged. "I'm certain he loves you."

"And I'm equally persuaded he does not." Rose hoisted her skirts, ready to leave. "Until someone convinces me otherwise—"

Her sister and friend stood helpless, unable to do so.

"—I intend to live my life without him."

Then Rose edged past the alcove and headed downstairs.

Standing alone on the banks of Morrow Creek, Will held his lantern aloft. Its light penetrated only partway into the forest surrounding him, offering glimpses of ponderosa pines and oak trees…but no sign of the unknown person he'd followed.

He glanced around, then down. His light illuminated a series of perfect hoofprints in the creekside mud. The sight jolted Will back to reason. He did not have time to chase after a mysterious figure. He had to pack. He had to find the runaway horses, get back to camp and strike the trail before sunup.

Decisively, Will turned. He tracked the hoofprints farther, but made it only a few steps before a puddle made him stop. It looked nearly the size of a human foot. A feminine foot. A foot unaccustomed to hard walking, slippery rocks or—

"Mr. Gavigan, you don't have a moment to waste."

In the dimness, he jerked up his head.

A well-dressed woman stood before him, dripping on the leafy ground. Inches from her lay more puddles, and a trail of soggy leaves. She seemed pale but determined…and strangely familiar, too.

"You're wrong about Rose," she said.

On the verge of asking who she was, where she'd come from and how she knew his name, Will stopped. He recognized this woman. He'd seen her with Rose at nearly every sunset for days.

"Tell me," he said grimly. "Tell me everything."

Chapter Seven

Morosely, Rose plodded downstairs. She didn't know where to go or what to do or how to behave. With a wry twist of her lips, she realized that she didn't even know if she had a bed to sleep in for the night. Her usual bunk was probably partway across Arizona Territory, now that Will Gavigan—driver, bagman and all-around Johnny heartbreaker—had assumed ownership of the Tillson medicine show.

With one hand on the banister, she glanced down at the Gala, still proceeding with full joviality. Fiddle music rose to meet her. Partygoers mingled in her path. Laughter surged, wholly incompatible with her mood. And just as Rose glimpsed a passage to the foyer, her father stepped forward.

"Rose, my sweetest of sweet!" He hugged her on the landing, possibly a bit tipsy from the hard cider the men preferred. "How did you find Mrs. McKenzie? She's an angel! I know she is."

"I liked her, Papa. But right now I simply must—"

"I was introduced to her by the renowned matchmaker of Morrow Creek. Whose identity is a secret, of course." With a confiding air, her father put a finger to the side of his nose. "One I'll never divulge. But Helen is not the only reason I've decided to stay here in town. No, sir. You're also the reason. You and Viola.

I've been unfair to you all these years. I've never considered what you were giving up by being on the road."

"Oh, Papa. I never felt I gave up a thing! I—"

"Tsk! I won't hear any arguments. I know you've put on a good show of enjoying our travels, but town living can offer you so much more. I know that now." He paused, smiling. "Anyway, I'm too old for the medicine show. It's high time I enjoyed retirement. That's why I told Will I'd sell him the show."

"I know, Papa. Will told me."

"He told *me* a few things, too. About you, and how much you fancy Morrow Creek." Her father chuckled. "So don't bother denying it. We Tillsons are plumb smitten with this town."

"Oh, Papa." Rose sighed, suddenly overcome. "What has *happened* to us since we stopped in this place?"

Beneath her father's quizzical look, Rose slumped. Because of a single unwanted stop, in a single bucolic mountain town, her entire life had crumbled. Morrow Creek had bewitched her father, stolen her sister and turned her cherished if maddeningly platonic friend Will into a vagabond she would never seen again.

All at once it seemed entirely too much to bear.

"You look tired, Rose." Appearing concerned, her father patted her shoulder. "Why don't you get some rest? You can start your exciting new life tomorrow, when you're refreshed."

"I no longer have a bed. Remember, Papa? You sold the medicine show to Will, and our wagons along with it."

He laughed as though she were joking. "Only one of the wagons. The other Will is leaving at the campsite, packed with our things. I'll be headed out to collect it tomorrow. But I promise you won't miss that old wagon once you see the room I've booked us at the Lorndorff Hotel." Her father searched his suit coat, then pressed a key in her gloved hand. "Get some sleep, Rose. You'll see. Everything will come right in the morning."

"I don't think so. It truly can't. Not anymore."

He hugged her. "At the Lorndorff there are feather pillows

and perfumed coverlets. Yes—perfumed!" Squeezing her close, her father sighed. "Sleep tight, my sweet girl. I'll see you soon."

After writing down their room number, Papa bade her goodnight. Moments later Rose found her wrap and stepped onto the front porch of the house that had hosted the worst night of her life…uncertain, unhappy and entirely disillusioned on the subject of All Hallows' Eve and Hallowe'en magic in general.

With nowhere else to go, she found her way to the Lorndorff Hotel. She stumbled into the lobby, shivering with cold. Warmth struck her, along with dazzling light from the expensive chandeliers. Their brilliance made her look up…but their light made her dizzy. She was accustomed to moonglow and old lanterns, comfortable with open sky and fresh breezes. Here at the hotel all the radiance was artificial. All the air was stifling, perfumed like dried flowers.

Distraught, Rose put a hand to her neck. She looked down at the paper her father had given her, but the spots dancing before her eyes made it difficult to read the hotel room number.

Hauling in a deep breath, she squinted—and was instantly struck with the fragrances of tobacco and whiskey.

Wide-eyed, Rose glanced around. No one else seemed to notice the aromas. With gooseflesh rising on her arms, she looked this way and that, trying to identify their source. At last she spied a lone traveler—an older man—a few steps from her. He stood by the fire, doubtless drinking and smoking. But his hands were curiously empty, and no one else stood nearby.

As though sensing her scrutiny, he looked up. "Help you find your room, ma'am?" He smiled. "You seem a bit lost."

For the first time Rose noticed his bellman's uniform. It was different from those belonging to the other employees she'd seen during her tea with Mr. Vance. This bellman's uniform was shabbier, with a tear in the jacket and smudges of dirt.

Nevertheless, he appeared friendly. Rose crossed the lobby.

"I'm Mr. Rupert—at your service." He doffed his hat, then

peered at her paper. "Room two-thirteen. That's one of our best. You'll find it at the top of the stairs, third from the left."

"Thank you, Mr. Rupert." Rose lingered, warming her hands. Those peculiar smells still hung in the air. If anything, they seemed stronger here by the fire. "I'm obliged to you."

"It's my pleasure, ma'am. You'll want to mind the stairs, though." He pointed. "The fourth from the top is tricky."

The fourth step. That was strange—the fourth hotel stair was problematic…just like Mrs. Brown's troublesome fourth stone….

"I'll be careful," she assured him. "Thank you again."

With great reluctance, Rose surveyed the stairs. At their peak lay four close walls, a perfumed coverlet…and loneliness.

"Er…if you don't mind my saying so," Mr. Rupert said, "you don't seem the type to bunk down at a fancy place like this."

Surprised, she stared at him. "I don't?"

He shook his head. "Don't get me wrong, but I saw the way you looked up at those chandeliers."

In unison, they directed their gazes upward.

"Some people don't want ceilings and wallpaper and plush carpets," Mr. Rupert mused. "I reckon you're one of them."

Rose frowned. "You're certainly the first to think so."

"Well, it might not be my place to say." He took off his cap, then turned it in his hands. He glanced at the portrait over the mantel, exactly as he'd been doing when she'd entered the lobby. "I'm sorry if I offended you. I didn't mean to."

"No, you didn't offend me." It was ironic that the one person who didn't know her seemed to understand her the most. "I *don't* want ceilings and wallpaper and plush carpets, but no one will believe me. And I certainly don't want perfumed coverlets!"

"I thought so." Mr. Rupert nodded. "I guess maybe that's why you remind me of her." He gazed longingly at the portrait. "She couldn't be contained, either. Couldn't be conventional."

Stricken by his obvious affection, Rose barely glanced at the picture before smiling at him. "You knew her, then?"

"More than most people ever did. There never was a more enterprising woman nor a more fine and generous person than Maude Brown. Why, in her day she set the standards."

Startled, Rose looked up. Through the alchemy of oil paint and canvas a familiar face gazed back at her, filled with wisdom and secrets. *Maude Brown.* This was *her* Mrs. Brown!

"We were an odd pair, I reckon," Mr. Rupert said. "A highfalutin' lady and a bellman didn't have much chance together. But I've been waiting a long time now. I don't intend to quit."

Feeling her gooseflesh return, Rose gazed at him curiously. "If I might ask—how did you tear your jacket, Mr. Rupert?"

"Ah. Now, *that's* a story to tell—it involves that dodgy fourth stair and a whole lot more." Shaking his head, the bellman slipped a cigar from his jacket. He peeked at the hotel's front desk, to confirm no one was watching them, then lit up, sending smoke into the air. Rose could have sworn she glimpsed a whiskey flask in his pocket. "Do you have a little while to spend?"

All of a sudden, Rose knew she did.

With everything finally collected, boxed and set to rights, Will climbed into his wagon's seat. He'd recovered the lost horses, gotten two of them in their tracings and packed the other show wagon. Now all that remained was leaving.

Drawing in a reluctant breath, he gazed over the campsite. In this clearing between the trees he'd finally come to see Rose Tillson for the woman she was. He'd come to appreciate her, to kiss her…to love her. He knew he'd never forget this place.

Which was all the more reason he had to move on.

"Let's go. Giddap." Will set the horses in motion. The medicine show wagon jerked and rolled, lumbering over the mossy ground with far less alacrity than it had displayed when arriving. But surely that was a whimsical notion? "Get on, now."

The horses snorted and blew, pulling onto the road. They heaved against their tracings, trying to head into town.

"Oh, no, you don't. This way." Brusquely, Will aimed the creatures in the opposite direction. All of fate was conspiring to take him back to Morrow Creek tonight. He was having none of it.

Will clucked at the horses. They picked up speed.

He jounced in his seat, frowning as he held the reins in uncaring hands. The Hallowe'en breeze swept past his face, not affecting his stony countenance. He couldn't shake the memory of the conversation he'd had with the woman by the creekside.

You're wrong about Rose, Mrs. Brown had said.

But Will couldn't allow himself the luxury of believing it.

She loves you, Mrs. Brown had pressed.

But Will already knew that. It didn't change a thing.

And you love her, the damnable woman had continued.

But Will had packed up all the same. He'd packed up, he'd gotten ready and he'd ridden away. Even now the wagon wheels churned beneath him, taking him far from Rose— maybe forever.

If I knew how to find the one I love, Mrs. Brown had persisted, *nothing on earth could keep me from running to him.*

"I guess Rose doesn't feel the same way," Will groused to himself now. But all the same he stopped the wagon.

Because, like a lightning bolt, the truth had struck him.

Maybe Rose didn't feel that way…but Will did.

"Mr. Rupert, that is a tragic story." Eyes widening, Rose frowned at him. "You agreed to meet Mrs. Brown at the hotel and elope—but she never arrived and you never saw her again?"

"Not that night nor any other. I just keep waiting."

"But you don't know if she'll ever come?"

"She's missed all our meetings so far, it's true."

"Maybe Mrs. Brown is waiting somewhere else."

"She said she'd come to me." Mr. Rupert raised his chin. "If I leave, I might miss her! No, ma'am. I'm not budging."

Rose shook her head. Mr. Rupert had told her of a clandestine love, a romance divided by class and distance and propriety. "There must be some misunderstanding between you."

"All I know is she lets me wait." Mr. Rupert puffed his cigar. "Maybe she never wanted a bellman for a husband at all."

"But that can't be!" Impassioned, Rose flung up her hands. "I'm sure Mrs. Brown loves you! Something must be keeping her from telling you—something dire. Because if I loved a man that much, I'd—" Suddenly stricken, Rose stopped.

"You'd…?" her new friend prompted.

Unable to say more, Rose gaped at him. Because something dire *was* keeping Mrs. Brown from meeting her beloved—those slippery stepping stones and that rushing creek.

But *she* had no such impediments. "I'm sorry. I have to go."

Then Rose clutched her wrap and raced from the hotel, hoping against hope that she wasn't too late.

When Will first glimpsed the woman running down the center of the road leading away from Morrow Creek, he thought she was that interfering busybody Mrs. Brown, come to pester him again.

But, since he was already nearly to the creek bridge, he decided to ride right on past. He had more important business to deal with tonight than a nosy woman—beginning with finding Rose and ending with telling her that he *had* been wrong.

Traveling man or no, he did not need freedom more than he needed love. He needed Rose. That was all. If being with her meant suffering through mercantiles and millineries and stultifying conversations about local politics, then he'd put up with those things. Someday he might even learn to embrace them.

Ahead on the road, the woman stopped. She lifted a lantern. Will recognized her. It couldn't be, but it was.

Rose. She started running full chisel, skirts flying. He knew it was her for certain when she dropped her wrap and kept coming. The lantern in her hand joggled crazily. "Will!"

"Rose!" Without thinking, without hesitating, Will jumped

from the wagon. It was a miracle he didn't land slap on his face, so eagerly did he leap to the ground and run. "Rose!"

Will shed his coat and ran faster. Behind him, the horses' harnesses jingled eagerly. It took an eternity to reach Rose.

She held up her light. "Will! Is that really you?"

Panting, Will clasped his hand over the lantern handle. In its glow Rose's face looked beautiful, like a dream. He took the lantern from her, then set it on the road.

"What are you doing?" She gawked at him. "How can I see?"

"You don't need to see. Just feel." Will straightened and cupped her face in both hands. He lowered his mouth to hers, hardly able to believe he was holding Rose again at last.

Their kiss lasted forever…and it wasn't long enough.

Mostly because Rose wriggled free.

"Will, I've got to tell you—you can't leave without me!" Her earnest gaze met his, her words tumbling over each other in their haste to be spoken. "I don't want Morrow Creek. I don't want it at all! I thought *you* did, so I pretended to like it."

Dubiously, Will angled his head. "It's a nice town, Rose."

"But I don't care! I'm not a town kind of woman!" Rose grasped his lapels. Unbelievably, she shook him. "Listen to me. I want grass and trees and the moon overhead."

He covered her hands with his. "I want you."

"I want a road to somewhere new. Do you hear me?"

"I love you, Rose. I've loved you for longer than I knew."

Carried away now, Rose scarcely paused. "I want all those things, Will, and I want stars to light the way! You must bel—"

"I love your smile." Tenderly, Will kissed her again. "I love your laughter. I love your way of burning biscuits. I love your eyes. I love your mouth. I love that you pretend to be examining the show accounts when you're really daydreaming."

"You…" Breathlessly, Rose paused. "You knew that?"

"I know more than you realize." He smiled. "I always have."

"You didn't know that I don't fancy life in town." Wearing a sassy look, Rose poked him. Then she sobered. "It's a nice place to visit, Will, but *please* don't ask me to stay there."

"I won't." Another lingering kiss. "I swear it."

"But I would," Rose said. "If you insisted. If you really needed town living, I would do my best to still my wandering feet. But the truth is I'm a traveling kind of woman, Will. You're going to have to accept that about me."

"I accept that." Hell, he was over the moon about that. "Ah, Rose. I never thought I'd find someone like you."

"That's because you didn't know how *much* I love you." Wearing a beaming smile, Rose gazed up at him. "But I do, Will. I love you with all my heart and soul, and I promise to tell you that every single day. Forever. No matter what. You will never, ever forget how much I love you."

"I will never, ever try." Will tipped up her face, then kissed her again. With his cheek pressed to her hair, he finally dared to release his pent-up breath. "You're *sure,* then?"

Rose shifted in his arms, trying to glimpse his face.

Knowing her intention, Will resisted. He feared she would laugh at him. Feared she would see through the formidable face he offered the world and know him for the lonesome soul he was.

Finally, Rose looked straight at him. For one terrifying instant she did see him. All of him. The comprehension was plain in her eyes…but so was the love that overlaid it.

"About you? I have never been more sure of anything. You can't leave me behind because I'm right here." She pressed her palm to his heart, then smiled. "And I'm never leaving you."

"Good." Gruffly, Will cleared his throat. He blinked away what in a lesser man might have been considered tears of joy. He took Rose's hand. "If you want stars to guide the way, Rose, you'll have them. Tonight you'll sleep beneath the Hallowe'en stars, and every night afterward, too, if that's what you dream."

"I dream of you." Rose kissed him. "*And* stars."

Joyfully, Will pulled her into his arms. This was where he belonged. With Rose. And this was where she belonged, too.

"Well, now," came the sound of a contented voice behind them. "I'd say this is more like it. True love reunited."

Breaking apart, Will and Rose both swiveled.

"Mrs. Brown!" Will gawked at her, seated pretty as you please on the wagon's bench seat. "What are you doing?"

"Doubtless she needs a ride." Happily, Rose waved to the woman. "And seeing as how Mrs. Brown was essential in our coming together tonight, I think we should give her one."

Atop the bench, the woman nodded. "At least as far as the Morrow Creek bridge, up ahead. That's as far as I've been able to go for years. But tonight…maybe things will be different."

Too happy to question her appearance there, Will did not resist when Rose took his hand, scooped up her lantern and wrap, then led him to the wagon. They clambered into place, with Rose in the middle and a satisfied Mrs. Brown sequestered on the end.

"I'm so sorry about your campsite, Mr. Gavigan," she said by way of greeting. "I'm afraid I got carried away with trying to delay your departure for dear Rose's sake. But all's well that ends well. That's what I always say." She smiled placidly.

Will gave her a suspicious frown, but his misgivings had no chance of sticking. Not when Rose sat by his side, pert and pretty, and filled with a hearty dose of Hallowe'en cheer.

"That's what I say, too, Mrs. Brown," she said.

"Indeed. You're a peach of a woman, Miss Tillson."

Smiling despite himself, Will drove on, urging the horses to go faster. Soon he'd be alone with Rose—alone and likely married before long, too. As far as proposals went, sooner was definitely better than later. He'd ask Rose to be his beneath the stars, in an outdoor proposal with all the trimmings.

"I do appreciate all you've done, Mrs. Brown. You've been

most inspirational to me." Rose leaned sideways to pin the woman with a knowing look. "Oh, and by the way—did you know there's a gentleman waiting for you at the Lorndorff Hotel? A certain Mr. Rupert, who says you're the most fine and generous woman he's ever known. He's *sure* you were supposed to meet there—"

"We were supposed to meet at the *creek!*" Mrs. Brown disagreed. "He never came. I thought he'd given up on me."

"Not at all." Rose kept chattering. "I spoke to him, and—"

Whatever else she said to Mrs. Brown was lost on Will. He was caught up in reveries of wedding vows, of Rose in a fine dress…and himself helping her *out* of that dress and into his waiting arms. Maybe he was a marrying kind of man, too, Will decided. With Rose at his side, anything was possible.

Shortly the businesses and houses of Morrow Creek came into view, heralded by pinpoints of lamplight and assorted jack-o'-lanterns on nearby stoops. Late revelers from the Hallowe'en Gala filtered through the streets, Jack Murphy's saloon appeared shuttered for the night, and moonlight peeked from behind the clouds to illuminate the homey scene.

Will put his arm around Rose. "We'll come back here on our new medicine show route. Don't worry about that, Rose."

"I'm not worried about a thing," she said.

"Mrs. Brown, where shall I take you?" Will asked.

There was no reply. Will glanced to the side. To his surprise, the wagon seat held only him and Rose.

"Where is Mrs. Brown? I've been moving at a fast clip for almost a mile. She couldn't have just disappeared."

"You'd be surprised." Rose's smile turned enigmatic. "I was telling her about a man I met at the Lorndorff Hotel tonight, and Mrs. Brown developed a powerful need to go creek-hopping."

Perplexed, Will stared at her. "Creek-hopping?"

"Yes. I have a feeling that now Mrs. Brown knows someone is waiting for her, she'll develop the confidence to leap across those stepping stones, lickety-split."

"Stepping stones?"

"You won't believe this, Will, but…she's a ghost."

He scoffed. "Just like that ghost cat of yours, I imagine?"

"Well, yes." Rose lifted her chin. "Exactly. And just like her friend Mr. Rupert. They've been separated for ages now. Mrs. Brown was on her way to meet him when she slipped and fell, hitting her head on the creek stones. She never arrived at their meeting, and poor Mr. Rupert never knew why. It was wrenching for them both! Especially after Mr. Rupert tripped and fell to his demise down the hotel stairs. But all's well now…partly thanks to us." She eyed him inquisitively. "You honestly can't tell me you didn't see the leaves and mud in Mrs. Brown's hair, can you? Have you no Hallowe'en curiosity at all?"

This was too much for Will. "Humph. Three ghosts?" He aimed a nod at the wagon's interior, protected by the drop-leaf behind their seat. "Tell that to little Chester back there. I reckon he'll feel real enough to you."

"Will! You didn't?" Looking delighted, Rose reached behind the seat, her skirted rump waving. She emerged with a tiny black, *non*-ghost kitten in her arms. She cooed. "Chester, eh?"

Firmly, Will nodded. "It's time we started putting down roots. Settling in. Getting busy with making a family."

Rose gave him an alarmed look. "I thought I told you—"

"*Our* way. Together, on the road, beneath the stars."

"Ah." Wearing her spooniest expression of all, Rose cradled the cat. "That sounds like a lovely way to have a family to me."

"Me, too." Drawing her nearer, Will kissed the top of her head. "But you'll have to stop that nonsense about Mrs. Brown."

"Very well. I'll stop for tonight."

"Good."

Rose pointed. "Just as soon as you look over there."

Game enough for anything now that he had his beloved by his side, Will turned his attention in that direction. At the same moment two people emerged from the entryway of the Lorndorff

Hotel. One was a woman dressed in a fine silk gown. The other was a man dressed in…

"Is that a bellman's uniform?"

"Absolutely." Rose squeezed his arm. "It is."

"That's peculiar. A fine lady and a bellman together."

"It's not peculiar at all. It's true love."

"Wait." Will peered closer. "That's Mrs. Brown."

"Yes, and her dear Mr. Rupert—together at last."

"But how can they be…?" Will trailed off, watching as the couple *drifted* down the street—both of them a good six inches above the ground—then vanished through the walls of the vicar's house. Spooked, Will rubbed his eyes. "Did I just see—?"

"You saw Hallowe'en magic at work." Smiling, Rose turned his face firmly to hers. "True as we're here together right now. Now look at me, Will, because there's more magic to come."

She kissed him then, and he knew it was true.

* * * * *

WEDDING AT WAREHAVEN

Denise Lynn

Dear Reader,

Hallowe'en, All Hallows' Eve, Samhain…doesn't it conjure images of treats, tricks, dark nights, leaves on the ground and magic? For a few hours, the curtain between the physical and the spirit world thins, leaving the air laden with the possibility of endless magic.

At Warehaven in the twelfth century, summer's crops have been harvested, the livestock herded to their winter grazing ground and the larder filled. The cold bite of winter rushes toward the inhabitants, making them anxious about what the future might bring.

What better time to gather with loved ones, friends and community to share food, drink, music and the glowing warmth of a roaring bonfire? Especially on this one night when the dead could return to celebrate with them.

From today back to ancient times, people have believed that this night is filled with magic that makes it possible to see our beloved dead and to cast spells enabling us to peer into our future. It was an ancient fire ritual that would expose the face of a true love that forms the basis for *Wedding at Warehaven*.

After the treats have been passed out, after the house is dark and the children are asleep, curl up with this book and walk with us into the magic of romance and Hallowe'en.

Denise

This story is for Kathy Carmichael and Elizabeth Vaughan. Ladies, you make wonderful cheerleaders and even better friends. And, as always, for my love, Tom.

Chapter One

October 27th, 1117—Warehaven Keep on the Isle of Wict

Clouds streaked steadily towards the near-full moon like ghostly fingers reaching across the sky. Sir Randall FitzHenry, bastard son of the King, waited silently beneath the towering oaks.

Soon the pale glow would go dim. Then, under the cover of darkness, he and his men would swarm Warehaven Keep.

As he had done many times this last hour, he stared across the narrow field separating the heavy woods from the keep. Through the open gates Randall could see the still roaring blaze of the bonfire in the bailey.

For three successive nights the shouts and laughter of those dancing around the fire had drifted across the field. Behind the voices beat the rhythmic pulse of the tabor drums.

The first part of his mission would be easy. There'd been no battles on the isle since his grandsire's day, so the keep was lightly guarded—as evidenced by the open gates. Warehaven would be conquered before the inhabitants knew they were under attack.

His spies had done their jobs. They'd brought him the layout of the keep, the names and descriptions of those in charge and the plans for each night's *festivities*.

He looked up at the sky. This task had been blessed—proof was in the clouds straining to douse the moon's light. Randall knew his advance men were in place. As soon as darkness overtook the sky, they would see to the men guarding the gates.

He nodded at the joyous shouts of Warehaven's celebrants. Let them make merry now. For this would be the last night they practised their pagan rites.

No more would they shamefully cast aside their inhibitions to dance and mingle so brazenly in the open before the fire.

And no more would they enact some Wild Hunt. A shiver traced down his spine at the memory of gazing upon the woman they'd sacrificed. Bruised, torn and broken, she'd died in agony, her unseeing eyes open wide, a scream frozen for ever on her lips.

Aye, he would find this stag of the forest—this supposed pagan god and his followers. He would end the vileness plaguing Warehaven once and for all. Those tasks he would accomplish without fail and without remorse.

The last task his liege, his father the King, had commanded—the one that left a bitter taste in his mouth—he would begrudgingly fulfil. He would ensure the keep's loyalty by for ever binding Warehaven's unwed witch to the crown.

Shadows inched across the field as the moon disappeared behind the encroaching clouds. Randall raised his hand, holding it steady above his head until darkness overtook the last glimmer of light.

He lowered his arm, silently waving his men forward.

Chapter Two

'Father will flay us alive if he learns of this.'

At her sister's hushed rebuke, Brigit of Warehaven forced her attention away from the fire. Ailis, the oldest, wrung her hands, while Mathilda, the middle sister, kept looking over her shoulder.

At times Brigit could hardly believe she was the youngest of the three. The other two were far more timid than she could ever be.

While Ailis was correct, and their father would be outraged by this reckless behaviour, Brigit had no desire to run back to the keep like a coward. Instead, she advised, 'Then perhaps, Ailis, we should not tell him.'

'He'll find out.'

'What matter does that make to you? Besides Simon, I am the only one still living under his roof and rule.'

'True enough,' Mathilda countered. 'But do you think our husbands would approve of this, either?'

'None of us will suffer censure if all goes well.' Brigit pulled Ailis's hooded mantle tighter around her sister's shoulders and tucked a wayward braid further inside the hood. 'We need only stick to the plan. Keep your hood pulled low over your face and nobody will pay us the least bit of attention. If we're not seen, there'll be nothing to tell.'

'I don't know, Brigit—'

She shot a glare towards Mathilda. 'Not you, too? I thought you were set on casting your spell before the bonfire this night?'

When Mathilda dragged the toe of her shoe back and forth across the dirt without answering, Brigit prompted, 'Does Daniel's attention matter so little to you after all?'

Mathilda squared her shoulders. 'Nay, I need to see this through.'

It was all Brigit could do not to roll her eyes at her sisters' indecision. They each had a mission tonight. Their father, brother and two husbands were gone from Warehaven, hunting and seeing to the nearby fields.

Sir Geoffrey, the man their father had left in charge of the keep, had taken it upon himself to call for an early start to the annual All Hallows' Eve festival. A bonfire had been set in the middle of the bailey for the last three nights in a row now. With the Lord absent, people had taken advantage of the merriment until morning light broke the night's darkness.

Each evening the three of them had willingly locked themselves into a secure chamber rather than fall prey to some rowdy guard who'd imbibed too much to remember his place.

Brigit chafed at being so confined. So, yesterday morning she'd devised a plan to see if the spells she'd heard the midwife talk about for years would work. Her sisters had begged and pleaded with her not to be so foolish. When Brigit had refused to change her mind, they had decided to accompany her and had chosen their own spells to cast.

Ailis carried her husband's first child, and she wanted to know how many babies they would have. She was determined to stand before the bonfire and twist an apple on its stem while counting the turns before the fruit snapped free. Supposedly, each turn represented a child for her and Robert.

Overly concerned that her new marriage seemed lacking, Mathilda was anxious to cast a spell of desire upon her husband, Daniel. She'd plucked stray hairs from his garments and braided them with some of her own. It was said that if she tossed the braided lock into the fire, it would make the owners of the hair burn for each other.

Since Brigit was the only one still unwed, her sisters insisted that she must see a vision of the love that would come to her during this next year. To do so she had only to walk away from the bonfire and glance over her shoulder to see his image in the flames.

She'd worked hard at restraining her reckless nature of late. The sheer excitement of doing something Brigit knew they shouldn't was far too seductive to let pass.

'Are we ready?' Ailis didn't sound eager, and Brigit knew if she gave either of them the slightest chance, they would try to drag her back inside the keep.

'Aye, 'tis time.' Brigit motioned for the others to adjust their hoods before leading them towards the fire. They stayed close enough behind her that she heard Mathilda's nervous giggle and Ailis's hiss of reprisal.

'Ho, what have we here?' A guard staggered towards them. The stench of ale reached them first.

Brigit pulled a dagger from beneath her cloak and pointed it towards the man's groin. 'Keep your distance.' To her surprise the order sounded steady. She'd feared that the heavy pounding of her heart would make her words falter.

And to her relief the man actually listened. He stared at the knife, before turning round to find a woman more willing to share his company than they were.

'He recognised us.' Ailis tugged on Brigit's cloak. 'Did you hear me? We are lost.'

'Stop it.' Brigit swatted at her sister's hand. 'Did you not smell the ale? He wouldn't have recognised his own mother.' She didn't bother to add that he wouldn't have recognised his wife, either, but his unfaithfulness was none of her concern.

'What are those?' Mathilda's half-gasped question brought all three to a halt.

Brigit followed the direction of her sister's trembling finger. Uncertain, she slowly moved towards the objects stacked a slight distance away from the growing fire.

Ailis reached past Brigit and fiddled with some loosely tied leather thongs, permitting one side of the object to fall open. 'Cages?'

Brigit picked one up and turned it round. Reeds were woven into the crude shape of…a cow, perhaps? Another appeared to be…a pig. She set the cage down, wondering, 'Aye, but for what purpose?'

A woman unfamiliar to Brigit hurried towards the oddly shaped reed cages, carrying a chicken by its neck. Without a word she stuffed the squawking hen into a cage, tied it shut, then carried it back to the fire.

Mathilda grasped Brigit's sleeve. 'They aren't going to…?'

The woman tossed the cage onto the roaring fire, stopping Mathilda's question.

'Oh, Dear Lord.' Ailis crossed herself and muttered what sounded like a prayer before grabbing Brigit's other arm. 'We need to leave this place.'

'This place?' Brigit shook herself free from her sisters' hands. 'This is our home.'

'I meant the bailey. Brigit, we shouldn't be here.'

'You knew that before we left our chamber.'

'But we didn't then know they were practising pagan activities.' Fear sent Mathilda's pitch higher, and louder.

'Keep your voice down.' Brigit leaned towards the other two. 'What did you think they were doing? The two of you infants can run back inside if you wish. But I am going to finish this.'

The fire burned hot against her back. Shouts and laughter from the revellers rang loud in her ears. The steady beat of a tabor drum, along with the keening lull of a flute, urged her closer to the devilish merriment.

While a part of her feared for the safety of her soul, her curiosity to know what the people of Warehaven were doing was strong. The seductive pull of the music and the wild, unrestrained dancing was stronger.

'I am *not* an infant,' Ailis huffed, then headed towards the fire. To Brigit's relief Mathilda followed. They elbowed their way through the crowd to the edge of the roaring blaze.

Ailis opened the pouch hanging from her waist, retrieved her fruit, then stepped forward. She twisted the apple on its stem, and twisted and twisted again.

By the sixth time her eyes were nearly as large as the apple. 'Oh, no, please, no,' she wailed, before giving the apple one more hard spin.

The stem broke free and Ailis stumbled backwards nearly screaming. 'Seven?' she said, before smacking Brigit's arm. 'This is your fault!'

'Yes, of course it is. I forced you to twist the stem so lightly that it took so long to break.'

Mathilda pushed between them. 'Now 'tis my turn.' The flickering blaze gleamed in her eyes.

Suddenly a finger of ice cut through the warmth of the fire to trail down Brigit's back. The fine hairs on the back of her neck rose and, sensing someone watching her, she turned to see who it might be. She found herself staring at Warehaven's captain, Geoffrey. Taken aback by the hard-focused intent glimmering in his eyes, Brigit stepped away from the unspoken threat.

Why was her father's man looking at her as if he'd like to devour her…or worse? His heavy-lidded perusal was out of place and unwelcome. Instead of enticing, she found his silent invitation repulsive.

Even with the thrum of the music, the heat flowing through her veins and the rampant wickedness surrounding her, Brigit had no desire to be caught up in the throes of wildness with Geoffrey.

She turned quickly back to her sisters, hoping he would understand the rejection.

A gloved hand grasped her shoulder. 'I am honoured that you

have graced us with your presence.' His hot breath blasted against her ear. 'But surely you did not come out here only to watch?'

Shocked by Geoffrey's boldness, Brigit fought to ignore him, hoping he would soon leave her alone. If she turned on him with the outrage burning in her chest, it would only cause a scene and draw attention to her and her sisters. Thus far no one else had made any comment about their presence, and she wished to keep it that way. Brigit forced her attention on her older sister.

Mathilda and four other women seemed to compare their braided charms before tossing them into the bonfire with a joyous shout of glee and then spinning away to giggle their way back into the crowd of onlookers.

Brigit shrugged Geoffrey's hand off her shoulder and moved between Ailis and Mathilda. To her relief he did not follow. But neither did he move away.

'Well?' Ailis asked, her growing excitement obvious in her racing questions. 'Did it work? Do you feel any different?'

Mathilda stretched languidly, like a satisfied cat, inching her hands up her body. Then she reached briefly for the star-dotted sky before crumpling into laughter. 'Oh, aye. I'm sure it did. I feel…I feel…different. More alive. More alluring. I'm certain Daniel will burn for me.'

Brigit knew that with the music and dancing, the roaring fire and the general mood of the gathering, any woman would feel more alive and alluring. But she wondered if the spell-casting had added to the emotions coursing through Mathilda.

'Your turn, Brigit.' Mathilda grasped her wrist, pulling her from their circle.

Ailis laughed before pushing her forward. 'I can't wait to see who it will be.'

From the corner of her eye Brigit saw Geoffrey retreat. To her dismay he headed around the fire. Had he guessed at their plans? Seeing one's true love in the fire was a common old wive's tale.

Was he somehow going to ensure he was the man she'd see through the flames?

She shook her head. It made no difference. Even if she did see him through the flames, he'd not be her true love. She had little liking for Geoffrey, let alone love. He was arrogant, over-bearing and too full of himself. And, more than his general bearing, there was something sinister lurking behind his brown-gold gaze. Something that made her blood run cold.

Let him do as he wished. She'd no fears of becoming his wife or love. She'd see him dead first.

Brigit put Geoffrey from her mind and hesitantly approached the fire. Each step closer made her heart pound faster. The warmth flowing through her limbs grew hotter. As if of its own accord her body swayed to the beat of the incessant drums.

Two young women from Warehaven's village joined her. The three of them laughed nervously, then tossed their heads in unison before falling into a rhythmic step towards their vision of the future.

Brigit untied her red cloak and tossed it behind her to her sisters. Then she mimicked the women on either side of her. Shoulders rolling suggestively, swaying hips and tapping feet drew ribald shouts from the men and encouraging cries from the women in the gathering.

Unable to ignore the heady sensation racing through her, Brigit closed her eyes, threw caution to the wind and gave herself over to the beat of the music.

Two steps forward, one back. A turn, a twist, then a tap of the toe brought them another step forward.

The crackling rage of the fire roared in her ears, shutting out any other sounds. Its burning heat ate away her inhibitions. She ran her hands down her body. The curves and swells tingled to life beneath her touch.

The three women repeated their seductive moves and came another step closer to the fire.

Primal heat licked at Brigit's flesh. An unbidden longing to feel a man's arms around her, to writhe naked beneath him, flared to life with an intensity that drew a moan from her parted lips.

Another round of twisting and turning steps brought them to the edge of the fire. With a flourish, the two women from the village turned, then swirled laughingly away from the blaze and into the open arms of their waiting men.

Left alone to finish the dance and complete the spell, Brigit tossed her head. Curious to see who the fire would show her, she looked over her shoulder.

The shouts of the gathering turned suddenly to screams of fear and horror, freezing her in place.

The pounding in her chest was no longer from excitement. A bone-chilling cold crashed into her stomach as a horse catapulted through the flames to land and then rear up before her.

Fear of the pawing hooves a mere hair's breadth from her face forced her back a step.

Certain that Satan would be seated on the horse's back, Brigit slowly craned her neck to look up at the rider.

Chapter Three

Sapphire-coloured eyes rimmed with anger and searing with the rage of battle burned into her, as if seeing her very soul. If this was not the devil himself, it was one of his closest dark lords.

Brigit turned and raced towards the safety of the keep. His deep, enraged shouts to stop bounced off her back. *Stop?* It was not likely she'd stop to converse with this dangerous stranger invading her home.

Quickly catching up with her hysterical sisters, Brigit grabbed their hands, nearly dragging them inside. Before closing the door, she glanced back over her shoulder at the bailey.

Her throat tightened with tears she refused to shed. Warehaven's men were being herded like animals to the centre of the yard. The women and children gathered together in a tight knot closer to the wall. The keep had been lost before they had even known it was under attack. How had this happened?

Brigit closed the heavy door and joined her sisters, now huddled by the fire. Ailis rocked back and forth on a small bench, her arms wrapped around her stomach as if protecting the child within. Mathilda stood behind her, trying unsuccessfully to soothe the distraught mother-to-be.

Brigit knelt alongside Ailis and clasped her hand. 'Hush, all will be well. They are not harming our men, only detaining them, so this is not an act of war.'

'Then what is it?' Ailis cried, 'What do they want?'

'Leave that to me.' Brigit brushed a tangle of hair from Ailis's damp cheek. 'You need to calm yourself. Think of your child. What would Robert do if he knew you were this upset?'

Ailis shrugged. 'He would—'

Her words were cut off by the crashing of the door as it slammed open against the wall.

Brigit rose. Putting herself between the approaching stranger and her sisters, she took a deep breath, then asked, 'What do you want? Why have you attacked Warehaven?'

The man's dark eyebrows rose briefly as he looked around the Great Hall before sheathing his sword and riveting his stare on her. 'I come for Warehaven's witch.'

Brigit's spine stiffened at his ludicrous response. 'Warehaven has no witch.'

'The activity outside suggests otherwise.'

With as much conviction as she could muster, she explained, 'We did nothing but celebrate.'

'Celebrate?' He nodded. 'Aye, it was obvious by the frenzy that it was nothing but a celebration.'

She wanted to argue, but how could she? Had she not thought the gathering wicked?

'You've nothing to say.' It wasn't a question, so she remained silent. He continued, 'I want the person in charge of the…gathering.'

His steady gaze seemed to question and condemn her. He thought *she* was in charge?

Mathilda whispered just loud enough for Brigit to hear, 'He means you.'

Unable to speak, Brigit nodded in agreement.

Her sister quietly urged, 'Run. Our husbands will protect us. Go, Brigit. Run.'

There was a small measure of logic in her sister's suggestion. If the man gave chase, it would enable her sisters to run for safety. Brigit whispered back, 'Seek your chamber and lock yourselves in.'

The man came another step closer. 'You waste your time plotting.' He shook his head. 'You cannot fight me.' He slowly drew his gaze the length of her body, then once again met her stare. 'And your dancing feet cannot move fast enough to outrun me.'

He had seen her. Brigit fought to ignore the humiliation heating her cheeks. She forced herself to hold his steady look. 'Again I tell you Warehaven has no witch. What else do you seek?'

A commotion by the door drew his attention long enough for her to make her escape. She raced towards the narrow hall connecting the Great Hall to another section of the keep. He quickly followed.

While he was stronger, and undoubtedly faster, he didn't have her knowledge of Warehaven Keep. Her father had constructed this abode with his children and their safety in mind.

Much like the underground tunnels in large castles, long, sometimes narrow and crooked hallways snaked off the Great Hall. They led to smaller chambers. Those chambers had a second door that opened out to yet another hallway. From the tallest tower, this one-storey part of the keep looked more like a rabbit's warren than a dwelling.

A warren she knew well. As children, she and her sisters had spent many an hour chasing each other around and through these corridors.

'Do not make this worse, Brigit.'

She nearly stumbled at his use of her name, but darted quickly into a small room, then out through the opposite door. If she could make it to the chapel, Brother Peter would see to her safety until her father returned. Or, if need be, there was a door in his private chamber that led out to the rear of the keep. A few steps to the postern gate would take her to the thicket beyond the wall.

Either way, instinct warned her that she needed to do all in her power to keep away from this man. She frantically reached to open the door to another chamber. The loose handle caused her to fumble, giving her a moment of panic before the door finally opened. She cursed silently at the door's creaking groan.

The sound of pounding feet warned her that the man had heard it, too. Brigit paused long enough to grab a bench and toss it against the closed door before exiting through the other side of the chamber.

If she could just stay ahead of him for a little while longer she would be able to make it to the chapel. Surely he would do nothing to disgrace the holy room or himself?

A crashing noise behind her was punctuated by a loud curse. Apparently he'd stumbled over the bench.

'Brigit, I know you can hear me. If you do not cease this childishness, I will be forced to go back for your sisters.'

She hesitated for a heartbeat, before resuming her race towards the chapel. He was but taunting her, seeking her easy surrender. Without pausing, she responded, 'Holding my sisters in my stead will gain you only an aching head.'

Once through the next chamber she did pause—long enough to throw the bolt on the door. With the chapel in sight, Brigit gathered a second wind and rushed for the sanctuary Brother Peter could offer.

She dropped to her knees before the altar as the sound of a door splintering beneath her pursuer's blows reached her ears.

Within mere heartbeats she heard his footsteps fall behind her. 'I hope you are praying.' His heavy breathing made his tone hoarse. 'You will need all the help you can get.'

Brigit unfolded her hands, then started to rise. 'I *was* praying until you barged in here.'

'What is this?' Still setting his robe to rights, a dishevelled Brother Peter emerged from his private chamber. He wiped at his eyes, then stared from her to the stranger. 'Who are you?'

The man slowly removed his mailed gloves and dropped them on the bench behind him. He took off his nasal helm, then unlaced and pushed his coiffe from his head.

There was a strong, hard line to his jawbone, as if he clenched his teeth. His lips were drawn tight in anger. A slight dent in his otherwise straight nose took nothing away from the chiselled strength evident in his features.

Over-long hair, as dark as a moonless night, fell across his face. He brushed it away before answering, 'Your new lord and master.'

Brigit gasped, and rushed behind Brother Peter. 'I bid you protect me.' She rose up on her toes and looked over the good brother's head. 'Warehaven already has a lord.'

The churchman ordered, 'Hush, child.' He then addressed the stranger. 'Do you have a name?'

Brigit realised this stranger was tall enough, large enough, that he could smash Brother Peter with little effort. Had she unwittingly put the cleric in danger?

The man answered, 'Sir Randall FitzHenry.'

'And what business have you here?'

'I'm here to end Warehaven's pagan activities. Something you seem to have been unable to stop.'

'There's no pagan…' Brother Peter hesitated. 'Oh, you refer to the harvest-end festival?'

Brigit defended Warehaven's people. 'There was no harm meant. It was nothing but a bonfire.'

'The dancing, and the burning of livestock is not harmful?'

'No.' She shook her head. 'We did nothing but cast old wive's spells.'

'*We?* My lady!' Brother Peter's eyes widened. 'You were in the bailey this night?' He took her non-answer as a yes. 'What were you thinking? You know you endanger your soul, and—'

FitzHenry interrupted the cleric's lecture. 'It seems I am here to assume command of Warehaven none too soon.'

'This is my father's keep.' Brigit stepped forward.

Brother Peter turned an exasperated stare towards her. 'Hush.'

'Let her speak. This involves her, too.'

She knew he was going to once again call her a witch, but for reasons that lacked any logic or common sense she wanted to see his full lips form the words. She wanted to watch the movement of his squared chin as he spoke, so she asked, 'How so?'

FitzHenry spread his long legs and crossed his muscular arms against his chest. His arrogant stance did not bode well. A smile…a smirk, perhaps…tipped up one corner of his mouth. 'You are to be the Lady of Warehaven.'

'I already am…' Brigit's wits caught up with her tongue. She took a deep breath to help calm the sudden warring of her heart. 'Oh, no—you can't mean—you have truly misplaced your mind if you think—' She grasped Brother Peter's arm. 'I refuse to wed him.'

'Or I could toss you into the bonfire. The choice is yours.'

In unison, she and Brother Peter shouted, 'What?'

'Shall I repeat myself?'

Brigit gained the ability to speak first. 'Aye, please do.'

Instead of recognising her tone as a challenge meant to distract him, he calmly repeated himself. 'I am here on my sire's orders to end the pagan activities around Warehaven. I am now the holder of this keep. Furthermore, I am charged with wedding the witch of Warehaven to ensure the keep's loyalty—or I can put her to death.'

He pinned Brigit with a cold stare. 'Since you are not unpleasant to look at, I will wed you.'

Shocked into momentary silence, Brigit tried desperately to gather her swirling thoughts. Pagan activities? Holder of Warehaven? Wed her or kill her? Not unpleasant to look at? The keep's loyalty?

'Since I am not this witch you seek, I need not concern myself with this matter.' She narrowed her eyes. 'And even if I were this witch, I would find your offer of marriage repulsive. To be honest, I find you—'

'Cease,' Brother Peter muttered under his breath. He grabbed her arm and forcibly shook her. 'Do not make this worse. Let me try to make this right.'

She clamped her lips together and nodded. If the cleric thought he could change matters, then so be it.

'My lord FitzHenry, am I right to assume your sire is the King?'

Brigit swallowed hard when the man nodded. She'd not re-alised he was *that* FitzHenry. It was rumoured that this bastard of King Henry willingly served his sire as an executioner. Re-gardless of the highly sensual effect his dark and handsome visage had on women, no lady in her right mind would wed him.

Brother Peter asked, 'And the King has reason to believe pagan practices are taking place here?'

'Lord Baldwin has brought the King proof enough. When Baldwin fell ill before setting out to oversee this matter himself, I was charged with the task.'

Brigit groaned. The Lord of the Isle, Baldwin, was her father's liege lord. She knew not what proof he'd taken to the King, but it must have been of great import that he had gone directly to the King.

'What proof?'

FitzHenry's glare was like ice. She forced herself not to tremble.

'A sacrifice. A human sacrifice.'

Brother Peter slapped his hand over his heart. 'Oh, Dear Lord.'

Brigit gasped. Surely Baldwin didn't think her father was in-volved? 'But how does that involve Warehaven?'

'The trail led here.' FitzHenry turned to the cleric, asking, 'You have not yet been informed of this by your elders?'

The flush racing up Brother Peter's face drew a groan from Brigit. The cleric had a bad habit of not reading or responding to directives from the Church in a timely manner. She was certain that the missive in question was tucked away in a pile on his table, waiting for a cold and rainy day.

'Ah—I may have misplaced that message, my lord.'

FitzHenry reached down inside the neck of his tunic and

pulled out a scroll. 'To ensure you do not misplace this one, you will act upon it immediately.'

Brigit tried to peer over Brother Peter's shoulder to read the missive, but the cleric moved away to finish reading it alone. When he had finished, he turned back to her and shrugged. 'There is nothing I can do, child.'

She shook her head in confusion. 'What do you mean? Nothing you can do about what?'

FitzHenry grasped her hand and pulled her to his side. 'Our marriage.'

'No.' She tugged in an attempt to free her hand from his hold. But he only tightened his grasp. 'Let me go.' She pulled harder. 'I am not going to marry you.'

'I think you would find that death by fire is not pleasant, Brigit.'

She froze. This had to be a nightmare. 'You would not dare.'

'You have no idea what I would or would not dare.'

Brigit tried to swallow her building fear. Unable to dispel the dread racing down her spine, she pleaded with Brother Peter. 'You can't let this happen. Not while my father is gone. Not like this.'

The cleric offered her the rolled-up missive. 'See for yourself. I have no choice in this.'

She knocked the scroll to the floor. 'I don't care what that says. I'll not wed this man.'

FitzHenry released her hand. Before she could flee, he pulled her hard against his chest, holding her firmly in place with his arms.

Neither her anger nor her fear was enough to stop her body's awareness of their closeness. Her bewildered mind cried out for her to feel revulsion, to be repulsed by the solid muscles pressed so tightly against the softness of her curves. Instead her blood warmed and her knees weakened.

FitzHenry ordered the cleric, 'Other tasks require my attendance. Bless this union and let it be done.'

Let it be done. The words roared in her ears, blocking out all other sounds, all other thoughts. *Let it be done.* Brigit closed her eyes, wishing the floor would swallow her as the cleric blessed their union. *Let it be done…*

FitzHenry brushed a hand across her cheek before sliding his fingers through her hair. 'Look at me, Brigit.'

His harsh tone had gentled slightly. While there was still a hard edge to his words, they didn't sound quite as cold or impatient.

''Tis nearly finished. You are my wife in the eyes of God. Be warned, before this night ends you will be my wife in all ways.'

She opened her eyes and glared up at him, promising, 'I will hate you until the day I die.'

'Good.' He lowered his head to brush his lips against hers. 'It will serve you well in the days to come.'

Chapter Four

Randall watched Brigit run away from him and regretted letting her out of his arms. Her slight form had been soft and warm against his chest. The brief contact had reminded him of how long it had been since he'd enjoyed something other than battle.

He hadn't lied. She wasn't unpleasant to look at. Light from the fire had danced on her burnished gold tresses. The gentle waves had clung softly to his fingers.

However, he didn't for one heartbeat think that their marriage would prove gentle or soft. A glimmering spark in her leaf-green eyes had warned him that this new wife of his would give him grief aplenty.

He'd expected her to fight this union. No woman would ever love a man who'd become little more than the King's cold-blooded killer. It didn't matter that the task set upon his shoulders had been to mete out justice, not murder. Or that his reputation was nothing more than tales told out of jealous spite. Those tales had done their job.

While there were plenty of women who would eagerly share his bed, none would ever discover if he owned a heart. He'd travelled that road once before. Deceit, betrayal and finally his own humiliation at being manipulated so easily had left a bitter taste in his mouth.

No matter. Whether their life together ever became easy was the least of his concerns. Either Brigit accepted her lot or she didn't. Right now he needed to discover where the male members of her family were, and who was in charge of the pagan rites.

Both Lord Baldwin and King Henry wanted the demonic activities ended. Permanently. They wanted the leaders rounded up and dispatched before anyone else at Warehaven was harmed.

It was their responsibility, their duty to their people, to ensure the safety of all. And it was his charge to ensure that duty was carried out.

He wondered if Brigit was truly one of the leaders. Would she have run so easily to the chapel if she were? Or had she done so knowing it would raise doubt as to her involvement? It mattered not. The King had provided a writ for their marriage, certain it would help quell the situation. From the way she had defended her sisters and those of Warehaven, Randall agreed.

Practising the old ways had not caused any trouble until lately. But when Baldwin had learned a Wild Hunt had taken place on his lands, and discovered the woman's body, he'd decided enough was enough and taken the issue to the King.

Hunting humans as if they were animals, simply for the thrill of the kill, was more than disgusting. It was surely the work of madmen. The fact that the *kill* had been a woman pointed to the devil's involvement. This, indeed, was the work of a demon.

And discovering Brigit in the gathering around the fire hadn't gone far in proving her claim of innocence. If she wasn't a witch, if she wasn't participating in pagan rites, what had she been doing there?

He headed towards the maze of hallways and chambers, hoping to find his way back to the Great Hall and his men. If they couldn't find the men of this family, they'd interrogate the men captured at the bonfire.

With a little coaxing one or more of them would talk. He hadn't come to this isle to be defeated.

Randall slammed a door closed, only to find himself back in a chamber he'd already come through a moment ago. With a frustrated curse he walked back into the hallway and tapped a knuckle along the wall. Finding a section of the wall that appeared to sound less solid than the rest, he slammed his nasal helm into and through the wall.

Cool night air rushed in around him. He kicked and punched the hole until it was large enough to pass through, then gratefully stepped out into the bailey.

'My lord?' His surprised squire was at his side immediately.

Before answering the young man, Randall looked back at the hole he'd made in the wall. Once the pagans were routed from Warehaven, he would tear down this dwelling with his bare hands and rebuild one that more resembled a keep than a warren.

'He did what?'

'Wed you?'

'When?'

'Why?'

'Without us?'

'Brigit, how could you?'

'Stop! Stop!' Brigit waved her hands at her sisters. 'I can't answer anything if you both talk at once.'

Once Ailis and Mathilda had calmed down they sat on either side of her on the bed. Mathilda urged, 'Tell us what happened.'

Brigit shrugged. 'It seems I am wed to the monster.'

Ailis rested a hand on Brigit's shoulder. 'How?'

'By the King's order.'

'Why?'

'They think we are holding pagan celebrations here.' She frowned, still trying to make sense of what had happened. 'And he thinks I am somehow involved.'

'We never should have let you attend the bonfire.' Mathilda sighed, before asking, 'Did you tell him of his mistake?'

'Of course I did—for all the good it did. He said I could either wed him or he'd toss me into the fire.'

'No.' Her sisters gasped. 'Surely he didn't mean that.'

'I think he did.'

Ailis grasped her hand. 'Brigit, we need to set this right.'

'How?'

'Father will know.' Mathilda rose to pace the floor. 'He should be back within days. You need to find a way to keep this FitzHenry from…' She hesitated. Her face flushed as she rushed on, 'From claiming you.'

'Claiming…?' Puzzled, Brigit leaned forward. 'And how do I do that? He has already promised to make me his wife this night.'

Ailis suggested, 'It should be easy. If you can't talk him out of it, tell him you are ill. Tell him it is your womanly time. Do anything, say anything, to keep him from your bed.'

'Lie to him?' Always a poor liar, Brigit wasn't certain if she could.

'It's that or you will find yourself well and truly wed.'

'Unless you think perhaps that is what you want?'

'No!' Brigit pointed at the door. 'Go—leave me be. I need to think.'

Once her sisters had left the chamber, she paced the floor. Could she lie to this FitzHenry? It would be an easy thing if his stare were less intense, if it didn't make her feel as if he was looking at her soul.

He knew her not, but when he turned that cold, piercing glare upon her, she had the feeling that he was seeing her very thoughts.

Brigit crossed her arms before her, hugging her body's warmth, trying desperately to chase away the sickening chill turning in her stomach.

Randall paused outside the door to his wife's bedchamber— *their* bedchamber. It had taken some rather intense interrogation to gather the information he needed. But he had eventually discovered that Warehaven's men were not at the keep. All four of them had gone to the outlying farms, seeing to the fields, and then planned to spend a few days hunting.

He'd split up his guard, sending half to find the missing men and ordering the other half to ensure the safety of this keep.

Now all he desired was to spend what little was left of the night getting to know this wife of his. His thoughts these last few hours had repeatedly strayed to the gentle swells and curves of her body, wreaking havoc on his concentration.

Unbidden desire had clouded his mind while he had interrogated the men—something that had never before happened. Now he wished to discover if she would be as passionate in truth as she was in his thoughts.

Randall drew in a breath and opened the chamber door.

He'd expected there to be no fire in the brazier. Brigit would not willingly offer him any measure of comfort. What he hadn't expected was to find the chamber empty.

He stormed out of the room and grabbed the first servant, demanding, 'Where is she?'

'My lord?' The older woman shook beneath his hold.

'The Lady of Warehaven.' Randall relaxed his grasp. 'Brigit. Where is she?'

'In her chamber?'

'Nay.'

A sigh escaped the woman before she pursed her lips. 'Then you'll find her out on the wall walk. She goes there to be alone.'

The wall walk. Of all the places for her to go this night. Her keep had been attacked and taken. Had she no sense? What was she thinking to put herself amidst armed men who were essentially strangers—nay, enemies to her?

He strode purposefully out to the bailey, his attentive glare sweeping the walls. One of the men posted at the gate tower nodded to his left.

Randall looked in that direction and found what he sought. He quickly climbed the ladder, pausing at the top to calm his sudden rage at her thoughtless actions.

Quietly, intentionally without warning, he came up behind her and, with an arm on either side of her, pinned her against the wall. 'What are you doing?'

She'd obviously heard his approach, because she didn't jump, or appear startled in the least. 'Waiting for you, I suppose.'

'On the wall?'

'I thought it better than my bed.'

He pretended to misunderstand. 'You thought the wall walk would be a better place for our marriage night than the privacy of a bed?'

She shook slightly against his chest. 'I am glad to know you possess a sense of humour, my lord.'

What game did she seek to play? Uncertain whether she shook from suppressed laughter or fear, he asked, 'You think I am jesting?' To get his point across, he wrapped one arm around her waist, pulled her hard against his chest and lowered his lips to her neck. 'I care not if all watch, Brigit.'

Shocked at the tingling sensation his touch against her flesh caused, she pushed her head against his shoulder and tried to twist away from his teasing lips. 'Let me go.'

He did. But only long enough to turn her around, so her back was now against the wall. She stared at his chest. His solid, hard, wall-like chest.

'I am not going to harm you. Look at me.'

The deep timbre of his voice beckoned her to comply. She lifted her face and squeezed her eyes shut as he lowered his head. He once again brushed his lips across hers, pausing to whisper, 'Be still.'

She didn't want to be still. Didn't want to feel this warming in her limbs. But when she parted her lips to say so, he captured them in a kiss.

He traced his tongue along her lips, making her gasp in surprise. And when he boldly caressed her breast, sliding the pad of his thumb across the sensitive tip, a shiver raced all the way to her toes.

Brigit's heart fluttered in rising panic. Her sisters had been wrong. This would not be easy. She pushed against his chest and tore her lips from his. 'No. Please, do not.'

He stared down at her. 'This is our wedding night. Did I not warn you what would happen this night?'

To her horror, her throat tightened. She swallowed hard, fighting her fear of the unknown. 'I…I do not feel well.'

Ignoring her claim, he slowly stroked a thumb across her lower lip. 'Have you never been kissed by a man, Brigit?'

'No.' She shook her head. 'Of course not.'

When he sighed, she expected him to demand his rights. But instead of demanding anything, he stepped back and offered her his hand. 'Let us retire.'

Stunned, she hesitantly took his hand. 'Retire?'

'Sleep, Brigit. I will not force you to become my wife this night. But you will sleep in the same bed with me.'

Something in his words, something in his tone, led her to believe him. It made little sense to her. 'I swore to hate you for the rest of my life. Why are you being kind? What trick do you play?'

'No trick.' He chuckled softly to himself before turning to lead her along the wall. 'I am being kind now because, my lady, you will have ample time to truly hate me during our very long life together. We need not spend this night wrapped in anger and disdain.'

With a nod towards the crowd gathering, he added, 'At least not with the entire keep in attendance.'

Brigit stood rooted to the floor of her chamber while she watched this stranger, this conqueror of Warehaven, this man she had been forced to wed, as he lit an oil lamp and then made a fire in the brazier. Without a word he turned down the covers on the bed, removed his clothing and climbed into *her* bed—naked.

'Get undressed and come to bed.'

With difficulty she prised her tongue from the roof of her dry mouth. 'You said…you said you would not…' She wanted to scream in frustration at the flush heating her face.

'What? Claim you? Take you? Make you my wife in truth?'

Unable to speak past the thickness in her throat, Brigit nodded.

'And I won't.' He patted the bed next to him. 'At least not this night. However, you are not going to stand there the rest of the night with your mouth hanging open. It would keep me awake.'

She snapped her lips together, crossed the small chamber and sat on the edge of the bed to take off her soft boots.

But when she turned round to pull the covers down, he slapped a large hand over them. 'Take off your clothes.'

She jerked back in shock at his suggestion. 'No.'

'It wasn't a request. Take off your clothes.' He didn't move. He didn't raise his voice. He simply stared at her as if he was ordering one of his men and expected to be obeyed.

Slowly reaching for the ties of her gown, Brigit closed her eyes. 'You promise not to…?' She trailed off, unable to put words to her question.

His sigh echoed in the chamber. 'It has been a long day, and an even longer night. I want only to sleep. I will do nothing you do not wish.'

She let her gown and undergown fall to pool at her feet, wondering why his promise sounded like a double-edged sword. With her back to him, she sat on the edge of the bed again, hesitating before slipping off her stockings.

Could she do this? She had grown up in the keep of a warrior. She'd seen naked men before. She'd helped her sisters bathe visitors of rank. But then there'd been nothing personal, nothing remotely intimate about the act.

Now…she glanced over her shoulder. FitzHenry's eyes were closed, his breathing even. Did he already sleep?

Exhaustion seeped into her limbs. She, too, needed the comfort of her pillow. She swung her legs onto the bed and leaned back into…his arm.

Before she could jerk away from his hold, he pulled her to his side. 'Hush.' With little effort he rolled her onto her side, her breasts pressed against the side of his chest. 'Now, go to sleep.'

How did he expect her to sleep like this? She tried to push out of his hold, but he only flexed his arm and draped a leg over hers. 'You aren't going anywhere. Go to sleep.'

'Go anywhere? I can hardly breathe, let alone go anywhere.'

He relaxed his arm slightly, but didn't release her.

Brigit's flesh burned against his. Her head spun from the rapidness of her pulse. Seeking to cajole him into freeing her, she quietly said, 'Instead of feeling like a new bride sleeping in her husband's arms, I feel like a prisoner.'

His chest rose and fell with a measured breath. 'I'm thankful my new wife isn't lacking in sense.'

His unexpected comment gave her pause. 'I am your prisoner, then?'

'Yes. Unless you've suddenly developed tender feelings towards me or changed your mind about sleeping.'

The heat now firing her chest wasn't from such close contact with his flesh. A prisoner? In her own keep? Her own chamber? Her own bed?

She gritted her teeth and answered, 'No. Neither.'

'Then go to sleep.'

Brigit held herself stiff, trying to keep their skin from touching as much as possible. She closed her eyes and fumed. She would get no rest this night.

Chapter Five

October 28th, 1117

Brigit's lover trailed his fingertips down the length of her spine. He stroked her flesh slowly, as if committing each inch to memory.

On a sigh, she leaned into his touch, wanting to prolong the pleasure of this sensuous dream for as long as possible.

Her cheek rested against his chest. His heart beat fast and hard, echoing her own building excitement. His ragged breath rushed hot across her ear, and she smiled with the knowledge that she alone was the cause of his desire.

She brushed her lips against his chest, tasting the saltiness. He caressed her hip, his hand possessively stroking and kneading the curves.

Brigit snuggled deeper into the covers…and frowned. This was nothing but a dream.

Why, then, did this growing heat feel so real that it nearly singed her flesh?

How did a mere dream call forth this desperate need fluttering beneath her heart and tightening low in her belly?

And why did it feel as if her breasts were pressing against hard muscles instead of the softness of a bed?

Impossible.

She shook her head to clear the confusion, and in the process brushed her nose across hair-covered flesh.

Brigit held her breath. Slowly opening her eyes, she lifted her head. An amused gaze met her shocked stare, prompting her into frenzied action. She scrambled to push herself up from her position atop him. How had she ended up sprawled across his chest?

The sudden widening of his eyes and the sound of his sharp gasp made her pause. She'd pushed herself upright in an attempt to get off his chest, and had straddled him on her knees instead.

It didn't take much thought to understand the direction his mind had taken. The darkening of his hooded eyes and the firm grasp of his hands on her thighs made it plain.

Brigit glanced down and realised they were less than one motion away from making this marriage valid. She lunged sideways onto the mattress, then rolled from the bed.

'What were you doing?' She dragged a cover from the bed and wrapped it around her. 'How dare you?'

'Spare me your hysterics.' Randall sat up, swinging his legs over the side of the bed. 'If anyone should be affronted, it is I.'

'You?' Brigit hugged the cover tighter to her body. She bit the inside of her lip, hoping the sharp pain would slow the hard pounding of her heart.

'Yes, me. I was sound asleep when you decided to seduce me. You should be thankful I realised you were still sleeping and did not take advantage of your dreams.'

She wasn't certain what angered her more—the sickening fact that he was most likely correct, or the wicked grin curving his lips into a smile as he dressed.

He paused to look at her. His intense perusal made her pulse jump even faster.

'Although I must admit, Brigit, for someone who claims to be unused to a man's kiss, I find the direction of your dreams… interesting, to say the least.'

It was a shame that she *wasn't* a sorceress who could spin magic out of nothing. For if she could, this barbarian would find himself smirking with his maker.

Brigit pointed at the door. 'Get out.'

To her amazement, he strapped on his belt and headed for the door. 'I have tasks to attend to this morning, and have not the time to be concerned for your whereabouts.' He opened the door, but before leaving added, 'Since you have nothing to wear, I can be certain you will remain here until I return.'

Brigit stared at the closed door for a moment, before looking down at the empty floor where she'd left her clothing last night.

Forcing her feet into action, she raced across the chamber. She bunched the thick, heavy cover in one hand and jerked the door open, to find him leaning against the wall opposite her chamber.

The urge to wipe the expectant leer from his face made her fingers itch. 'Where are my clothes?'

'I had them removed while you…slept.'

She stepped into the hallway, but Randall moved forward, quickly forcing her back into the chamber. He nodded towards the men flanking her door. 'In case you somehow conjure a gown from the air, they will be here to keep you inside.'

'So I truly am a prisoner?'

'A prisoner?' He traced a finger along her jawline, lowering his hand when she turned away from his touch. 'No, you are *my* prisoner.' He leaned closer and whispered, 'There is a difference. One you will soon understand.'

Once he had left the chamber, Brigit dropped down onto the edge of the bed. His unspoken threat should have had her heart racing in fear. Instead it beat strong and steady with anger.

She should be worried about what this day might bring. But she was more concerned about what this man had planned for Warehaven. While she had nothing to hide, she didn't want him snooping around her father's keep alone.

It was doubtful if either one of her sisters would think of

accompanying him. They were most likely still cowering in their chambers.

She slammed a fist onto the bed. At least they had clothing to wear.

The chamber door creaked open. Brigit rose, grasping her covers tightly. Surely his men wouldn't think to come in here?

'My lady?'

She breathed a sigh of relief and met the elderly servant half-way across the room. 'Mabel—yes, I am here.' Brigit took the tray laden with food from the panting woman, set it on a small table near the bed, then led Mabel to a chair. 'Sit. Why did they make you bring this up here? Have they no sense?'

Once the woman had caught her breath, she waved a hand weakly in the air. 'Oh, I but carried it into the chamber. One of the boys…young Walter, I believe…brought it up the stairs for me. He awaits me on the landing.'

'There are servants aplenty to do this work. Why you?'

Mabel shrugged. 'Because his lordship was certain I'd be no help to you, my lady.'

The man used his head far too well. He could be more dangerous to her and Warehaven than she'd first thought.

Brigit walked to the narrow window opening and looked down at the bailey. Already he was surrounded by some of Warehaven's men. She couldn't hear them, but their motions, their nods, let her know that they were readily conversing with the enemy.

She needed to be out there—needed her father's men to see her, if only to remind them to whom they had sworn their allegiance. And she needed to make her presence known before the men unwittingly gave FitzHenry information he could twist to fit his purpose.

Her fingers tightened on the covers. But she couldn't go out there naked. She needed to find a gown. And she needed to devise a way past his guards.

Mabel rose, placed a hand on her back and stretched. 'My lady, I should return below stairs.'

Brigit's eyes widened in surprise at the obvious answer before her. She smiled at the servant. 'Mabel, how would you like to prove his lordship wrong?'

'Now they are caught, lock Warehaven's sons-by-marriage in a chamber with their wives.'

'My lord?' Randall's captain questioned the order. 'Would it not be easier to secure them in a cell?'

Randall had been waylaid by Brigit's sisters earlier, as he'd left the keep. Both had been hysterical and highly unreasonable. While it would be easier to hold the men in a cell, being confined with their wives might convince them to more readily supply the answers they'd refused him this morning.

It might also remind them of what they stood to lose. Especially since one woman was carrying her husband's first child.

He repeated his order. 'Lock them in a chamber. Make certain at least two men guard the door at all times. And put two more at the head of the corridor to that wing.'

While watching his man leave to do his bidding, Randall's attention was drawn to a small gathering at the well house. Six of Warehaven's men surrounded the elderly servant he'd sent to Brigit's chamber.

It was normal for the men to be asking about Warehaven's lady, so he thought little of it. He would give them a few moments to learn of her well-being before breaking up the group.

His main concern wasn't the gossiping men around the well, it was centred more on the tall, hawk-nosed man watching his every move. Randall's spies had already informed him that this Sir Geoffrey was the man Warehaven had left in charge of the keep.

Since he'd not come forward as being Warehaven's captain, Randall didn't trust him. An honourable man would have come

forward. He would have accepted responsibility for the keep and
its inhabitants.

Instead, Geoffrey had kept as far away as possible. Yet
Warehaven's men still sought him out. Randall knew it would
behove him to put Sir Geoffrey in a cell, keep him away from
the men. But something told him—the man's furtive actions,
perhaps—that allowing him a measure of freedom might force
his hand. If he'd been involved with the recent happenings at
Warehaven, he would eventually do something to implicate either
himself or the person truly in charge.

Randall headed slowly towards the well house. The men had
had more than enough time to learn of Brigit's welfare.

A glimmer of burnished gold peeped out from beneath the
hood of the elderly woman's hood.

He stared at her and held his breath. Surely he was seeing
things? A light breeze lifted the edge of the hood, causing Randall
to quicken his steps.

The men around her scattered just as he reached the group.
Before the woman, too, could make a quick escape, he grasped
her arm. 'Stay a moment.'

She kept her face averted.

Obviously she thought he completely lacked any wits. Randall
narrowed his eyes. He'd play along…for a time. Loosening his
hold slightly, he asked, 'Did you have any difficulty taking the
food up to Lady Brigit?'

She shook her head.

'Good. I had feared she'd try talking you into helping her escape her chamber.'

Her arm tensed, but she made no other movement except to
wrap her free arm around her waist. She wriggled her hips a little
and shrugged her shoulders.

He frowned, before glancing down to see the corner of her
bedlinen dragging on the ground from beneath her gown. It was

all he could do not to laugh at her sad attempt at making herself appear larger by apparently wrapping the covers around her body. He shifted a foot onto the edge of the blanket.

Randall released her arm. 'I won't keep you any longer. Have a pleasant day.'

Her soft sigh reached his ears as she walked away. Two steps later she froze in place.

'Something wrong?'

She slowly turned around, then glared down at the cover now stretched from the toe of his boot to the ground at her feet.

'How long have you known?'

He scooped up the cover and tossed it to her before closing the distance between them. 'From the moment your hair fell from beneath your hood.' Randall reached up and tucked the telltale strands behind her now reddening ear. 'Have you always disobeyed orders?'

She kept her face averted as she shook her head, but the flush on her cheeks said otherwise.

'How did you convince the maid to give up her gown?'

Brigit lifted her chin to stare directly at him. 'Magic, my lord. I conjured a spell she could not resist.' She tilted her head. 'After all, am I not the Witch of Warehaven?'

Her answer nearly took his breath away. Lord, this wife of his was bold.

He cupped her cheek, grasping her chin when she tried to turn away. 'Have a care of that tongue, my lady. Someone not as understanding as I might order it removed.'

'Understanding?' Her voice rose in what he assumed was surprise before she narrowed her eyes and said, 'No one would be that cruel.'

He leaned closer, placing his lips against hers as he warned, 'Don't be too certain of that.'

Brigit gasped, and he took advantage of the opportunity to taste her parted lips. She didn't move. Not to return his kiss, nor to struggle against him. He pulled her closer, silently cursing the covers in her arms that kept their bodies from touching.

To his satisfaction, she tentatively returned his kiss. The warmth of her tongue sliding over his quickened his pulse.

Autumn's chill fell away. The sounds of bustling activity in the bailey faded. A rushing warmth flowed into his limbs.

He wanted to tear the blanket from her arms and the gown from her body. He longed to feel her against him, soft curves against hard muscle, flesh against flesh.

In his mind he saw her writhing naked beneath him, gasping his name, eyes shimmering, arms reaching out to hold him close, legs parted—Randall dragged his mouth from hers and stared down at her. He'd not entertained thoughts this vivid since he'd been an over-eager lad.

This loss of control, this unbidden longing, wasn't normal. The intensity of the feelings buffeting him, leaving him unable to think clearly, could not possibly be caused from anything other than bewitchment.

'You truly are a witch.'

Brigit blinked. A blush tinted her cheeks. She pushed away from him. 'And you, FitzHenry, truly are a fool.'

Chapter Six

If Brigit knew nothing else, she knew without a single doubt she was no witch. How this man could call her such was beyond her understanding.

She'd merely teased him about conjuring a spell against Mabel. He'd deserved such a response for thinking to confine her naked in her chamber.

A sudden chill lifted the fine hairs of her neck. The breeze, while cool, was not cold enough to prompt the unease building in her chest.

She glanced around the bailey, searching for the cause of her distress. The raised eyebrows directed towards FitzHenry and her were not out of place. After all, she'd been compliant in the enemy's arms while he'd ravished her mouth in public.

All seemed normal. Still, a tingle of warning urged her to keep looking. Brigit swept her gaze around once again—and froze upon meeting Sir Geoffrey's angry stare.

He had no reason to look at her with such blatant rage. His glare silently promised harm. Instinctively, she stepped closer to FitzHenry.

He lightly grasped her arm. 'What is wrong?'

'Nothing.' She shook her head, trying unsuccessfully to shake away the fear creeping up her spine.

He slipped his arm across her shoulders, pulling her against his side. For some reason his protective stance gave her a measure of peace from Sir Geoffrey's unspoken threat.

'Who is that man? What is he to you?'

Sir Geoffrey turned away, and she wondered if FitzHenry's attention had made him uncomfortable. 'My father left him in charge, but he is nothing to me.'

'Was he responsible for the revelry?'

'I…' She paused. Long-ingrained training, obedience to her father, duty to her people, urged her to protect Warehaven's man regardless of his transgressions. It was her sire's right, not FitzHenry's or even hers, to deal with this man. 'I am not certain.'

The arm across her shoulders fell away, permitting the chill again to trip down her spine. FitzHenry moved away, warning, 'Do not think to lie out of some misplaced sense of loyalty.'

'Misplaced?' She swung her gaze to his, shivering at the icy coldness in his eyes. 'Protecting Warehaven is not misplaced loyalty.'

'True. As long as you remember that Warehaven is no longer under your father's command.' He leaned closer. 'Protect Warehaven all you wish—for me.'

Before she could respond, he took the covers from her arms, then tossed them atop a barrel sitting next to the well house. 'Come.' Entwining his fingers around hers, he tugged her forward. 'Show me around *my* keep.'

The near-full moon glowed brightly against the dark, cloudless night sky. Brigit leaned over a lower section of the wall and breathed in the crisp air.

FitzHenry had done his best to infuriate her. And he'd failed. She corrected her thought. By all outward appearances he'd failed.

He'd easily set her blood to raging more than once. But after his comment about Warehaven being *his* keep she'd forced herself not to argue with him about anything. Instead, she'd pinned a polite smile on her lips and shown him around Warehaven, introducing him to those they happened upon and pointing out minor things of interest.

Naturally she did not think it would interest him to know about the tunnel running behind the keep from the kitchen to the other side of the wall. Nor did she think he'd be interested in knowing where the extra cache of arms was hidden in the stables.

And she was certain he'd not find the small workroom where she dabbled with herbs and spices to be of any importance.

To her relief, she now had her clothing back, and the guards at her door had been dismissed. All in all the day had gone well.

Until this evening's meal. Talk had turned to plans for tearing down Warehaven's warren-like keep and rebuilding next spring. Before she'd let herself shout that this was her father's keep, and they had no right to make such plans, she'd fled the table and taken refuge outside. To her grateful amazement FitzHenry hadn't followed.

The creak of a board drew her attention to the figure approaching. Again icy-cold dread crept up her spine, warning her to be wary.

'Do you see them?' Her instincts had been correct. Sir Geoffrey stopped alongside her and nodded towards the woods. 'They are out there.'

Brigit scanned the line of trees. Even with the light of the moon she was unable to see anything. 'Who is out there?'

'The dead souls of the brave, waiting for the god of death to lead them across.'

What he said made no sense—dead souls waiting? Sir Geoffrey had moved so close while speaking that Brigit could feel his hot, rancid breath on her cheek. She backed away. What had happened to rob him of all ability to reason?

He stared at her, his eyes gleaming with a light so unholy she silently prayed for divine protection. '*He* is coming for them. No one, not even FitzHenry, can stop him.'

'Who is coming?'

'Woden.' Sir Geoffrey leaned closer. 'You above all should be honoured.'

The man thought a pagan god was coming? The god of death? FitzHenry had mentioned a sacrifice—a human sacrifice. Had Sir Geoffrey been involved? Had he been responsible for such a gruesome act?

Unable to swallow her gasp, Brigit quickly tried to cover the sound with a cough before asking, 'Why…why should I be honoured?' How could her father have left this man in charge of Warehaven?

'Because you have been chosen as his mate for this season.' Sir Geoffrey grasped her arm above the elbow. 'You must save yourself for him. But not for much longer. He will come for you in three nights.'

She tried to pull free of his bruising hold. 'Take your hand off me, Sir Geoffrey.'

He did as she demanded, but trailed a finger down her arm. 'It is good that you tremble in anticipation.'

Anticipation? It was more in fear than anything else. But ingrained self-preservation warned her not to let him know that.

'You will enjoy pure ecstasy beneath the rutting stag.'

Sir Geoffrey had not simply lost the ability to reason. He spoke of pagan gods and mating stags as if they were one and the same. He'd become possessed by something dark and evil, and she worried for the others of Warehaven. Because her father had ordered it so, they listened to this man; they followed his bidding.

Brigit tried to back further away, bumping into a corner of the wall instead. FitzHenry was inside the keep, and he believed she was responsible for the recent goings-on. The men currently patrolling the bailey were complete strangers to her. The men of her family were absent from Warehaven. Who would come to her aid?

Her father's man caressed her shoulder. 'Do you know why you were chosen above all others?'

If she wished to leave this wall unharmed, she knew her safety depended on her ability not to anger Sir Geoffrey.

Forcing herself to remain outwardly calm, she said, 'No. Tell me why.'

He brushed the back of one finger across her cheek. She turned her face away and bit her lip to keep from crying out. 'Because you are still pure and worthy.' He lifted a strand of her hair. 'You *are* still worthy, are you not? I have seen no bloody sheets, nor heard any cries or groans of lust come from your chamber.'

How long had he been watching her so closely? Should she lie, or speak the truth? Which would bring less harm? Brigit's impulse was to lie to him. But she feared doing so would enrage him. He was obviously unstable, and she'd no wish to be forced into defending herself against him.

Meeting his wild stare, she forced herself to answer. 'Yes, I am still worthy.'

'Good.' The word rolled slowly from his mouth. He stroked her arm. Taking her wrist, he turned it over and placed a key on her palm. 'Your brothers-by-marriage need to participate in the hunt. Release them tonight and I will see them to safety.'

He stepped away, giving her heart a chance to resume a more normal beat. When the haze of fear lessened, she asked, 'Release them?'

Sir Geoffrey looked at her. After the wild shimmer in his eyes had disappeared, he frowned. 'Aye. They are held prisoner in your sisters' chamber.'

Guilt assailed her. She'd been so intent on keeping FitzHenry busy with trivial things that she'd not given her sisters more than a brief thought. She'd thought they stayed there of their own volition.

She was angry at FitzHenry for not telling her. But her hopes rose at the notion of the men being at Warehaven. 'Daniel and Robert have returned?'

Sir Geoffrey's frown deepened, bringing his eyebrows together. 'Were you not aware they were captured and questioned early this morning?'

'Nay.' Relief flowed warm through her. Daniel and Robert could be counted on to rescue her if need be. 'Are they well? Were they injured?' Her breath caught. 'What about my father and Simon?'

'Your father and brother are still free.' A strange expression twisted his face into a mask she couldn't read. 'I am not certain Daniel and Robert are unharmed.' He glanced away a moment, as if seeking words.

'Are they…are they alive?'

'Aye, they'll live. The King's executioner would gain no pleasure if they died too soon.'

Dear Lord, would FitzHenry be that cruel? Brigit wasn't certain. And that uncertainty froze the blood in her veins.

Sir Geoffrey spoke again. 'Remember, release them tonight and send them into the forest to the oak ring clearing. You will not like your fate if you fail.'

'But…' He walked away before she could ask anything else. It would be near-impossible to get past FitzHenry's guards long enough for the men to exit Warehaven. And the clearing Sir Geoffrey spoke of was at least a day's walk.

She closed her fingers around the key and headed back to the keep. She couldn't decide who best to trust—FitzHenry or Sir Geoffrey.

It was obvious that Sir Geoffrey, in his madness, would prove dangerous whether she deceived him or not. The danger might be great, but it would only be a danger to her.

Eventually someone at Warehaven would realise his mind was possessed by a vile sickness, and he would either be somehow cured or meet his end. Hopefully before he caused too much havoc.

FitzHenry, however, was a threat not only to Warehaven but also to her family. The danger from him came not from an unstable mind fraught with evilness, but from his strength and loyalty to his sire.

If he believed her family—her father, in particular—was involved in what he considered pagan activities, he would see them dead…or worse. Already the ownership of Warehaven had been stripped from her father's hands.

Brigit crossed the Great Hall and climbed the steps to the upper level with leaden feet. Her mind and stomach twirled in circles, each one spinning faster than the one before.

Never in all her years had so much responsibility or so great a decision rested on her shoulders.

It was all she could do not to drop to her knees sobbing.

She desperately needed to talk to someone. Not Brother Peter. He would not argue the points with her. He would not give her the opportunity to choose as the Lady of Warehaven should.

Instead he would choose for her and then, as he would a child, tell her what to do.

She was no longer a child, and she did not want or need anyone telling her what to do.

What she wanted was to talk to her sisters. Aye, they were high-strung and mindless at times. But once they gave their emotions a chance to subside, they were quite capable of arguing with her.

At the landing, she turned towards her sisters' shared chamber and stopped halfway down the corridor. Two guards flanked the door to the chamber.

When they saw her, they both took up a position in the hallway, effectively blocking her from reaching the door.

'My lady, you need retire to your own chamber.'

She wasn't going to be put off that easily. 'I want to talk to Mathilda and Ailis.'

'We have our orders and we can't allow that.'

Brigit knew the answer, but asked, 'By whose order?'

'Mine.'

Surprised, she spun around to face FitzHenry, dropping the key in the process. It clanged onto the wood floor.

Before she could retrieve it, he bent over and snatched it up. 'What is this?'

Why did he ask such an obvious question? 'A key.'

He glared at her. 'To what?' Before she could answer, he shook his head. 'No. Don't answer.' He tossed the key to a guard and nodded towards the door.

She stared at the floor. Her heart lodged in her throat as the key grated in the lock and the door momentarily opened, then closed.

After taking a deep breath, she began, 'I only wanted—'

He curled his fingers around her wrist, turned and headed in the opposite direction, dragging her along.

'What are you doing?' She prised at his fingers with her free hand. 'Let me go, FitzHenry.'

'Oh, I will. But not here.'

Brigit dug in her heels and jerked her arm as hard as she could. 'I said, let me go.'

FitzHenry spun round and pulled her against his chest. Glowering down at her, he warned, 'You do not want to do this in front of my men.'

She swallowed past the lump in her throat, but dared to ask, 'Do what?'

Another one of his infuriatingly wicked smiles curved his lips. 'I can't decide if I want to beat some sense into you or make love to you. Either way, I don't think we need an audience, do you?'

Unable to form a coherent word, she shook her head.

Chapter Seven

Once they reached her chamber, he pushed her inside before slamming the door closed behind them.

'Where did you get that key?'

Brigit moved to the other side of the chamber, hoping that by putting some distance between them she'd be better able to think clearly. 'I'm the Lady of the Keep. I had it.'

'No, you didn't. I went through your things and took all the keys from your chest and from the maids.'

The empty space separating them filled with a heavy silence. Not knowing what to say or what to do, she watched him, wary of what he might do.

He was so much bigger than she was, stronger, and from the frowning glare creasing his forehead and darkening his eyes she realised he was more determined to get answers than she was to lie.

Unable to choke down her building fear, she stiffened her spine, hoping a show of bravado would see her through. She kept her gaze averted, and finally answered, 'Apparently you missed one.'

She heard his deep sigh before he said, 'You are far from stupid. So do not for a moment presume that I am.' When she didn't respond, he said, 'Brigit, look at me.'

He spoke her name softly. It fell from his lips like a caress against her cheek. She looked up at him. 'I… I…' Dear Lord above, who should she betray?

FitzHenry slowly closed the distance between them. Each step brought him nearer, making her heart race a little faster.

'Do you think you were on the wall without my knowledge? Do you imagine I wasn't informed the moment Sir Geoffrey joined you?' He stopped before her, his thighs pressing lightly against hers. 'Do you believe I remained inside the keep, leaving you alone with another man?'

He trailed a finger up her arm, caressed her shoulder, then brushed the back of one finger against her cheek, repeating the same movements Sir Geoffrey had made.

Yet FitzHenry's touch did not frighten or repulse her.

No. Instead his warm touch made her feel as if she had stepped backwards off the edge of a cliff and fallen helplessly into the abyss. Much to her disquiet, she found the feeling pleasant.

'Where did you get the key, Brigit?'

She hesitated. He already knew the answer, so why did he ask?

FitzHenry slid his hand to the back of her neck. His palm, warm on her skin, sent flashes of ice and fire to prickle against her scalp.

He had no reason to act with such kindness towards her. What was he planning? Brigit shivered. What he plotted would not bode well for her.

She tilted her head back to look up at him. Her wisest course of action would be to tell him what he wanted to know. But sometimes the wisest course could prove more dangerous. Instead of answering him, she asked, 'What are you doing?'

He breathed against her ear, whispering, 'Am I not making myself clear enough?'

To remain upright on her wobbly legs, Brigit clung to his shoulders. She tried to turn her head away from his teasing lips. Unable to do so, she knew she needed to order him to stop.

'FitzHenry, please.' Her entreaty sounded more like a breathless plea than an order.

'Randall.' He gathered her into his arms. 'My name is Randall.'

The tiny part of her mind that did not hunger for what he seemingly offered warned her to be careful. He was after answers, no matter what it would cost her.

Unwilling to pay the cost, she pushed weakly against his shoulders. 'I know what your name is, FitzHenry. Release me.'

He loosened his hold slightly, but said nothing. Unable to quell the worry building in her stomach, she studied his face. A burning hunger darkened his gaze, replacing the frowning glare.

Brigit closed her eyes and turned her head away. What had she done? She should have pushed him away sooner.

He threaded his fingers through her hair and then turned her head back towards him. 'Look at me.'

After she opened her eyes, he asked, 'What do you fear, Brigit?'

She parted her lips to say she feared him, then closed them against the lie. It was not fear of him that caused this weakness in her legs, the spinning of her mind, the quickness of her heartbeat and the heaviness settling low in her belly.

It was fear of her own weakness. Fear of her building need, the hunger for his touch, for his kiss. Fear that she could so easily succumb to him.

He was the enemy. He'd attacked her home, taken it from her father. He'd called her a witch.

What was wrong with her? How could she feel anything for this man except hatred?

She willed her heart to harden against him, clenched her jaw and said, 'I fear nothing, FitzHenry.'

He lifted one eyebrow. 'Is that so, Lady FitzHenry?'

'Don't call me that.'

'But that is who you are, Brigit. You are wife to one of the King's bastards. Not even your father can change that.'

She gasped.

'That's what I thought.' He shook his head. 'Listen to me. If you thought you could hold me off until your father returned and he'd have this marriage annulled you are wasting your time. Not even he can save you from what you seem to think a dire fate, Brigit. Only one person can do that.'

Before thinking, she asked, 'Who?'

'You.' He released her and walked towards the bed. 'Only you can change your fate.'

She swallowed, then licked her suddenly dry lips. 'How?'

'Where did you get the key?'

'I am to betray Warehaven's people to save myself?' She shook her head. 'I will not do that.'

'Then do not.' He unfastened and removed his sword belt, then placed it on the chest at the end of the bed. She watched as he pulled off his tunic and shirt before sitting down on the edge of the bed. 'Come here.'

Her pulse raced. 'No.'

In little more than the blink of an eye, he had crossed the room, scooped her into his arms and headed back to the bed. 'I did not *ask* you to join me.'

'You will force an answer from me?'

'No.' He dropped her onto the bed. 'Get undressed.'

She scrambled to the far side of the bed. 'So you plan to rape me instead?'

'Rape you?' To her amazement, he laughed. 'I may be the King's bastard, and his well-paid executioner, but I do not rape women.' He sighed, then repeated, 'Get undressed.'

Uncertain what he planned, she hesitated—which only prompted him to ask, 'Would you prefer I tear the clothes from you?'

Brigit stood up and turned her back to him. Her fingers trembled as she removed her clothing as quickly as possible. Once naked, she almost dived beneath the bedcovers.

FitzHenry blew out the candles and doused the oil lamp. In the darkness of the chamber she heard the brushing of fabric as he removed the rest of his clothing before climbing into the bed with her.

But instead of settling himself onto the mattress, he tore the covers from her and dragged her to his side.

'You said you did not rape women.' She held her body stiff against him.

'And I don't. Not even my unwilling wife.' He trailed his fingertips along her arm. 'I will not harm you. I won't even take your precious maidenhead this night.' He rolled onto his side and lowered his lips to her ear. 'But I will touch you, and I will kiss you, Brigit. 'Tis time you faced at least one of your fears.'

She crossed her arms tightly over her breasts. 'I fear nothing.'

'So you say.' He stroked a palm across her arms. 'Then why are you so tense? Why do you seek to keep yourself from me?'

Intentionally trying to anger him, she said, 'I wish not to be touched by someone I so dislike.'

Instead of anger, she knew by his low chuckle that she'd only aroused his mirth.

'That is the irony of flesh, Brigit.' While talking he slid a hand across her belly. 'The body does not care about feelings.' His touch trailed down her leg. 'It will respond to a soft touch or to the rush of warm breath.' To lend credence to his words, he breathed against her ear, lowered his lips to the side of her neck.

To keep from gasping in pleasure at his touch, she bit her lower lip. Her body warred with her mind. She hated him. She longed for him.

He lifted his head and ran his tongue across her lips. 'Ah, Brigit, it is a war as old as time.' He touched her forehead. 'Your mind hates me.' He placed his hand on her trembling belly. 'But your body says otherwise.'

How did he know this? Was he truly able to read her soul, her mind? And he dared call *her* a witch?

FitzHenry gently curled his fingers around one of her wrists and tugged lightly. 'Come. I will not hurt you. Hate me. Hate what I've done and what I will yet do to Warehaven. But trust me on this, Brigit. I will not harm you.'

She wanted to scream. She wanted to cry. Worse, she wanted to throw herself against his chest and beg him to make all of this go away. In hope that he would leave her alone, she blurted out, 'Sir Geoffrey gave me the key.' To her horror, her voice broke on a sob.

He paused a moment, before releasing her wrist. For a single heartbeat she thought he would roll away now that he had the information he wanted. Instead he cupped her face, brushed away a traitorous tear, then covered her lips with his.

At first his kiss was gentle, lightly stroking and coaxing her lips apart. She closed her eyes and prayed he would keep his word not to harm her.

As she relaxed into his kiss he deepened it, demanding more until Brigit was certain fire flowed through her veins. A cry caught in her throat. He'd been right. Her body didn't care if she liked him or not.

Unable to deny the desire and the heat racing along her spine and limbs, she uncrossed her arms and wound one around him to pull him closer.

Without breaking their kiss, he stroked a hand along her neck, across her shoulder and over her breast. She leaned into his touch. Her eyes flew open and she gasped in surprise when he traced a circle around one taut tip.

He'd touched but one small part of her body, but the sudden flash of pleasure and need raced clear to her toes.

FitzHenry lifted his head. 'Do you believe me now?'

When she didn't respond, he drew another gasp from her by thumbing another sensuous circle. Brigit sighed before admitting, 'Yes. Yes, I believe you.'

'There is no need for us to like each other. But our marriage would go smoother if we could at least trust each other, Brigit.'

She reached up and stroked his cheek. The stubble of his unshaven face was rough against her palm. 'FitzHenry—'

He growled low in his throat. 'I have a name.'

'Randall, we are enemies. How can we ever trust each other? You didn't even tell me that you'd captured Robert and Daniel. Why should I trust you?'

He moved his hand and covered her stomach. His touch was hot against her skin. 'Just as you did not find it necessary to show me the tunnel beneath this keep, or the cache of weapons hidden in the stables.'

Now her cheeks burned hotter than the flesh beneath his touch. It wasn't the heat of her cheeks that pricked at her heart. It was the knowledge that he'd not truly wanted her or her body for anything other than to gain the upper hand.

'Nor did you think to show me the workroom where you mix herbs and potions.'

She grasped his wrist and pushed his arm away. 'Is that what this is all about, FitzHenry? Punishment for not freely giving you all of Warehaven's secrets?'

Without saying a word, he reached down and pulled the covers over them, before rolling onto his back.

Brigit turned onto her side, facing away from him. She cursed the unwarranted pain in her chest and wiped angrily at the silly tears falling unbidden down her cheek.

She hated him. She hated herself more. How could she have been so foolish as to believe he'd wanted her?

'For the love of God, woman.' He rolled onto his side, slid an arm around her and pulled her hard against his chest. 'Is it that impossible to believe that I desire you? Countless men would envy me my wife. While she may not be gently spoken or obedient, she is lovely to look upon. Her skin is soft, her breasts are the perfect fit to my hand, and her lips are warm beneath mine. Why would any man, friend or foe, not desire you in his bed?'

His hoarsely spoken admission took away her ability to think and to speak. She sniffed and wiped at her eyes again.

Chapter Eight

October 29th, 1117

Randall pulled a stool closer to the bed and stared at his sleeping wife. What on earth was he going to do with this woman his sire had bade him marry?

He sat down and traced the outline of her jawbone. Her skin was soft and pliant—unlike her temper. She blew hot and cold faster than the changing seasons.

Aye, she was young, and obviously well sheltered by her father: a grievous mistake on Warehaven's part. The man should have known better than to shield his youngest from coming of age.

Randall brushed a lock of hair from her face. Her sire could not be held solely to blame. Brigit was no longer a child. She knew her place, but willingly chose to defy him.

Oddly enough, he was able to somewhat overlook her stubborn defiance because she did it out of a sense of loyalty to Warehaven. That was worth much. Did he honestly want her to break that loyalty?

No. There was nothing wrong with honouring her duty to Warehaven and its inhabitants. Far from being wrong, it was admirable in a female so young and inexperienced. However,

Randall did want her to learn how to discern loyalty to Warehaven versus loyalty to an individual.

She was wrong to trust and protect Sir Geoffrey. The man was obviously up to no good, and was likely the cause of Warehaven's current predicament.

He would discover that today. Some time during the night Sir Geoffrey and a handful of Warehaven's men had left the keep and hadn't yet returned.

When he'd gone down to the Great Hall this morning to break his fast, he'd found a charm hanging on a cord from the back of Brigit's chair at the high table.

Randall hadn't thought anything about it until Mabel had dropped a platter of food upon seeing the item. She'd wrung her hands as she nervously explained that it was an old charm. The triple interlocking triangles signified that its owner was ready to give his life to the god of death.

In this case Randall feared the owner was meant to be Brigit. But who had put the charm there?

He'd questioned the servants and the men milling about the hall, only to discover Sir Geoffrey had visited the kitchens during the night. The servants' fearful reactions upon seeing the charm led him to believe none of them had placed it on Brigit's chair. And he knew his men hadn't done so.

That only left Geoffrey. It appeared the man was up to something that would not bode well for anyone. All Hallows' Eve was two days away. Randall wanted Geoffrey and his followers caught and confined or, if necessary, killed before then. And he wanted Brigit at his side when the men were captured.

Not just to ensure her safety. She needed to know, to see for herself, that her father's man wasn't worth protecting.

He rose and pulled the covers from her. 'Come, Brigit, we have a long day ahead of us.'

She briefly opened one eye, while grabbing at the blankets. 'It's still dark. The day hasn't yet arrived.'

'It has if one is hunting.'

'I do not hunt.'

He grasped the blankets, but before he could strip them back, she rolled them around her and moved down further inside her makeshift cocoon. 'Go. Feel free to enjoy your hunt.'

Randall knelt on the bed and leaned over her. 'I could stay here with you instead.' He nuzzled his cheek across the top of her head. 'We could spend the day in bed…together, getting to know each other better.'

Instead of lunging from the bed, as he'd expected, she wriggled her fingertips at him from the edge of the blanket. 'As you wish, my lord. But find your own covers.'

He wasn't about to waste any more time with words. He grasped the edge of the bedlinen and tugged hard, unrolling her in the process.

Before she could scramble back into the warmth of the bed, he picked her up and deposited her on a stool near the open window. Randall wickedly hoped the autumn breeze was ice-cold against her skin.

'FitzHenry!' Brigit wrapped her arms across her chest, shivering.

'Randall—my name is Randall.' He tossed her clothes at her. 'Get dressed.'

She grumbled. 'Get undressed. Get dressed.' Pulling her gown over her head, she added, 'You need to make up your mind, Randall.'

'I would prefer you naked, but the men might find it distracting.'

'Aren't you amusing at this early hour?' Brigit glowered at him as she laced up her gown. 'What are we hunting?'

'Sir Geoffrey.'

Brigit tried to hide her shock, but she knew by the harsh, questioning look on Randall's face that she hadn't schooled her own features into a mask of indifference fast enough.

He walked to the window and pulled the skin shutter closed before crossing his arms against his chest and staring down at her. 'What aren't you telling me?' His lighter, more playful tone of a moment ago had gone.

Brigit rose, then turned to head for the door. 'Nothing. Are we ready?'

He caught her arm, leaned past her, snatched something from the chest behind her and nearly slapped it into her hand. 'Here— this was found hanging from the back of your chair at the high table. I can only imagine it's a gift from your Sir Geoffrey.'

She looked down at the cold metal in her hand and instantly let it fall to the floor. She lived on an isle where pagan beliefs and Christian faith had intermingled freely without harm. Until recently. It would have been odd had she not recognised the symbol.

Unlike the almond shape of the pendants in her jewel chest, this was made with the sharp corners and straight sides of a triangle. This was a death knot. Was this what Geoffrey had meant when he'd called her the chosen mate? Was she to be the next sacrifice?

Brigit swallowed before asking, 'The sacrifice you mentioned—was it a man or a woman?'

Randall tightened his hold on her arm. 'A woman. She died with her eyes wide open in fear and a scream on her lips, Brigit. She'd been tortured. But you knew that, didn't you?'

'Dear God in heaven, no.' She swung her head to stare up at him. 'No, I didn't know. Nobody at Warehaven would condone such an act.'

'No? Then why were you conversing with Geoffrey? What did you discuss? Why do you protect him still?'

Heaven help her, she'd not meant her uncertainty to go this far. She never meant for FitzHenry to think her truly evil, or a partner with Sir Geoffrey. She'd only thought to protect Warehaven.

How was she going to find the words to undo this?

Without breaking eye contact, she lifted her chin a notch and raised her hand to rest it against his heart. 'I swear to you,

Randall, I am no pagan witch. My only sin is that I thought my loyalty to Warehaven more important than anything else. My dancing around the fire was a lark—only a lark. We—my sisters and I—were bored, and I convinced them to perform some old wives' tales for entertainment. That is all.'

His one eyebrow rose in question. 'Old wives' tales?'

'Aye. Mathilda tossed a braid of her and Daniel's hair into the flames to renew the fire of their marriage. Ailis twisted an apple on a stem to see how many children she and Robert would have.'

'And your spell?' A twitch at the corner of his mouth made her wonder if he thought her explanation nonsense.

She shrugged. 'As I walked away from the fire I was to look over my shoulder and see a vision of my true love.'

He relaxed his hold on her arm. 'And did you?'

'You bolted through the fire on your horse before I had a chance to see anything.' She couldn't help adding, 'And now it seems to matter not at all.'

'Why is that?'

'It would be pointless to seek my true love while I'm wed to another.'

The moment the words left her mouth, Brigit wished them back. It was beneath her to be that cruel. He was her husband, no matter what she thought of their marriage.

If he gave any thought to her statement, he didn't show it. Instead he asked, 'What did you and Geoffrey discuss?'

Brigit glanced around her chamber. Every item she saw reinforced her loyalty to Warehaven. The chest for her clothes, the bench behind her and her bed had all been made by Timothy, the woodworker. The cloth for her gowns and the curtains surrounding the bed had been woven and dyed here by Mabel and her daughters.

The tallow for her candles, the food she ate, the herbs that scented her chamber and bath—someone from Warehaven had made each item that bettered her life and made it more pleasant.

How could she betray any of her people? Her life was already in jeopardy. When Daniel and Robert failed to show up at the clearing, Sir Geoffrey would know she'd betrayed him. But if she told FitzHenry about Geoffrey, she would in effect betray everyone.

If Geoffrey thought for a moment that she'd given him up to his enemies, how many of Warehaven's people would suffer and die? She could not live with herself if that happened.

She was certain FitzHenry and his men would capture Geoffrey, thus saving her the need to betray the people of Warehaven.

FitzHenry tightened his hold on her arm and shook her. 'Listen to me and listen well. Do not misplace your loyalty in this. Freely protect those who serve you well. But do not think to hide a murderer behind your skirts. It will not bode well for your claim of innocence if you do.'

His evenly spoken words made her feel sick to her stomach. To combat the churning, she gave her anger free rein. 'What will you do, FitzHenry? Find me guilty and kill me, too?'

'I will do whatever is deemed necessary. Do you understand me?'

Shock at his softly spoken threat froze the words in her throat.

He released her. 'Finish dressing and meet me outside.' Before reaching the door, he paused long enough to add, 'You have family here. You might want to consider their future, too.'

Brigit stared at the closed door. Had that been a threat? Would he do something to her sisters or their husbands if she refused to tell him what he wanted to know?

From what little she knew, his reputation as the King's executioner was well deserved. But surely he wasn't so vile that he'd harm or kill innocent people?

The thought gave her pause. What if she was wrong and he *would* go that far? She quickly finished getting ready. The sooner they found Sir Geoffrey, the sooner everything could be put right.

* * *

Brigit squinted against the sunlight flashing through the gaps in the trees. They'd followed the path east for a couple of hours, and the sun was now at the perfect height to glare directly in her eyes when not shaded by the forest.

She shifted in her saddle and jerked the hood of her cloak further down her face. At any other time she'd enjoy the warmth of the sun. Today, however, her anger, worry and indecision pounded like hammers against her temples.

'Are you unwell?' FitzHenry slowed his horse until he rode next to her on the trail.

'I'm fine.'

'Good. Then you won't mind continuing our discussion.'

The last thing she wanted to do was discuss anything with him. In truth she wanted to slide from this bouncing horse, curl up under a tree and be left alone.

When she didn't answer, he asked, 'What did you and Sir Geoffrey discuss?'

Without lying, she replied, 'We didn't *discuss* anything.'

He took the reins of her horse and brought both animals to a halt. Waiting until the others were a slight distance ahead, he turned to her and cupped her chin in his hand. 'The time for word-games is at an end.' His thumb trailed lightly across her lower lip, making her shiver slightly. 'What is he planning?'

While his hold didn't hurt, she couldn't turn her face away from him. 'FitzHenry, please. You don't understand—'

The blaring sound of hunting horns broke through the forest. Animals scurried through the underbrush, shaking leaves and branches in their wake. Birds took flight, crying out as they left their nests and perches in the trees.

FitzHenry frowned. 'What—?'

The horns blared again. But these horns did not call the start of a normal hunt. This was a signal to begin something far more sinister and demonic. Brigit's throbbing temples threatened to burst. She closed her eyes, swallowing against the pain and the sudden chill making her tremble with a sick, cold dread.

'We need to leave this place.'

Before she could explain why, FitzHenry's men had turned around and surrounded them, their swords at the ready.

She tore her horse's reins from FitzHenry's hand, and over the din of the charging horses and weapons being unsheathed, she shouted, 'It is a call for the hunt to begin, and we are the hunted.'

Chapter Nine

'Close ranks!' Randall stood in his stirrups to see over the heads of the guards tightly surrounding him and Brigit. He'd been told about this Wild Hunt. So the sight before him shouldn't have taken him by surprise.

About fifteen half-naked men, dressed in nothing but animal skins and dye markings on their flesh, rushed towards his group. Their unintelligible shouts sounded as crazed as they looked.

They were men possessed. And at their lead was Sir Geoffrey. The skin of a gutted stag covered his head, shoulders and back. Multi-coloured ribbons fluttered from the antlers. A chain clasped on either side held the skin on like a cloak.

Randall glanced at Brigit. The look of terror on her face wasn't fake. It answered most of his questions. She wasn't involved with Geoffrey's plans.

About twenty paces away, the huntsman stopped suddenly. Geoffrey rose up in his saddle to shout, 'Give me my woman.'

Randall's sword arm ached to drive his weapon through Geoffrey's black heart. Unfortunately he'd have to deny himself the pleasure. He didn't have enough men here to fight and protect his wife at the same time.

Without moving, he whispered to Brigit, 'Say nothing until I give the word. Then turn around and ride for your life. I will be right behind you.'

To his men, he ordered, 'When I give the signal, open ranks behind me. Hold them off as long as you can without risking your life. Take no prisoners.'

'Did you hear me, FitzHenry? Give me my woman.'

'Your woman?' Randall pretended to look around in confusion. 'I see no woman here except my wife.'

Sir Geoffrey laughed. The high-pitched vile sound turned Randall's stomach. Had he not guessed at the man's insanity before, this noise would have made him wonder.

'Your *wife*?' Geoffrey's horse reared at the man's shout. Jerking on the reins, he yelled, 'Have you yet validated it with a joining? I've seen no proof.'

The man referred to the absence of bloody sheets hanging from their chamber window opening. But Randall wouldn't tell Geoffrey or any of the other men the truth of his marriage. That was between him and Brigit. Instead, he said, 'The proof was sent to my sire.'

'Nay. The King would not care whether his bastard spawn wed a maiden or not. But it will be easy enough for Woden to tell if you lie.'

'Woden is naught but a myth created by madmen.' He intentionally sought to anger Geoffrey enough that he would make a fatal mistake.

Once again Geoffrey's manic laughter screeched through the forest. 'You will see, and then you'll believe.'

'Show me.'

'Be patient. Soon. He will arrive soon. Right now I need ready his chosen mate. Give me my woman.'

'Come and take her.' Randall raised his sword in the air. 'If you can.'

As Geoffrey and his men charged forward, Randall urged Brigit, '*Go!*'

The men behind them opened ranks, permitting him and Brigit to exit the circle and tear back down the path. Shouts punctuated by the clanging sound of sword meeting sword rang like music in his ears.

He didn't fear for his men. There were nine of them, and each was well trained enough to deal with Geoffrey's force. Had Brigit not been present, he'd have stayed to take down Geoffrey himself. He would not risk her falling into that heinous villain's clutches.

Brigit hung on to her horse's reins for dear life as its hooves quickly ate up the ground, putting more and more distance between them and Sir Geoffrey. The throbbing against her temples had lowered to her chest. She gasped for breath against the frenzied pounding of her heart.

She should have told FitzHenry sooner, and not debated with herself so long. But she had thought she'd have time. She had thought he and his men would capture Geoffrey. If they failed to kill him, how would he retaliate?

'Brigit, slow down.'

FitzHenry rode alongside her. 'Give the horses rest.'

She kept her gaze trained on a spot between her horse's ears, waiting for him to say something.

Finally he kneed his beast closer, until his leg touched hers, and broke the silence. 'Anything you'd care to tell me?'

'I am sorry.'

'Of course you are. But that's not what I meant. Did you know that you were Woden's chosen mate?'

Brigit flinched at his tone. She couldn't blame him, but it still chafed. 'Yes.'

He ducked to miss hitting a tree branch on the narrow path. 'Did you plan to let him kill you rather than tell me anything?'

'Yes.' But she'd believed, hoped, that he'd capture Geoffrey before it came to that.

His curses rang in her ears. Once he'd caught his breath, he asked, 'Has everyone on this isle lost the ability to reason?'

She didn't think he truly wanted an answer, but she said, 'I thought it would be better for me to be the object of his madness rather than the people of Warehaven.'

'How noble of you. I had no idea that I had wed a martyr. Did you give any thought to what *I* might do to Warehaven once you were dead?'

No, she hadn't thought of that. 'I didn't think you'd do anything if I died. I worried more about what you'd do if you knew that one of Warehaven's people was responsible for the problems of late.'

'You didn't think I would—?'

The sound of hunting horns cut off his question. Brigit gasped as if someone had struck her in the stomach. 'They're still after us.'

He caught her arm. 'Hush.' Turning his head, FitzHenry listened to the horns. The sounds seemed to come from three directions, as if one horn answered another. 'They've cut us off from Warehaven and Carisbrooke.' He nodded towards the east. 'Earl Baldwin said there are caves by the coast. Do you know where they are?'

Brigit nodded. 'But we are hours away, and there are chalk fields between here and there.'

'We have to find somewhere safe. We'll worry about the fields when we get there.' He released her arm, then paused long enough to lightly stroke the side of her face. 'You were wrong. I would be outraged if anything happened to you.'

Surprise and confusion kept her speechless as he turned and rode ahead.

Brigit wiped the sweat from her forehead, dropped the saddle roll she carried, and sat down on a semi-flat boulder. 'Please, stop a moment.'

After turning the horses loose, they'd crossed the chalk fields on foot. By some miracle she hadn't broken her ankle. Although it hadn't been easy—one footstep would find solid purchase, while the next would hit a spot that skittered into pieces beneath the lightest step—it was still easier than climbing down a rocky cliff.

'We're almost there. You can rest then.' Randall extended his arm, took her hand and pulled her back onto her feet. 'Come on.'

She groaned while picking up her supplies. 'You said that hours ago.'

'Hours ago we were still on horseback.' He tugged her arm gently, coaxing her to follow him. 'I never would have guessed you were weak.'

'I am *not* weak. I haven't eaten today. I haven't slept well. I—'

'You haven't slept well?' He stopped, then turned around to look at her.

Brigit shook her head at the foolish comment that had her cheeks burning with embarrassment. 'I feared waking up and finding myself on top of you again.'

'That would have been terrible.'

'Yes, it would have been—for me.'

He ignored her comment and climbed down another boulder. 'Here.' He readjusted his saddle bag and helped her down.

The mouth of a cave gaped just a few feet away. To her relief, the narrow ledge leading to it was flat. Brigit looked down and saw nothing but a sheer rockface and the sea far below.

'Are you going to join me? Or are you going to stand there all day?'

She shook the dizziness from her head and ducked into the cave behind him.

The sun had already started its descent, so the cave was nearly dark. Randall dug through his saddle bag and retrieved flint. 'See if you can find something to use for a fire.'

Brigit felt around with her feet, locating the remains of what appeared to have been a campfire. 'Someone was here before us.' She brought him the half-burned wood and unused branches from a nearby pile.

'Let's hope they aren't still here.' He gathered some of the branches into a makeshift torch. After a few tries they had enough light to make their way further back into the cave, where he made a small campfire while she unpacked their meagre supplies.

'What are we going to do now? We can't stay here for ever.'

He unbuckled his sword belt and placed it on the floor of the cave, next to the blanket she'd unrolled. 'We'll stay here for the night. If we set out early in the morning, we can make our way along the coast, then cut in towards Carisbrooke.'

Suddenly nervous about being alone with FitzHenry, Brigit looked around the cave. It was too small. Too confined. And far too isolated.

'Brigit, come here.' He closed the space between them and pulled her into his arms.

She kept her body rigid, her arms frozen at her sides. She longed to relax against his chest and return his embrace, but she knew that was what he was after. He wanted her to let down her guard. And, even though she had to eventually start trusting him, this deserted cave wasn't the place to begin.

'Are you afraid I'll make this marriage valid? Or do you fear having to tell me what you know about Sir Geoffrey and his plans?' he asked softly.

Brigit looked up at him. The fire's light glittered in his eyes, and for a moment she thought she saw a twinge of regret, of pain. She sighed and looked away. 'Both. I fear both. I fear you.'

He walked away, but turned around suddenly and stared at her. She cringed at the rage etched across his face as he shouted, 'I have done nothing to you. Nothing to make you fear me. Your life was mine to take or to keep. I chose to keep it. Does that count for nothing?'

Brigit opened her mouth, but no words formed in her mind. She had no answer for him.

'Warehaven is mine. You cannot change that, Brigit. But you are still its lady. I gave you that boon, thinking it would quell the worry and fear of the future for you and your people. Yet you hate and fear me so much that you can't even bring yourself to call me by name.'

Shame overwhelmed her. She reached towards him, drawing her arm back when he stepped further away. Knowing she was wrong, yet not knowing what to say or what to do, Brigit grabbed the torch and ran further inside the cave.

She needed to get away from the angry hurt on his face and in his voice. Anger and hurt that *she* had put there—unfairly.

Randall let her go. He ran a hand down his face. She was driving him out of his mind. Never in his life had a woman affected him so.

And he didn't like it.

He didn't like the way his stomach had knotted when Geoffrey had threatened her. He didn't like the way his heart pounded when he held her.

And he most certainly didn't like the way she roused his temper with nothing more than a look.

All this after only knowing her for a little over two days. What would it be like a month from now? A year from now?

He laughed weakly. He'd be a babbling idiot by then.

Maybe he should let her father have their marriage set aside. His chest tightened at the thought.

No.

Randall dropped down onto the blanket. He should go after her. Neither one of them knew this cave. She might get lost, fall into a crevice.

Or, worse, find an exit and leave.

'Randall!'

He jumped to his feet at her scream. It echoed off the wall of the rocky chamber.

'Randall!'

He grabbed his sword, lit a brace of branches, then headed towards her terrified screams.

The light from her torch glowed from around the bend. He raced forward and saw her frozen against the wall of the cave.

'Brigit.' He pulled her into his arms. She shook from head to toe. Tears streamed down her face. 'What is it?'

Beyond the ability to speak, she made a moaning sound in her throat and buried her face against his chest. Finally catching her breath, she raggedly gasped, 'A dragon.'

Chapter Ten

A dragon?

While he'd long heard tales of dragons, he doubted they were anything more than a myth. But whether she had actually seen a dragon or not wasn't in question. Her wide-eyed unseeing stare told him that her terror was real. She'd seen *something*.

'Where?' Randall tried to prise her away from his chest, but she curled her fingers around his tunic and clung for dear life.

'Brigit, I need to look.'

'No. Don't leave me.'

He hadn't believed it possible for her to press her body any tighter against his. But somehow she'd managed.

And the feel of her wild pulse against his chest took his mind in directions it shouldn't be going. At least not at this moment. If he did discover something beyond the next bend, he needed to have his wits fully about him—and not focused on thoughts of her naked flesh pressed seductively against his.

Randall groaned in frustration. 'Brigit, I am only going around the next bend. You stay here.'

When she shook her head, he grasped one of her wrists and gently pressed his thumb into the soft underside until she released his clothing. Thankfully, she relaxed her other hand of her own accord.

He pushed her against the wall of the cave. 'Don't move.'

He took three steps before realising she'd followed him. It would be no use ordering her to go back. She was beyond listening.

Cautiously he peered around the next turn. No sound broke the heavy silence of the cave. Randall extended the torch to shed more light into the darkness.

Whatever hulking beast lay just beyond the wavering shadows, it didn't appear to move.

'Is it still there?' Her voice shook.

'Something is there.' He didn't add that the something was large. Extremely large. While he didn't relish the idea of facing the beast, the thought that it might surprise them in their sleep necessitated he deal with it now.

'We should leave here.'

'And go where, Brigit? Night will soon fall. I have no desire to be in the forest at night with some pagan devil hunting us.'

'What if…what if you get killed by the dragon instead?'

It was something he hadn't considered—nor would he. 'Have a little faith.' He didn't want to stand here discussing this. Their voices might awaken the slumbering behemoth.

The idea of the beast awakening caused him to consider something else. He could die in this cave. If that were to happen, Brigit would be so panicked, so terrified, that she would not think to run for her life.

He needed to soothe her—quickly. Needed to lessen her paralysing fear. He quickly pulled Brigit against his chest and caught her surprised breath with his lips.

It would not be such a bad thing to die with the taste of her on his lips. Under the spell of their shared kiss, the tenseness of her body eased. When she finally leaned against him on a shuddering sigh, he spun away, leaving her to stand alone.

Hopefully it would take a few moments for her to clear her

head before she followed him into the beast's lair. And even though their kiss made him burn for her, he had to confront the monster in its den to keep her safe.

He crept up on the sleeping dragon as silently as possible. He tightened his hold on the makeshift torch and adjusted his grip on his sword.

Less than two steps away he held his breath, raised his sword, then lunged towards the beast, slamming his blade into its skull.

He stumbled, but regained his footing as his weapon sailed through the beast as if hitting air. Randall pulled his blade back and frowned.

Even had it been unable to attack, an animal would have roared at the moment his blade struck. He lifted the torch and stared down at what was nothing more than a pile of bones.

Amazed, he walked the length of the beast. What had once surely been a magnificent creature when alive, was now about twenty feet of bones. Apparently it had come into this cave to die.

'Brigit, come here.'

'Is it dead?' Her voice drifted weakly from around the corner.

'It has been for quite some time.'

She joined him. Her eyes grew larger as she held her torch higher and studied the skeleton. 'Do you think there are any more?'

'How many animals this large has your father brought home from a hunt?'

'None.'

'Then I'd say this was probably the last one.'

She leaned against him in relief. 'I didn't realise it was dead.'

'Had I happened upon it unarmed, I most likely wouldn't have taken the time to determine that, either.' Randall doused his torch, then put an arm around her. 'Come, you need to rest before morning. I can return with a few men some other time.'

He wanted to study this creature a little further, and wanted to retrieve what he could of the skull. But that was something he could do another time.

They walked back to the front of the cave in silence. Brigit chewed on her lower lip, wondering what to say to this man who'd come to her rescue without hesitation. That was not the action of a man bent on harming her.

But how many times had he told her he wouldn't hurt her? And how many times had she not believed him?

She'd only known him two days. In that time he'd taken her father's keep, captured her brothers-by-marriage, forced her to wed him and kissed her until her toes curled.

He'd yelled at her, ordered her about, threatened her, taken her clothing away and stoked fires of longing in her belly with nothing more than a look or a gentle touch.

He'd called her a witch and gently cupped her cheek.

Her throat tightened with emotions she didn't yet want to name but could no longer ignore.

When they reached their camp, Randall took the torch from her hand and doused it before pulling his tunic off then stretching out on the blankets she'd spread on the cave's floor.

He laced his fingers behind his head and stared up at the ceiling. A frown marred his forehead.

She was a woman fully grown. It was time she acted like one. Brigit dropped to her knees at his side. 'Randall…I…am sorry.'

A surprised look wiped away his frown. She'd expected him to comment on her free use of his name. Instead he lifted a hand and traced her lower lip with his thumb. 'For what, Brigit?'

She fought to ignore the way his touch warmed her. 'For not believing you. For not telling you about Sir Geoffrey. I could have prevented all of this from happening had I simply told you what you wanted to know.'

He slid his hand around her neck and pulled her steadily closer. Just before his lips touched hers, he whispered, 'Then we would not have found a dragon together, would we?'

Together. His words brushed sweet and gentle against her heart. She had a good idea of where returning his kiss would lead.

But his touch carried her to a place that promised safety. His kiss chased away the coolness of the cave and warmed her.

Brigit sighed, then parted her lips.

Without hesitation he swept her into his arms and pulled her on top of him. His body cushioned hers from the hard stone beneath them.

His gentle kisses and light touches only served to fan the building frustration gnawing at her. She craved something more, something less…gentle.

Brigit threaded her fingers through his hair and slanted her mouth more firmly over his. A soft moan of longing worked its way free from her throat.

He cupped the back of her head and rolled them onto their sides, facing each other. Breaking their kiss, Randall asked, 'What do you seek, Brigit?'

He would make her ask? Force her to beg him? Since she'd done her best to avoid this moment, she couldn't blame him. But she wasn't quite certain what to ask for.

Brigit closed her eyes and took a slow, deep breath. So be it. Meeting his heavy-lidded gaze, she said, 'I seek to be your wife, Randall.'

This time when he covered her lips it wasn't with gentleness. Nor did his kiss promise safety or simple warmth. 'Twas more of a fierce storm swirling around her than safety. And the warmth quickly grew to a blazing fire.

While his mouth filled her with anticipation, his hands made quick work of unlacing her gown. She slid her hands beneath his shirt and marvelled at the heat of the flesh covering the muscles of his back. Except for a few puckered scars his skin was smooth under her fingertips. She traced the ridge of his spine, wondering at the shiver chasing her touch.

Had she caused such a reaction? Did he feel the same flashes of fire and ice she did?

He reached beneath the skirt of her gown to caress and stroke her thigh. Brigit trembled at the intimate contact.

She kneaded his shoulder blades, ran her knuckles down his side, before dragging her palm up towards his chest. Her thumb brushed across a flat nipple, and when it swelled beneath her touch, she gasped, unable to contain her surprise.

Randall broke their kiss on a groan. He sat up, pulling her along with him. Without a word, he tugged both of her gowns over her head before removing his shirt and tossing the garments atop his previously discarded tunic.

They sat thigh to thigh, facing each other on the blanket. He reached out to cup her breast and thumbed a circle around the nipple. Brigit shivered at the sensation. He grasped her wrist and placed her hand on his chest.

She mimicked his motions, delighted to realise that, aye, he did feel the same flashes of fire and ice.

Following his lead, she learned his body while he learned hers. Her tentative touches grew bolder to match his. Stroking, kissing, memorising gentle curves and hard muscles, until Brigit wanted to scream at the relentless hunger clawing low in her belly.

Randall caressed her cheek and drew her towards him. Meeting her halfway, he slanted his mouth over hers as he slid a hand down her torso. His touch burned a trail lower, sliding over her stomach to settle against the need pulsing between her thighs.

The steady contact, light and slow at first, grew firmer, until she gasped at the dizzying promise beckoning her towards bliss.

She clung to his shoulders. Her fingers curled into his flesh. His hot breath against her neck fanned the flames already licking at her skin.

Unable to contain the storm thundering through her, Brigit cried out, 'Randall, please.'

He nudged her down onto her back, tore at the ties securing his braes, then knelt between her legs.

She reached for him, but he pushed her hands away, intent on heightening the storm to a wild tempest. She strained against him, arching her hips, seeking something she couldn't identify.

Her legs trembled. He leaned over her and gathered her into his arms before pushing the tip of his erection past her thin barrier.

Brigit froze at the unfamiliar intrusion. The pain she'd expected was nothing more than a small twinge of discomfort that disappeared as quickly as it had begun.

But the longing, the hunger remained. She tilted her hips and he pushed into her, filling her. Her eyelids fluttered. She held on to him tightly to keep from falling alone into the storm.

She wanted to weep at the exquisite completeness overwhelming her. Her body raced towards fulfilment. Unable and unwilling to stop it, she cried his name, and through the fog clouding her senses heard her name leave his lips.

Randall collapsed on top of her. But his weight was a welcome closeness. She groaned in complaint when he rolled them onto their sides.

He held her in his arms, his chin resting atop her head. She burrowed her face against his chest.

Once her pulse and breathing had slowed to more normal levels, she tilted her head back and glanced up at him. 'No wonder Mathilda wishes to renew the fire of her marriage.'

Randall's chest shook with suppressed laughter.

Just saying her sister's name made her wonder about her family's future. 'Randall?'

'Hmm?'

'Now that you know Sir Geoffrey is responsible for Warehaven's troubles, what will happen to my family?'

He tightened his embrace, forcing her head to rest back against his chest. 'Now is not the time to discuss what will or won't happen. Can we not simply share a night of peace between us?'

She frowned. If he was going to let her family go, would he not have said so? Did that mean he still intended to carry out his sire's orders?

She squeezed her eyes shut and forced her mind away from her dark, frightening thoughts. Aye, she could give him this one night of peace.

She wanted more. She wanted a lifetime of days filled with peace and nights spent crying out in shared passion. But she feared this one night might be all they ever shared.

Chapter Eleven

October 30, 1117

Randall sat up and stretched the soreness from his back and neck with a heavy groan. He must be growing soft; sleeping on the hard ground had never bothered him before.

He turned to wake Brigit, but found an empty spot next to him. His light mood evaporated. Where was she?

Her clothes were missing. Had she left? He leapt to his feet and gathered his own clothing.

'Brigit?'

She stepped into the opening of the cave. 'Good morning.'

Tugging on his clothes, he asked, 'Where were you?' Appalled at the angry tone of his voice, he explained, 'I was worried that something had happened to you when I didn't see you here.'

'The *bed* was too hard, so I was sitting outside in the sunlight.'

He arched his back. 'Aye, rock makes for little comfort.'

She pulled salted pork, bread and cheese from the saddle bag. 'Hungry?'

'A little.' Actually, he was more anxious to set out, but knew he should eat something first.

She bent to roll up the blanket. 'I have already eaten.'

He leaned against a large rock and quickly filled his stomach as he watched Brigit stow their few belongings. Her short, to-the-point sentences, the way she avoided looking at him, told him that something was wrong.

After last night they should be close, more open with each other. What had built this cold wall of silence between them?

Then he remembered their conversation before falling asleep. She feared for her family. But if they were not involved with Geoffrey, why would she worry so?

Randall washed down the bread and cheese with a swig from the wineskin before packing the remaining food away.

'Ready?' Brigit waited by the cave's entrance.

He didn't answer her. Instead, he pulled her into his arms and lowered his head to kiss her.

She turned her face away. 'We should set out.'

Their one night of shared peace had apparently been their last. 'What is this? What is wrong?'

She shrugged as if nothing was amiss. 'Nothing. I just wish to spend tonight in my bed.'

'You are a poor liar, Brigit.'

She stared up at him. Tears clung to her eyelashes. 'What will you do to my family?'

As much as her tears pained him, his first duty was to his sire. He released her, grabbed the saddle bags, then stepped out of the cave. She was right; they should be on their way. The sooner this was over with the better.

'I need to know, Randall. I may have become your wife, but that does not mean I have forsaken my family. What will you do to them?' She followed him out into the sunshine and along the path leading to the base of their ascent.

He'd rather ignore her, but knew full well that she would plague him with questions or beleaguer him with her temper until he gave her an answer.

Randall took her hand and helped her up to a boulder. 'It depends on their guilt.'

Scrambling for purchase, she said, 'I have already told you they had nothing to do with Geoffrey and his men. They took no part in yesterday's hunt, nor will they be involved in the one tomorrow night.'

He stared down at her. 'Tomorrow night?'

'Yes. I told you… Oh.' She squinted her eyes shut and shook her head before meeting his stare again. 'I meant to. I was distracted.'

Distracted? Lives were at stake and she had been distracted? A myriad of unsettling thoughts buffeted him. Had she intentionally set out to waylay him, effectively taking him away from Warehaven?

Had he let a pretty face and sensual curves divert him from his mission? Was Brigit that calculating?

His heart believed the answer was a resounding no. But his warrior's sense urged caution. There was a way to discover the truth.

He tossed the saddle bags to the ledge above, then not so gently pulled her up to join him on the boulder, pinning her against the cliff. 'Have you betrayed me, Brigit?'

'Betrayed you?' She blinked the confusion from her eyes before narrowing them to slits. 'Is that what you think I have done?'

'You told me nothing about Geoffrey's plans. You kept me at arm's length while your father's man plotted mayhem. What should I think?'

She shouted at him in return, 'You attacked my home. You forced me to wed you against my will and expected me to become the meek, obedient wife.'

Intentionally feeding her anger, he nearly snarled his reply. 'I expected you to act as the Lady of Warehaven and do what was best for your people—not set out to keep me from fulfilling my duty.'

'Did I lure you into the forest for Geoffrey to hunt like an animal?' She smacked his shoulder. 'Did I lead us on this unpleasant trek to the caves to spirit you away from Warehaven?

Did I spread my legs and play the whore to keep you from your father's task?' She curled a hand into a fist and struck his chest. 'Let me go.' Her voice broke and she tried to push him away. 'Let me go. Get away from me.'

His experience as an interrogator told him that she hadn't betrayed him—her rage and shock were genuine. Relief eased the tightness in his chest. But the task now before him seemed daunting. How was he going to soothe her justified anger?

It would take much more than sweet words and gentle kisses. They had not the time for either. Still, he owed her something in way of explanation.

He grabbed a handful of her hair and pulled her head back. 'No. I will not let you go. Not now, or ever. You are my wife and I would have no other.' He silenced her outrage with his mouth.

She struggled against his onslaught, kicking ineffectively at his shins, pushing against shoulders, but he refused to let go.

He heard her sob and tasted the saltiness of her tears, and still he would not relent. Only when she ceased struggling and tentatively returned his kiss did he release his grasp on her hair.

Randall gathered her close in his arms and feathered his lips across her face, whispering, 'I am sorry. I had to know, Brigit. I had to know.'

'I hate you.'

Her voice was too soft and shaken for one who claimed such a thing. He brushed his cheek across the top of her head. 'I blame you not.'

'There was no excuse for treating me so. I will find a way to make you pay for such an underhand act.'

'I expect no less.' He chuckled before releasing her. 'Come, we need make haste now that you've kept us here so long.'

It seemed to Brigit that they'd walked for days instead of mere hours. They'd already cleared the coastline and cut inland towards Carisbrooke. Now they were nearly at the keep.

She was still vexed at the way Randall had chosen to test her loyalty to him. Her word should have been enough. It had been a nasty trick that she'd not fall for again.

To make matters worse, he still hadn't answered her question about her family.

Lost in her own thoughts, she stumbled in surprise against Randall's outstretched arm. He caught her around the waist to keep her from falling. 'Steady.'

'Why are we stopping…?' Her question trailed off when she noticed his tilted head. He was listening for something behind them in the woods.

She turned around and heard it, too. Twigs snapping and fallen leaves crunching beneath footsteps.

Randall pulled her off the path while unsheathing his sword. She took refuge behind him, peering around his shoulder to see who, or what, followed them.

The murmur of voices reached her, growing steadily louder, until she heard, 'You had better hope we are not lost. I swear, I will thrash you until my arm falls off.'

Brigit's heart leapt in joy at the sound. She bolted around Randall, dodging his grasp, crying, 'Father!'

Heedless of Randall's shouts, and the underbrush snagging at her gown, Brigit ran towards the approaching voices. With little warning, she launched herself against her father's chest.

He closed his arms around her as he staggered backwards a few steps before catching his footing. 'Brigit, child, what are you doing here?'

She felt his arms tense as he asked, 'Who is this man? Why does he chase you?' He pushed her to the side and pulled his sword free. 'Has he harmed you?'

'No.' Brigit laid a hand on his arm. 'No, father, do not. He is my husband.'

'*What?*' Her father and brother shouted in unison.

She held out her hand towards Randall. 'Father, this is Randall

FitzHenry. We wed three days ago. Randall, this is Arwel of Warehaven, my father, and my brother Simon.'

As her father stared at her, dumbfounded, her brother asked, 'The King's FitzHenry?'

Randall nodded. 'Aye.'

To Brigit's horror, Simon drew his weapon and pointed it at her husband. 'What are you doing here?'

Randall raised an eyebrow as he looked from the sword to Simon.

Even though only three days had passed since they'd met, Brigit recognised the threat in that cold, steady glare. Her smaller and weaker brother wouldn't stand a chance.

She quickly grabbed the hilt of Simon's weapon. 'What are you doing? I said he is my husband.'

Simon physically shoved her away, knocking her to the ground. Before the first cry of warning could leave her mouth, Simon had flown through the air and landed with a thud on his knees next to her.

Randall held Simon's weapon, the tip pressed against her brother's neck. 'Touch my wife again in such a manner and I will gut you.'

Her father stepped forward and cuffed the back of Simon's head. 'Have you not yet caused enough trouble that you seek to add to your sins?'

Randall handed Simon's weapon to the older man before sheathing his own sword. After helping Brigit to her feet and pulling her close to his side, he asked, 'What trouble has he caused?'

Chapter Twelve

'What *trouble* has he caused?' Brigit's father repeated as he looked from her to Randall, then to Simon and back. 'It seems there is more than one tale that needs telling here.' He settled his gaze on Randall. 'Why is the King's son on the isle, and how has he come to wed my daughter?'

Without formalities, Randall answered. 'I was sent here to take possession of Warehaven and quell the recent rash of pagan activities there.' He briefly squeezed Brigit's waist, adding, 'It was up to me to decide whether to kill the witch of Warehaven or wed her.'

To her utter shock, her father laughed before saying, 'She is not a witch, so I am grateful you did not kill her. Although at times you may wish otherwise.'

'That is all?' Brigit jerked out of Randall's embrace. 'I have been worried sick, have made myself look like a traitor by defying my husband, yet all you can say is that you are *grateful*? What about Warehaven?'

Her father shrugged. 'Brigit, I am old, and have longed to return home.'

She'd had no idea that he wished to leave Warehaven and return to the border lands of northern Wales. 'You have never said that before, Father.'

'What was there to speak of when I could not decide what to do with Warehaven? Robert and Daniel have their own keeps. Simon is not ready for the responsibility and may never be. As for you—until now I'd lost hope you'd ever find someone strong enough to wed you. I had come to believe I would never again see the land of my birth.'

Her sire turned his attention back to Randall. 'What have you discovered about Sir Geoffrey's activities?'

'I didn't mention Geoffrey.' Randall shot her a questioning look.

'You didn't need to.' Her father hitched a thumb towards Simon. 'This one waited until we were at the fields farthest from Warehaven and then let the horses loose. Robert and Daniel set off in one direction to find them, and we took the other. It wasn't until yesterday that he finally admitted Sir Geoffrey had put him up to the trick and was leading me around in circles.'

Randall grabbed the front of the younger man's tunic and jerked him forward. 'Why?'

Simon muttered something under his breath that nobody could hear and gained himself a good shaking.

'Answer me, boy.'

Simon swatted at Randall's hands. 'I am not a boy.'

'Then act like a man and tell me what has happened.'

Randall handled Simon with more patience than Brigit would have thought he possessed.

'He threatened to kill Ailis, Mathilda and Brigit if I did not do his bidding.' Her brother's eyes widened and he paled as he added, 'He…he described their deaths in great detail and I believed him.'

Randall asked, 'Exactly what was his bidding?'

'I was to set the horses loose.' Simon glanced at their father before admitting, 'And to make certain we did not return until after the All Hallows' Eve festival.'

Randall released Simon. 'Did he say why?'

Her brother shrugged. 'It made little sense to me, but Sir

Geoffrey thought it would appease the god of death if he were to hold a Wild Hunt in his honour.'

Her husband shifted his focus in Brigit's direction. 'See how easy that was?'

Her father's laughter made it that much harder to ignore Randall's teasing. 'Perhaps the two of you should have wed each other.' She turned her back on both of them and headed down the path.

Three days of fretting, worrying, arguing and fighting—for what? So the two of them, the former and current Lord of Warehaven, could laugh at her?

They could stand there and laugh by themselves. This path led directly to Carisbrooke. She could easily find her way alone.

'Brigit, wait,' Randall shouted at her.

Not wanting his company, she quickened her pace. And since they were well within the Earl's lands, she didn't need his protection. Earl Baldwin's men constantly patrolled the area. In truth, she was surprised that they hadn't already run into one or more of his guards.

'Brigit,' Randall called out again. 'I said *wait*.'

She turned around to say no—but the sight of Geoffrey and seven of his wild huntsmen blocking her path froze the word in her throat.

Before she could run, or scream or even force her mind into action, the men had surrounded her. Sir Geoffrey grabbed her and pulled her hard against his naked chest.

'My, my—what have we here? This is truly an offering for the god.'

Brigit found her voice and screamed, 'Randall!'

He heard her scream of terror and it took his breath away. There were no dragons in this forest, so what had brought about such fear?

Randall sprinted around the bend and came to a heart-stopping halt. Warehaven and his son jerked to a breathless stop beside him.

Sir Geoffrey held Brigit before him, with the flat of his sword across her throat and his free hand grasping a fistful of her hair.

'I told you to release my woman, FitzHenry. But you wouldn't listen.' Geoffrey jerked hard on Brigit's hair. Ignoring her scream of pain, he said, 'So now it comes to this.'

Randall gritted his teeth. Geoffrey would not get the chance to hold his hunt tomorrow night—he would die this day.

Arwel moved closer and rested a hand on Randall's arm as he addressed Geoffrey. 'This is how you repay me? You take my daughter prisoner?'

'Repay you for what, old man? You have given me nothing I did not earn.' Geoffrey bent his head and placed his lips below Brigit's ear. 'Although there was plenty more I wanted.'

Randall felt a growl of rage build in his chest, but he kept his tone steady and ordered, 'Release my wife.'

'Or what?' Geoffrey curled his lip and twisted the sword so the edge rested against her neck. 'Stay where you are, FitzHenry, or I will sacrifice her now.'

Not only would this spawn of the devil die today, he would die slowly and painfully.

'Sacrifice her?' Simon's question came out as little more than a squeak. He cleared his throat. 'You told me if I kept my father away, you wouldn't harm my sisters.'

'I lied, little man. While the other two are safe, this one is to be Woden's bride tomorrow night. She will be stripped naked and staked out for his pleasure.'

Geoffrey laughed softly, as if at a joke he'd just told. He released her hair, slid his hand down her arm, then reached around to cup a breast. 'She will discover pure ecstasy from his rutting.'

Randall's fingers curled in anticipation of sliding his sword into Geoffrey's chest and twisting it hard, through flesh, muscle and bone, to finally lodge in his demonic black heart.

First he needed to gain Brigit's release. With Geoffrey's unnatural state of mind it was impossible to guess the man's actions. But he had to attempt something.

Randall sheathed his sword and tipped his head in mock defeat. 'I salute your cunning. You have outwitted me.'

A sane man would have recognised the ruse for the lie it was. However, Geoffrey merely preened at the admission. He tilted his chin and looked down his nose at Brigit. 'I have, haven't I?'

Brigit frowned. What was Randall doing? He was plotting something. She kept her eyes focused on her husband.

Randall's shoulders drooped. He lifted a hand and wiped it down his face, pausing to rub at his temples. When he lowered his hand it was all Brigit could do not to gasp at the immense pain swimming in his eyes.

'Sir Geoffrey.' Randall stretched out his hands in supplication and took a step forward. 'May I bid my wife farewell?'

Geoffrey swung the sword away from Brigit's neck and pointed it at Randall. 'You may bid her farewell from—'

Everything happened in less than a heartbeat. Randall bowed, as if accepting Geoffrey's half-spoken order. But Brigit saw the lightning-quick movement of his hand as he pulled his dagger from his belt.

The very instant he stood upright she turned her face away. But she still heard the whoosh of the blade as it sailed past her head to land quivering in Geoffrey's neck.

The man holding her captive hadn't time to finish his sentence before his words gurgled to a stop.

In the next instant mail-clad men on horseback charged forward from the woods. Brigit screamed and spun away from the wide-eyed dead man still clinging to her.

Randall raced forward, drawing his sword, and dispatched two of Geoffrey's followers before pulling Brigit into his arms and against his trembling chest.

He held her close. Their hearts pounded against each other. Not trusting himself to speak through the lump in his throat, he simply held her tightly, eternally thankful for the opportunity to do so.

Dear Lord, when had he come to care so for this woman? How had she crept so silently and firmly into his heart? He did not like this caring—it frightened him far too much, and nothing frightened FitzHenry—and it made him take risks he never would have considered before.

She clutched at the fabric covering his back. 'I cannot breathe.'

He relaxed his hold slightly. 'I thought he would kill you before I could slay him.'

Brigit ran a hand through his hair. 'I did, too.'

'I don't know what I would have done.'

To his horror, his voice faltered. Brigit didn't move. She didn't say a word for a couple of heartbeats. Then, just when he hoped she'd let it pass without comment, she cupped his cheek and lifted her face to his.

'I love you, too, FitzHenry.'

He groaned. 'If this is what love is, I want no part of it, wife.'

She smiled and ran her thumb across his lower lip. 'I fear you have no choice, husband.'

A guard from Carisbrooke approached. He cleared his throat, then said, 'My lord FitzHenry?'

Once Brigit had taken her leave, Randall turned to the man. 'I thank you for coming here when you did.'

'One of your men came to the keep yesterday. We have been looking for you.' He nodded towards the forest, where other men led four horses towards them. 'We have extra horses for you, and men if you need them.'

'I foresee no need for the men, but we will take the horses. I'll see they're returned tomorrow.'

The man waved away the offer. 'Earl Bladwin has already sent word that we are to grant you whatever you require.'

Randall looked at the eight dead bodies littering the path. 'Have someone cart these remains to Warehaven.'

'Aye, my lord.'

Once the guards had left, Arwel joined Randall. 'Now what will you do?'

'Right now we need to return to Warehaven, to make sure all is well.' He wanted to make certain none of Geoffrey's followers still resided within its walls.

'What about my family?'

Randall held back his smile at the question, oft asked of late. 'That is something we need to discuss.'

'Well, then, I understand you control a keep with a fine cook and even better wine.'

'Do I? I've not had time to yet discover if that is so.'

Arwel slapped his shoulder. 'Ah, there are many treasures you've yet to discover. Come, I'll share them with you over a meal.'

Simon and Arwel mounted their borrowed horses and headed towards Warehaven. Randall helped Brigit onto another, pausing to caress her leg once she was in the saddle.

'Randall, what will you do—?'

He reached up and placed a finger over her lips. 'That is between me and your sire.'

'Fine.' She tossed her head, then tugged at her horse's reins.

He was tired of arguing and wanted no more of it—at least not today. So he let her go without a word.

They could argue tomorrow, or the next day. And he was certain they would.

Chapter Thirteen

October 31, 1117—All Hallows' Eve

Brigit stood in the gate tower, waving until she could no longer see her family. All of them—her sisters, their husbands, her father and brother—were leaving Warehaven.

That had been decided during last night's discussion. To her amazement, Randall had asked her to join him and her father while they talked of what to do next.

Brigit knew that Ailis and Robert wanted their baby born at their keep, not at Warehaven. Randall had agreed to see that the couple arrived home as quickly and safely as possible. He'd sent a midwife along, just in case, and Mathilda and Daniel were going with them.

The discussion had become heated when the topic of explaining everything to King Henry had arisen.

Randall had felt it his responsibility to speak with his sire. But Brigit's father had argued that, while he now had the chance to leave Warehaven in capable hands and return to his home, he'd not been to court since before she'd been born. He claimed that he truly wished to see his old friends once again before he returned to the land of his birth.

It had taken some coaxing, teasing and kissing on her part to convince Randall of the wisdom in her father's suggestion. After a while she'd realised that Randall had only prolonged the arguing to get more kisses.

Her family's innocence in the pagan activities was bittersweet. While they were alive, well and free of Geoffrey's influence, she'd not be there when Ailis gave birth. And there was a great chance that she'd never see her father again before he died.

To be honest, she hadn't thought of the last. Her father had, though, and he'd made her promise to spare him only a few days of grief when his time came. He swore his life had been wondrous, and he'd not have her wallowing in sorrow for months on end.

Her family no longer in sight, she rested her forehead against a wooden support beam.

Strong arms pulled her firmly against a warm chest. 'Are you all right?'

'Aye.'

She turned in Randall's embrace and laid her cheek against his chest. He rocked back and forth on his heels, and she closed her eyes, enjoying the soothing motion. 'I need to thank you for helping to prove them innocent.'

'You seem to have forgotten one little thing, Brigit.'

'What is that?'

'The moment Brother Peter blessed our union, they became my family, too.'

'Aye, but you still could have held them responsible for what has happened here. Especially my father.'

'Your father is old. Too old to oversee the running of a keep. I saw that within moments of meeting him.' He rubbed his chin across her hair. 'Besides, do you really think I could be that cruel? Did you truly believe I would have them put to death for Sir Geoffrey's crimes?'

She wouldn't lie to him. Not any more. 'Yes, I did.'

'Ah, Brigit, you have much to learn.'

'Are you not King Henry's executioner?'

'While it has proved useful at times, my reputation is unfounded. I did not kill for the sake of killing. I did not murder innocent men.'

'That is good to know. But still I need to thank you properly.'

He sighed heavily, and freed her from his embrace. 'Then do so, and let us never speak of it again.'

Brigit took his hands between hers. 'I am grateful for your kind fairness. I swear to you that I will prove my gratitude by becoming the good and obedient wife you deserve.'

Randall's eyes widened. His mouth opened, then snapped closed. He pulled his hands free, turned and then without a word he quickly left her on the wall.

She covered her mouth to keep from crying. What had she said? What had she done to upset him so?

'My lady?' Mabel called out as she entered Brigit's chamber. 'Why are you sitting here in the dark?'

Brigit stared at the unlit coals in the brazier. Night had begun to fall, and in her distress she'd not even noticed. Not once had Randall approached her since leaving her at the gate tower.

While she had seen his men come and go from the keep, she hadn't so much as caught a glimpse of him.

She looked at the servant. 'What do you have there?'

Mabel handed Brigit her red hooded mantle. 'His lordship has a message for you.'

To Brigit's surprise, the elderly servant blushed, but forged ahead. 'He says that if you wish to be a good and obedient wife you must stay here in this bedchamber and sleep alone.'

Mabel peered at her and asked, 'Child, what possessed you to wish to be something so silly?'

Brigit ignored the question. 'Did he say anything else?'

'Aye.' Mabel pursed her lips a moment before saying, 'He said that if you would rather be the Witch of Warehaven, you know where to find him.'

Brigit's heart nearly sang with joy. She grabbed Mabel's hands. 'Do you know where he is?'

'Of course I do.' Mabel tipped her head and smiled slyly. 'But I'm not to tell.'

'Mabel!' Brigit quickly paced the chamber, then snapped her fingers. 'In the warren?'

'No, my lady.'

The sound of a flute and tabor drums floated in through the window. Brigit smiled. 'He's at the bonfire.'

Mabel said nothing, but she blinked rapidly and shrugged her shoulders.

Brigit slipped into the cloak, pulling the hood over her head, and raced down to the bailey.

The fire crackled merrily in the yard. Since Geoffrey and his men were dead, and posed no danger, Randall had agreed to let the All Hallows' Eve celebration go on as planned.

Shouts and laughter from Warehaven's people rang loud in her ears. The steady beat of a tabor drum, along with the keening lull of a flute urged her closer to the gaiety.

She searched for Randall, scanning the throng of people, and noticed a tall, well-muscled man with an oddly familiar animal skull perched atop his head.

Brigit skirted the perimeter of the crowd, trying to get a closer look.

But the man seemed to know where she was, and he kept far enough ahead of her that she was unable to see more than quick peeks of his strange costume.

The crowd around her shifted until she no longer walked the perimeter but was swept into the celebration.

The gathering thinned, permitting a hand to reach out and untie the hood to her cloak before grasping her wrist and pulling her towards the fire.

Each step closer made her heart pound faster. The warmth flowing through her limbs grew hotter. She swayed to the beat of the incessant drums.

But this time it wasn't women from the village who joined her. It was a man—her man—wearing the skull from their dragon on his head.

Brigit pulled off her cloak and tossed it into the crowd. With her shoulders rolling suggestively, swaying hips and tapping feet, she gave herself over to the beat of the music and danced for her husband.

Two steps forward, one back. A turn, a twist, then a tap of the toe brought her against Randall's chest. With their bodies pressed tightly together, her back against his chest, they took another step forward as one.

The feel of his hard thighs pressed against her, and the sound of his heavy breathing burned hotter than the fire.

His nearness, his touch, ate away her inhibitions. She ran her hands down her body. His hands closed lightly over hers, the tips of his fingers stroking where her hands led. The curves and swells of her body tingled to life beneath their shared touch.

She and Randall repeated their seductive moves as one, and came another step closer to the fire.

Primal heat licked at her flesh. An unbidden longing to feel more than just his body press against hers, to writhe naked beneath him, flared to life with an intensity that drew a moan from her parted lips.

Another round of twisting and turning steps brought them to the edge of the fire. With a swirling flourish, Randall dropped a kiss on the side of her neck, then stepped away from the blaze, leaving her there alone.

She watched as he walked away, then looked over his shoulder at her as the crowd roared their approval.

A few nights ago she'd come to this very same spot and performed this same dance. She'd enacted an old wives' spell and seen what she had believed to be her enemy and the destruction of Warehaven.

Instead the spell had been true. She'd seen her love in the flames. Now he, too, had looked into the blazing fire, and in the depths of his eyes she saw that he'd also found love.

Brigit ran the few steps forward and lunged against his chest. Randall didn't stagger beneath her assault, as her father had. He lifted her easily into his arms and carried her through the parting crowd.

Once inside the keep, instead of heading up the stairs, he entered the warren and quickly carried her through a series of chambers and hallways until they reached one chamber awash in candle-light.

He set her on her feet and untied the laces holding the skull on his head.

Brigit rubbed her body against his. 'Where did you get that?'

'I sent a couple of men to the cave for it earlier.'

He caressed her breast. Even through the barrier of clothing his touch made her shiver. 'So you had this wickedness planned?'

Randall worked the laces on the sides of her gown free. 'After you thought to terrify me, by vowing to be good and obedient, I knew I had to do something to make you see reason.'

'You don't want a good and obedient wife?' She tugged his tunic over his head and tossed it on the floor. His shirt soon joined the pile.

He bunched the skirt of her gown inch by inch in his hands. His fingers grazed her flesh with each gathering of fabric. 'Being good is not always the best course of action.'

With a quick swipe he pulled the clothing over her head, leaving it wrapped about her upraised arms as he leaned down to trail his tongue around the peak of her breast, drawing it into his warm, moist mouth.

Brigit arched her back and struggled to free her arms. 'Randall, please.'

He lifted his head and pushed her back onto the bed. 'No. Obedience is for children and men at war.' He knelt on the floor between her parted knees. 'You are not a child.'

She lifted her head to stare at him. Candle-light danced in his eyes as he held her gaze captive. He leaned forward and laved her pulsing flesh with his tongue.

Shock made her heart jump. Pure carnal need wrapped her in its fiery heat.

He paused long enough to add, 'And you are definitely not a man at war.' He slid his hands beneath her, tilting her against his mouth.

She dropped her head down onto the mattress and closed her eyes. Lights danced against her eyelids. She'd wanted an all-consuming passion. Had wished for a lover to claim her completely. Had wanted to writhe beneath his touch.

She had all of that and more. She had a man who could protect her and keep her safe during the day. And a lover who could drive her wild and fulfil her at night.

Waves of pleasure washed over her, threatening to carry her away. She cried out his name and he covered her with his body, stripping the gown from her arms and then filling her until pleasure claimed them both.

Randall rolled onto his back, taking her with him. He cupped her face between his hands and kissed her chin, her nose, her lips. 'I love you as you are, Brigit.'

Unable to find words for the warm joy spreading through her, she turned her head and kissed his hand before feathering her lips against his cheek.

He threaded a hand through her hair and brought her head to rest against his shoulder. 'I have no need for a good and obedient wife. I would much rather have Warehaven's Witch at my side and in my bed.'

Brigit closed her eyes, trying to hold back the tears of joy seeking to escape. Against his neck she whispered softly, 'And you will always have her, my love.'

* * * * *

MASTER OF PENLOWEN

Christine Merrill

Dear Reader,

When my editors asked me to do a Hallowe'en story, I was beyond happy. Fall is my favorite season. It's a great time to enjoy the last of the good weather by kicking through some fallen leaves, choosing a pumpkin, or drinking fresh apple cider after a hay ride. And, of course, there are those bags of snack-size candy bars that never seem to last until the trick-or-treaters show up.

But by far, the best time of all is Hallowe'en. I knock down the real cobwebs on my chandelier and put up some fake ones, decorating my house with all the creepy fun of the season. Then I light the candle in the jack o' lantern, and settle down with a favorite ghost story or a monster movie marathon on the TV.

And this year, I was able to celebrate the season at work as well. I could sit down at the computer every morning, and lose myself in a dark and stormy night with a brooding hero, a plucky heroine and an old dark house with a secret.

Life doesn't get any better than that!

Christine

> *To Roger Corman and the late, great Vincent Price—*
> *who warped me for life.*

Chapter One

$\infty\!\!\!\infty\!\!\!\infty$

Arabella Scott rocked her body along with the swaying of the mail coach, trying to ignore the aching in her bones. She was a long way from London already, but still had far to go before she reached her destination. She told herself that the journey alone would be an adventure, and an exciting beginning to her new life. The rugged coast of Cornwall had been interesting in daylight. And the sunset, now that they were away from any town, was quite spectacular. But the crisp October air and the falling leaves reminded her that this was a season of death, not rebirth. Winter was coming, and it would be as cold and hard as her future.

Without warning she felt the coach lurch to a sudden stop, and heard the drivers shouting to each other. The vehicle shook as the horses shied and reared. There was the sharp retort of a pistol shot, and the cry, 'Stand and deliver!'

Highwaymen.

She had little to offer, should they accost her. Her purse was nearly empty, and she wore only the most simple jewellery. If there had at least been another passenger, she might have taken solace in shared misery, but she was alone except for the drivers. She held no romantic notions about the gallantry of outlaws. The men were little better than common thieves, and she doubted they would show respect to a lady with nothing to give them and no one to protect her. She pushed back into the darkest corner of the seat and out of line with the window, drawing the grey cloth of her shawl up to hide the whiteness of her face.

There was the sound of footsteps outside the carriage, and the body swayed as someone jumped onto the running board. A lantern swung past the window beside her. For a moment a dark shape blocked the moonlight from outside. And then it was gone.

The robbers seemed more interested in the drivers and the luggage on top of the box. She could hear curses and threats, and argument as the driver refused to leave his seat.

There was a loud bang, and a thump as a body fell to the ground at the side of the road. The other man jumped down from the seat, before he could be shot, as well.

Her heart hammered in her chest. The drivers were putting up little struggle, considering. There were outriders, were there not? Some kind of guard? There was supposed to be protection, for the coach often carried items of value. Perhaps the drivers did not struggle because they expected rescue to arrive.

But there was no sound of approaching horsemen, and she could hear the triumphant laughs of the highwaymen, climbing into the seat to take the reins.

Dear God, they did not mean to take the coach, horses and all? Surely someone would alert them to her presence, and they would put her out on the road.

But the drivers must be too frightened, or incapacitated. Or perhaps they had forgotten her. She heard no protest. There was another shot, and the crack of a whip. Then the horses danced again and sprang forward, throwing her back against the seat. She clung to a strap to hold herself in place as the coach tore down the road into the gathering darkness. The land was whipping past her window at an alarming rate, and the carriage was rocking from side to side. At this speed, to throw open the door and fling herself out would mean certain death—either from the fall or beneath the wheels.

After a few miles she felt their progress slow a little, and the horses lurched to the left, down a side road and away from the well-travelled way. She could feel the unevenness of the ground as the carriage bumped along. Branches slapped against its sides as the way narrowed and the going became more difficult. The robbers slowed the horses, making attempts at stealth, listening for pursuit.

But none came. She could see, to the rear of the coach, trees seeming to close behind them in a wall of green darkness as the narrow road twisted and turned through the forest. If people did not know to look for it, she suspected that they would have no idea where the stolen coach had gone.

And now, they had reached what seemed to be a wide spot in the road. Or perhaps it was a clearing, for she could see a glow in front of them that must come from a fire. The horses' gait fell to a walk, and then they stopped. She could hear a cry of greeting from someone ahead.

Her mind raced over the facts, searching for anything that might help her in her precarious position. She was alone, far from the common road. No one would even think to look for her until tomorrow, when she did not arrive safely at her destination. She had been brought to a place that was secret enough to conceal a band of thieves. If she could not manage to escape without calling attention to herself, she would be at the mercy of the highwaymen once they discovered her. She shrank further back into the darkness of the carriage and remained perfectly still, hardly daring to breathe.

Arabella could hear the men laughing outside, tearing at the baggage to get to the strong box. She counted three voices, and prayed that there were no silent observers to the looting, for her potential captors all seemed to be on the left of the coach.

She gathered her nerve and slid quietly across the seat, preparing to grab the door handle and escape from the far side, away from the fire and into the darkness of the forest.

But it was too late. There was a cry of surprise, and a man's laugh. Then the coach tilted with the weight of a body and the door opened. Rough hands reached for her, dragging her back across the seat and out into the night.

She had been right in one thing: there were three of them, and the black cloths that had served as masks were hanging loose around their necks. They made no effort to hide their identities from her. Her hopes sank at knowing they did not care if she saw their faces. Their plans would not include ransom, even if she had money to offer.

When her feet touched the ground, she set her heels into the dirt, trying to slow the progress of the man who held her. But she was no match for him. He had her about the waist, pinning one arm to her side and holding her tight to his chest. She could smell his stinking breath in her face. He was pushing her backwards, walking towards his companions and laughing as he went.

Her mind clouded with visions of what was likely to occur should she not escape. She screamed and redoubled her efforts, kicking against his legs and flailing with her free arm, hoping to throw him off balance.

He seized her wrist and tried to pull her arm behind her.

She struggled until she felt her sleeve tear at the shoulder, and for a moment the man lost his grip. She fetched him a cuff across the ear that was strong enough to daze him, and when his grasp loosened she slipped free, turning to run. She had managed only a few steps before another man caught her and hauled her back towards the fire.

It was over for her, then. They were stronger than she, and outnumbered her. No one knew or cared where she was. She was alone in the dark, and there was to be no brave rescue tonight. Dear God, she prayed, let it at least be quick. By the look of the men around her, it was likely to go worse for her the longer she remained alive.

Suddenly, there was a sound of hoofbeats behind them. A

horse and rider were approaching at full gallop. She felt the man holding her grow tense, saw the other two draw weapons and smile into the darkness, ready to greet the traveller with certain death.

She screamed to warn the man, whoever he was, so that he did not ride into an ambush. But the hoofbeats did not slow, and suddenly the horse was upon them.

The chaos of the next moments came at her in a blur. She had a glimpse of a dark man on an enormous black horse, charging into their midst. Then an arm came down upon the man holding her. A riding crop slashed past her ear, catching him in the face. The highwayman swore and released her as the leather cut his cheek to the bone. She barely managed to get clear of him before the dark horse reared and the sharp hooves struck him down.

The rider wheeled on the second man, drawing a great curved sword from under his cloak. The robber stood, too shocked to fire his weapon, as the rider finished him with a single cut to the chest.

The third man turned to run. And for a moment she thought that the rider meant to allow it. He made no effort to spur his horse, but went very still, wiping his blade and sheathing the sword.

The last highwayman must have thought the same, for he went only a few yards before turning back and raising his pistol to fire.

But the rider was faster, producing his own weapon and firing without hesitation. The last man went down with a ball in his head. The clearing was still as the echo of the shot died away.

'Here. To me.' The horseman gestured to her, and spoke as though he were calling a frightened animal. 'There may be others. We must go before they come searching for their friends.' He didn't dismount, but turned his horse towards her and offered an arm to help her up into the saddle with him.

But she was afraid to move. The shock of the evening's events caught up to her as she viewed the carnage at her feet, and she stepped out of his reach instead of towards him, almost stumbling upon the body of the man who had held her. She raised her fists to her mouth, to stop the scream that she knew was coming.

With a quiet curse he rode to her and caught her easily, scooping her up to sit before him so that she perched precariously on one hip. Then he rode to the front of the carriage and drew his sword. For a moment she was afraid that he meant harm to the horses. But he swiped down at the harnesses that held them, cutting them free and slapping the beasts lightly with the flat of the blade to urge them away from the yoke.

'Better they should find their own way tonight than spend it tied here,' he muttered. 'The storm is likely to break at any moment.'

And, true to his prediction, the first raindrops hit them, spattering against the oilcloth cloak he wore. He pulled it free from between their bodies and enclosed her in it as though it were a tent, pulling her body tight to his, clutching her to him with one arm and handling the reins with the other.

She could feel the hardness of his body: the immovable arm, the chest as solid as a stone wall, the thigh well muscled from too much time on horseback. There was a growing hardness pressing into her hip where the movement of the horse rubbed their bodies together. It occurred to her too late that she was in the arms of a man who had done cold-blooded murder to get her, and now held her prisoner just as surely as the others had. He was taking her to God only knew where. Her fate might be little different from the one she would have experienced at the hands of the highwaymen.

She struggled to free herself as the horse gained speed beneath her. He reined in, but when she sought to slide to the ground, his grasp on her only grew tighter.

She felt his response, as well as heard it, for the words rumbled deep in his chest. 'I can handle you, madam, or I can handle the horse. If you insist on fighting me, I will drop you and go on my way. If you are prepared to manage the cliffs of Cornwall on foot in the dark, then by all means, continue as you are doing.'

Arabella froze against him, imagining the alternatives. She was alone but for him, and had no idea how far it might be to the nearest inn or farm, or even which direction she would need to walk. She could be killed in a fall or freeze to death before morning. The heavens had opened and rain was pouring down on them, and through the gap in his cloak she could see the first flashes of lightning in the distance. She would be soaked to the skin in moments if she managed to get away. Even if she reached the ground, she could not very well outrun the horse, for the man rode like the devil and did not seem the least bit bothered by the weather.

She wrapped her arms tentatively around his waist to cling to him, laying her head against his chest and squeezing her eyes shut.

He opened his cloak and put a finger under her chin to tip her head up, so he could see her face in the darkness. Then he grinned down and stared into her eyes. His were dark, as black as the sky at midnight, flickering with the reflection of the lightning. She lost herself in them, and although her fear remained, nagging at the back of her mind, the will to escape faded. For better or worse he had her now, and would do as he liked.

He laughed as he felt her submit to him, and made the horse rear and dance under them. She held him even tighter in total surrender. She had never been so close to a man before, and her feelings veered from terror for her future to mortification that, even if she had nothing to fear from her saviour, someone might learn the details of her rescue and know how quickly she had abandoned propriety.

Once he was sure that he had won, he settled the horse and spurred it on, and they raced ahead of the oncoming storm in a mad gallop. She buried her face against him again, not wanting to see where they were going since she had no means to stop it.

The ride seemed to last for ever. Time slowed, and the scene in the forest grew more distant in her mind as her physical distance from it increased. A stupor came over her, winding through her mind like the tendrils of a vine, leaving her thoughts disjointed and jumbled. She wished the man who held her would pause long enough to let her change her seat and ride astride, for it would be no more unladylike than her current position, plastered against his body, and much less precarious. But he did not seem to notice, and held her even tighter as his speed increased.

She should at least introduce herself, she thought. Demand the man's name in return. Thank him for his help. And perhaps request, as politely as possible, that he put some space between their bodies to allow her a shred of modesty. But she felt almost too tired to move, let alone speak. She vowed that no matter what happened she would not swoon. But what harm could it do if she relaxed and let him hold her? She allowed her head to loll against his chest, feeling the hair on his body rubbing against her cheek through the open neck of his shirt. It felt strangely comforting, and…

Something else.

If she could pull her wits together, perhaps she would find a name for the unfamiliar sensations she was feeling as he held her. They were most assuredly wicked. She cursed her weakness, for had she been in whole possession of her faculties, she knew she would not be taking pleasure in them. Lord only knew if her rescuer was saint or sinner, but if her immediate future was ravishment, she could only hope that he meant to wait until there was a warm, dry bed in which to dishonour her. For she did not have the will to fight him.

At last she could feel their pace begin to slow, and when she forced her eyes open and peeped from under the cloak, she could see that they were approaching a manor house. The drive was long and curved, with over-arching trees that slowed the pace of the rain but gave the impression of a long, dark tunnel. Through the branches she got occasional glimpses of the house: a massive outline against the black of the stormy sky, its unlit windows glittering like obsidian against the dark grey stone of the walls.

He rode to the open iron gate and through, directly to the house. There were no lamps lit on the drive, nor footmen in attendance at the door, and no welcoming candles shone through the windows. There was no sign at all that she would be any better off inside than she had been in the wilds of the forest, surrounded by cut-throats.

He dismounted, pulling her down after him, and gestured to the door. 'Welcome to Penlowen. My home.' He opened it himself and waved her inside. 'I must see to my horse. Please wait here.' With no further welcome or explanation, he shut the door behind her, leaving her alone in the dead silence of the entry hall.

Chapter Two

Arabella waited, listening to the fading echo of the door slam, expecting to hear the approach of the servants. Surely someone would be along in a moment to offer her a hot drink, or at least a place by the kitchen fire? There must be someone to care that the master had gone out in a storm, and to wait eager for his safe return.

There was nothing. Her ears strained for any sound that would indicate life and activity, but she heard only the wind and rain outside, distant through the stone walls, softer than the scratch and gnaw of mice in the dark. She had the idle fancy that she could hear the footsteps of spiders on the walls, for there must surely be some. The room was barely lit, and she could not see the corners. The chandelier above her was dark, and the few candles in the sconces on the wall did not provide enough illumination to show her all.

She turned and looked around her. Other than the candles there was no decoration on the walls, which were the same grey stone as the stairs leading straight up into the darkness in front of her.

She reached up and lifted one of the candles out of its holder, trying to shed light higher. She got a murky impression of a gallery above her, and rectangular outlines along the walls, squares of deeper black that might be portraits or tapestries. She waved the candle to the sides. Corridors, as dark as caves, to the left and right of her. She moved a few steps down the one to her right and called hesitantly into the darkness, then waited for a response.

The silence echoed back.

This was ridiculous. It made no sense to be hanging on the doorstep when she was cold and tired and frightened. Surely her rescuer had not meant for her to do that? She had but to take a few steps into the darkness, open a door, and she would find a sitting-room fire. Then she could wait in comfort. She would leave the door to the room open, and her host would find her when he returned. If it was his house, then he would guess where she had gone.

Arabella carried the candle towards the corridor on the left, and felt darkness close around her like a blanket. The air in the hall was cold and damp, and she shuddered against it, taking an involuntary step backwards, towards the dimly lit entrance.

Then she scolded herself that it was nonsense to be afraid of the dark, and stepped forward again. After what had occurred already this night, she should know that there was no terror in being alone.

And yet she could not shake the feeling that she was *not* alone. There was no sound, but still…

She opened the first door wide, and was greeted by a darkness even deeper than that in the hall. The light from the candle struggled into the empty room, and the flame seemed to retreat back to the candle in despair. As her eyes adjusted to the gloom she could see the outline of furniture, draped in Holland covers, looming like ghosts in the darkness. An icy draught blew from the chimney of the unlit fireplace. That was what was making the candle flicker. She shook her head. If her host did not mean to keep a fire lit, then it was most foolish of him not to close the flue.

She shuddered again, as the damp in the room crept into her bones. How could the dark rider stand to leave the house in this condition? Although she could not yet smell mildew, the carpets and the furniture would soon be spoilt if he did not keep the windows closed and a fire lit. For now that she was away from the entryway the house felt every bit as damp as if she was standing on the cliffs of Land's End.

She turned and tried another door, to similar effect. There was the dim shape of an overturned chair, seen in a brief flash of lightning through the parted window curtains. But her candle did little to penetrate the darkness, and the air felt as cold and damp as a grave.

There must be some room in the house that was in use. Why else would he bring her here? But she could not shake the feeling that if she turned to examine the other corridor, she would find the same thing: darkness, silence, decay. Did her rescuer live in a mouldering ruin, with only a few candles for company?

Unless the house was not his at all, but had been abandoned by its owners. It would be an excellent place to choose to stop if he intended something other than rescue, and did not wish to be interrupted.

'You should not be here.'

She started at the sound of his voice, which echoed the sentiments of her heart. The candle flame jumped wildly as her hand shook.

'I asked you to wait for me in the entry hall. It is not safe in the darkness.' Her host stood behind her, and his presence cast an air of menace over the already unwelcoming hallway.

'I am only a few steps from there now,' she said, trying to catch her breath. 'It is not as if the hall is set with traps.' She waved her candle to shine its light upon the floor and tapped it with her foot. 'Solid enough, I think. Stone. A hundred years old, at least. I see no danger in a little darkness and a few empty rooms.'

He laughed without mirth. 'Then perhaps your nerves are stronger than mine. Please. Let us return to the entry.' He stepped deliberately behind her, as though he meant to guard her, and let her lead for the few paces back to the front door.

She wished that he had gone before, for it made her nervous to know that he was behind her, where she could not see him. As soon as she achieved the front hall, she turned round so that she could watch him. He walked past her, until there was a wall to his back, rather than the emptiness of the corridor.

Arabella held the candle up so that she could see his face. And she had to hold it high, for he was much taller than she: well over six foot, with the broad, well-muscled body she'd felt behind her on the horse. His clothes were still wet from the storm. Though he wore neither jacket nor waistcoat, he seemed oblivious to the chill in the air. The stark white of his shirt seemed to glow in the dim light of the hall, accentuating his complexion, which was tanned a deep brown. He ran a quick hand through his black hair, shaking the last of the rain from the shaggy locks, and stared at her with eyes equally black, unreadable in the darkness.

She wet her lips. 'I suppose I should thank you, for saving me, Mr…?'

'Lieutenant Richard Acherton, madam. Late of His Majesty's cavalry, now retired.' He bowed slightly, with military precision. 'Welcome to my home.'

She glanced around her, trying to imagine the building she had seen as anyone's home, for she found it as far from comfortable as any place in her experience.

He cleared his throat, and she looked back to him. 'Oh, yes, I am sorry. I quite forgot myself. My name is Arabella Scott. I was travelling towards St Ives when my coach was waylaid. The highwaymen came upon us suddenly, dispensed with the drivers, and took the reins. They must have thought there were no passengers. But when they found I was still within… I suspect they meant to…' The details of the evening rushed back to her. Her fingers went numb, and she dropped the candle she'd been holding, increasing the gloom around them.

The lieutenant stepped forward, stooped to retrieve it from the floor and took her by the wrist. 'I am sorry you were forced to experience what you did, Miss Scott.' He drew her forward until they stood near to the other light, as though he could pull her away from the memory. Then he relit her candle from one in a sconce.

'It is all right,' she said, although she could not give confidence to her voice. 'And I am most grateful to you for your aid. If you had not come when you did—'

'I often ride the land at night.' He interrupted her again. 'It helps me to sleep.'

He found galloping through the darkness to be restful? The man must be mad. She saw a haunted look in his eyes that she had not noticed before.

In return, he must have seen the doubt in hers. 'I know the roads well, as does my horse. I suspect we could ride some parts with eyes closed. A little moonlight is all I need to travel them safely.'

She doubted that she could call the trip they had made particularly safe. She broke the gaze to stare down at his hand, which was still holding her fast by the arm. Perhaps he meant to reassure her, but she wondered if he would release her should she resist.

As if he understood, he dropped his hand to his side, and muttered, 'Still, I must offer apologies to you for what has occurred. A gentlewoman should not have experienced such coarseness on a simple trip through the country. Not the violence against your person, nor my violence in stopping it.'

'You could hardly have predicted it, Lieutenant.'

'I feel responsible, all the same.' His tone changed as he spoke, until it was almost gentle. 'It is my property, you see, that those men were using for sanctuary. My family ignored the problem for far too long, and unsavoury elements have claimed much of my land as their own. I must work to restore order before I can truly feel at home here.'

He looked around them at the house and shook his head. 'I am sorry as well that I could not bring you to a more secure rescue. But with the storm about to break this house was the only refuge I could offer.' The gentleness had disappeared from his voice to be replaced by bitterness.

It was a surprising statement—for what could be more secure than the man's home, if the land outside was wild and beset with robbers? She glanced around in the dim light of the candle. 'I am sure it will be more than comfortable. And quite finer than what I am accustomed to.' But she could not hide the chill she felt as she thought of the empty rooms behind her, and she stepped closer to the candles.

'It is no place for a lady. I doubt there has been a female guest here for several generations.'

She smiled at the idea. 'You make it sound very monastic.'

'That was not my intention. I only wish to warn you that it is rough living, and to apologise for it.' He glanced at the dim flame in front of her. 'And I must ask you to be more careful with the candles. It would not do to be caught in the dark at Penlowen.' And then he looked into the shadows behind her, and his face held a curious dread.

It struck her as rather odd that a man so obviously without fear a few moments before, who could show no mercy when dispatching highwaymen and then ride breakneck through the night, would be afraid of the dark in his own home. For he *was* afraid. She was certain of it. When he did not think she was watching him, his eyes shifted uneasily about the room, and stared off down the empty corridors as though he expected to see something.

But if he was afraid, why did he not have more light? Perhaps he could not afford the candles. A large house did not always mean a large fortune. If there was no money for light or heat, than it would be most ungrateful of her to expect more comfort from him than he would take for himself. He had saved her life. She could manage for a night with a small amount of discomfort.

She smiled at him. 'As you wish, Lieutenant.' She took the candle from him again. 'I do not know the way around your home, and have already managed to blunder down an unused wing. I am sorry if I have imposed on your hospitality in any way. But I assure you, I meant no harm.'

'My dear Miss Scott, you have no reason to apologise. You are welcome to what comforts I can give you, while you are here.' His words were gallant, but he cast another nervous glance down the hall behind her. 'But they are unlikely to be found down that particular passage.'

'Would there be somewhere I could wait? Until you can find a servant to accompany me to an inn?'

When he met her gaze, he looked even more uncomfortable. 'I'm afraid a journey out will be quite impossible. The storm…'

'Then a sitting room, perhaps? I could wait until the rain has ended. Or until morning, if need be. If you could spare a maid to sit with me, I would be most grateful.'

He touched his hand to his forehead and closed his eyes before answering. 'Also impossible, I'm afraid. I blame myself for bringing you here, when I could just as easily have turned the other way and taken you to an inn myself. But it was farther, and I was unsure of the weather. At the time, I thought this the safer course.'

He opened his eyes again, as though forcing himself to acknowledge her presence. 'The truth is, Miss Scott, that I cannot offer you any company but my own. I have servants. There is a couple who are willing to do for me in daylight. But they are only two, and it is a large house. Only the most necessary rooms are open at all. And in any case, they cannot be persuaded to stay the night under the roof of Penlowen. It has not proven a difficulty until tonight. I am accustomed to hardship, and am growing used to solitude. But now, I fear, I have inflicted it upon you.'

'No servants?' Did he expect her to spend the night unchaperoned? If anyone learned the truth of it, she doubted that they would see her worth as a respectable companion.

He read her thoughts. 'Do not fear. No word of this shall reach beyond these walls. We will find a way to escort you back into society without incident once the storm breaks and the sun is up.'

This was something, at any rate. 'Thank you for your concern. Until then, where shall I…?' She gestured with the candle, and saw him flinch as the flame trembled.

'I have a kettle on the fire, and a light supper waiting upstairs. It is not much, but I am willing to share. If you will accompany me?' He held out a hand to the stairway and picked up the other candle, shepherding her ahead of him.

Arabella looked at his face, which was gracious but still unsmiling. There was no trace of the grinning horseman who had killed for her, then clutched her to his chest as they galloped. Her host was being as courteous to her as circumstances allowed. If things had been different, she might even have been flattered by his attention. She would have thought herself lucky, for he was a most handsome gentleman, and it was a rare day when such men even noticed her, much less expressed concern for her welfare.

But he was so sombre, and behaving so strangely, that she could feel the hair at the back of her neck prickling at his simple offer of tea. After a brief hesitation she preceded him, and did not stop until she reached the upper landing. She turned back to watch him climb the last few steps, and saw the darkness following close behind him. It was probably fatigue that made the shadows seem to roil as if something were alive in them, just out of the reach of the candle flame. She turned her eyes away from it to focus on the man approaching her, who grew more wary with each step into the house. He watched his surroundings as though he was heading into battle, not to tea.

But when he looked at her, he managed a hesitant smile. 'Almost there. The first door to your left.' He reached and caught the knob, and gestured to her again, urging her through and shutting it behind them.

It took a moment for her eyes to adjust to the brilliance of the room. On every flat surface there were candles. In sconces on the walls, set on tables, on wooden chairs and on the stone floor. Even on the mantelpiece, although it hardly seemed necessary, for the fire in the ornate stone fireplace was blazing uncomfortably warm. The only dark spot in the room was the one place too dangerous to hold flame: the large four-poster bed on the centre of the opposite wall.

It was a man's bedroom.

Chapter Three

Arabella stared at him in mortification, trying to decide if this was some strange joke or merely what she had expected when he had scooped her onto his horse: some attempt at rape or a perverse idea of seduction.

The lieutenant shrugged helplessly in response. 'It is all I have to offer.'

'And totally unacceptable. You cannot think that I am so simple as to remain a full night in the bedchamber of a strange man simply because he tells me there is no other room available?'

'But there is not.'

'Pull the other one, sir, for it has bells on. The corridor is lined with doors, and many of them must lead to suitable rooms.'

'They are not prepared.'

'I do not need preparation,' she insisted. 'I can sit on the floor in the dark, if need be, with the door locked. Or I can trust my fortune to the storm. Or even lie in the straw beside your horse if there is no other choice.'

She made to leave, but he caught her by the shoulders and turned her away from the door. 'You will do no such thing. That horse is a more dangerous companion than I, Miss Scott, for he was trained to fight on the fields of Portugal, and shows no mercy to those who fall beneath his hooves. He is a vicious brute.'

'Much like his master.' She struggled in his grasp and felt her ripped sleeve settle around her wrist and slip to the floor as his fingers dug into the bare skin on her arm.

He released her, staring in horror at the red marks of his fingers on the pale flesh of her arm. When he spoke, his voice was hoarse. 'Perhaps so. But neither of us is as dangerous as what waits for you outside this room.'

Then he retreated until his back was against the door. 'I am sorry, Miss Scott. But I must insist. You will remain here with me until the sun rises. The rest of the house is not fit for visitors.' He paused. 'It is not safe.'

'That is foolishness, sir.' But he was so adamant that she could not sound as sure as she felt.

'Perhaps. But remember, you have me to thank for your rescue. You did not think me foolish when I dispensed with your captors. And so you must indulge me in this.'

She squared her shoulders and glared at him, trying to appear as stern and unwelcoming as possible. 'I do not wish to appear ungrateful, Lieutenant. But there are limits to what I will do for you in thanks. What you are suggesting is little better than I expected at the hands of those robbers. I will not share a bed with you.'

His lips quirked in an ironic smile. 'I do not expect you to. I said we would share the room. The bed is yours, if you wish to rest. For myself, I sleep better in daylight. But if I must sleep tonight, it will be on the floor, between the bed and the door. In any case, the candles will be lit the whole time, so that you can see I mean you no harm.'

Did he seriously mean to sleep on the floor like a dog? There must be more comfortable places in the house, or even in this room, where he might lie. 'I do not understand.'

'And I cannot make it any clearer. I am sorry. You trusted me before. Please, trust me now.'

It was not as if she had much choice in the matter. In the hall below, she had almost forgotten her fear of him. But now, in the confines of the bedroom, he seemed even larger and more intimidating than he had when in the forest, and his behaviour did nothing to allay her dread. The man was clearly mad. He sought to confine her against her will, and she had only his word that what he did was for her safety.

If she tried to go around him, he could block her without effort, and she suspected that he would lay hands on her again if she persisted. Even if he meant her no harm, he might do her injury with his attempts to gain her obedience. She rubbed at the marks on her arm, where he had held her, and saw him colour in embarrassment.

'Please.' The word came from him in a broken whisper.

She stared up into his face and saw obvious distress, not malice or lust. Perhaps he was telling the truth as he understood it? In his mind, to wander the house alone was a greater danger to her person than the destruction of her reputation. If she was lucky, he was eccentric but harmless. As long as she did not challenge his delusion he would set her free in the morning. If not, then she had been carried from the frying pan into the fire, and there was little she could do but wait for the inevitable. For a moment the chill of the darkened rooms seemed to touch her again, and the hair on her bare arm bristled in response.

She put on a smile that she hoped was not too obviously false. 'How can I resist such hospitality?'

He smiled back, just as insincere. 'And now you will humour the idiot, will you? So as not to upset him? Very well. Perhaps I am mad. As long as you do as I ask, I do not care what you think of me.' He shot the bolt on the door behind him, and stared at her for a moment. His eyes seemed to linger too long on her ripped dress, and the body inside it. She tensed as he reached out to her. But he placed a hand very deliberately on the remaining sleeve of her gown, guiding her by the elbow to a chair by the fire. 'A cup of tea, perhaps? And a little food to raise your spirits?'

Arabella watched him move past her to kneel at the hearth, and considered for a moment making a run for the unguarded door. But what good would it do her? If he meant to have her, he would surely catch her before she could get more than a few steps. She had seen him act quickly and with no hesitation when circumstances called for it.

She was far, far away from anyone who might come to her aid, should she need help. But neither would the truth come out if she *was* ruined. Anything might happen, and no one would ever know.

The thought was all the more frightening for the trace of excitement she felt at the idea. She remembered how easy it had been to give in to him when he had demanded her obedience on the horse. Perhaps her brush with the highwaymen had unhinged her? For if the moment came when Lieutenant Acherton demanded his reward, she was not sure what she would do in response.

His posture seemed easier, now that the door was locked, and he poked at the logs in the grate, sending the fire under the kettle to blazing. He made a strange picture, for the carvings on either side of the fire seemed to loom over him. As he worked, he was flanked by two black stone angels, that were almost as tall as her host was when standing. They faced each other over the fire, backs hunched to support the mantel on their outstretched wings. Perhaps their poses were intended to appear welcoming, or to give some comfort to the owner of the room. But instead they seemed to threaten him, their fingers pointing in accusation, hands reaching to clutch and not to soothe.

No wonder her host was mad. If the rest of the house was decorated in the same vein, it must prey on his mind. It certainly did on hers.

He knelt at her feet, slicing bread and cheese, and then held it out to her, his head bowed. As he turned to prepare the tea, a lock of his hair fell over his face and he brushed it absently away. And she thought, should she wish to sketch it, that the scene presented was of an ordinary man overshadowed by forces beyond his control.

The lieutenant removed tea from a small tin box and steeped the leaves, then poured the result into a single mug. This time, when he looked up to offer her the tea, his eyes met hers. With the firelight shining on his damp hair, accentuating his fine chin and strong shoulders, he looked most handsome, and not the least bit threatening. She remembered the feel of his body against her cheek, and immediately wished she could forget it. It had been the most intimate experience of her life. Much more so than the few dances she had been able to attend, where there had been nothing so daring as a waltz.

He took her hesitation for reluctance. 'Again, I am sorry to offend you. But we must share the cup. There is only one.' For a moment, his face lit with a bemused smile. 'The last thing I expected on earth tonight was that I'd be entertaining a lady in my room.' He took a sip, and then held the mug out to her.

No poison, then, or drugs to render her helpless and at his mercy. She almost laughed at the lurid fantasies that had been forming in her mind. Suddenly it all seemed very innocent, and it was clear the situation was as awkward for him as it was for her. 'Believe me, Lieutenant, that is a comfort and not an insult. It would not have assured me of your intentions, had I found you well prepared to receive me.'

He offered the tea to her again, and bowed his head in deference. She took it, and felt her fingers brush his, ignoring the small thrill she felt in it. Then she took a sip and offered it back to him. He drank again.

'I swear on my honour that my intention tonight is the same as it is every night I remain here: to see morning. And then we shall get you back on your journey again, for I have no wish to detain you.'

The statement was odd, for she could hardly see how being safe and dry inside, while the storm raged without, would lead to such a dire description of the night. But his position at her feet made him look strangely chivalrous, and she could feel an embarrassing flush colouring her cheeks.

'It was not you who detained me. I think the blame for that lies with the highwaymen.' She shivered.

He looked up at her with concern. 'They did not hurt you, did they? I must say, you are taking everything surprisingly well. Some women would be rendered prostrate by the events that have transpired this evening.'

She thought back on what had occurred, as if seeing it through gauze: the sound of voices, the feel of hands on her body, and the blood and thunder of her rescue. Then she turned her mind's eye from it, before the details came clear. She did not want to remember. 'I suspect I shall give way to my emotions at some point. But now is hardly the time. You have done enough for me, sir. You should not have to contend with a hysterical female, as well.'

He shook his head in amazement and passed the cup back to her, then busied himself with the kettle. When he spoke, his eyes did not rise from his work. 'You are most unusual, Miss Scott.'

'I think not, Lieutenant. In any crisis there must always be someone who keeps their head, who can put common sense ahead of rash action or excessive emotion. That role usually falls to me. Not very interesting of me, I suppose. But I am sure that my employer will find it a most useful asset.'

He looked up. 'Employer?'

She nodded. 'I was headed west, to take a position as companion to an elderly lady in St Ives. I hope Miss Witherstone will understand the delay. When women reach a certain age, it can be hard to get them to listen to reason.'

He leaned closer to her, staring up into her face, examining her closely. 'You were to be a paid companion?'

She laughed. 'Believe me, sir, it will be far easier than being an unpaid one. I have been caring for an elderly aunt for quite some time. Although I loved her dearly, in the end I gained nothing for it. She left the house and what little she had to a family friend. There was no longer a place for me.'

He took the plate from her. 'And you have no other family?'

'None, Lieutenant. My parents died when I was but a child. My aunt was all I had.'

He looked at her even more closely. 'There are no friends that you could appeal to?'

'None that would wish me to live with them. I have no desire to be a burden on others until I join my parents and aunt.'

'You are all alone in the world, then? With no one to care where you have gone?' He was staring at her again, and made no effort to mitigate his rudeness.

As the silence lengthened between them, she wished that she had not been so open about her situation. For now he knew that if she disappeared while in his care, no one would think to look for her. 'Not completely alone,' she amended, with little conviction. 'But I have little experience other than what one might gain while caring for an invalid. Now that my aunt is gone, it makes sense to seek a future doing what one knows, rather than what one does not.'

'But as a paid companion? Forgive me for saying it, Miss Scott, but companions are normally whey-faced spinsters.'

She laughed back at him. 'I am six and twenty, Lieutenant Acherton. And unmarried. I think we can safely say that the term applies to me.'

'But you are beautiful.' He said it as though it was an overlooked solution to her problems, not a statement of opinion. Then he leaned towards her, so that the distance between them was unusually close.

She nearly spilled the tea they had been passing between them in her attempt to slide her chair away from him. 'If it were not obvious before, then I should take that as a sure sign that you have been no more in society than I. I am average, at best, and without fortune. I am unattached at an age when most other women have families of their own to care for. I am totally unsuitable, I assure you, for anything other than genteel employment.' She said it with as much finality as possible, hoping that her assurance would put to rest any ideas he might be having. 'I am sure that Miss Witherstone is eagerly awaiting my arrival, and will make an enquiry should I not arrive in St Ives on tomorrow's coach.'

He reached out and took the mug of tea from her hand, raising it in a mock salute to acknowledge her statement. 'I am afraid we will have to disagree on several of the points you have offered to support your decision. Because I think that there are other, more appropriate positions open for you than waiting hand and foot on some dried-up old maid.'

In a ballroom, she might have dismissed his words as idle flirtation. But in a bedroom, and accompanied by the intense look he was giving her, she suspected it was a less honourable suggestion. 'Perhaps, sir. But, as you have no say in my future, your disapproval of my choice counts for little.'

'Tonight you are a guest in my home, and thus you have little choice but to listen to me.' He smiled at her, gazing into her eyes as he had on the horse. And she remembered how easily he could control her, should he choose.

Without wishing to, she glanced at the door.

'Do not even think it.' She saw him tense almost imperceptibly, ready to rise and block her way should she try to leave. 'As I was saying, if you cannot manage to sleep, you will be forced to bear my discourse until morning. I may have no say in your future, but you have said nothing to change my opinion of it. You are describing a miserable existence, a life in servitude, as though it were your first choice and not your last.'

'It is an excellent choice, and one that I have given much consideration.' She lifted her chin in a show of pride. 'It is not as if I am to be a scullery maid, Lieutenant. A companion is not so low as all that. I have heard that some are treated more like a member of the family than a servant.'

He snorted. 'If being a Witherstone is such a great honour, than why do not other family members step forward to take care of their own?'

'Do you know them?' She leaned forward, hoping for some scrap of knowledge that would make her future seem less uncertain.

'No, I do not. But I know their kind, right enough, and can guess what awaits you in St Ives. I suspect when you questioned the family about the old lady they assured you that she is a fine woman, but that they seldom have opportunity to visit her?'

It was an accurate description of her interview with the lady's nephew in London, and she gave a slight nod of confirmation.

'But did you think to ask why they could not have brought her to London instead? I wager if you'd have heard them talk of her at home, they'd have let slip the words *"clutch pursed"* and *"sour"*. And they'd have expressed the fear that there is more stone than wither in the old hag. Whoever is set to watch her will spend the best years of her life on a hard job.'

It rankled to hear her worst fears voiced by this stranger, and she snapped, 'You speak of a lifetime's employment as a curse, not a blessing. At least I will have the happiness that comes with knowing there will always be a breakfast on the table in the morning, and a roof over my head at night. That is more than enough for contentment, and certainly as much as I deserve.'

His face twisted in a bitter smile. 'But for someone who yearns in secret for freedom, it is a death sentence. I should think, from the fervent way you defend it, that you enjoy being trapped.'

'I never thought of myself as trapped.' *Until you called me so.* She thought the last words, and then tried to unthink them before he read them in her face. Her spoken words were not true, in any case, for she *had* felt trapped—many times. And had learned that it did no good to think thus, for it did not change the facts.

'You lie.' He smiled. 'It does no good to dissemble with me, you know. You are as easy to read as an open book, Miss Scott.

Your eyes are most expressive.' He paused for a moment to look at her, and seemed to lose his train of thought. Then he said, 'The truth, please. You are young and spirited…'

'You make me sound like a horse.'

He laughed. 'Perhaps I have spent too much time outside of society, if that is the best I can manage in compliment. But you do have spirit, Miss Scott. It has been put to the test this evening. I have trouble imagining you sitting quietly at a bedside for the rest of your life, subjugating your needs to those of another. Did you not find the role of nurse to be confining? And, now that you are free of it, do you not wish for better?'

'Me, sir?' She looked down at the floor by her feet, for to look too long into his eyes was making her nervous. 'You have a most curious view of me to think that.'

'I suspect I have an accurate enough view of you, from where I sit.' Even without looking she could feel his gaze travelling over her with inappropriate intimacy. 'You appear to be an attractive woman who has set limitations upon herself, more through fear than necessity. You pretend to desire the life you have chosen, but in your heart you know you are lying. You want more. I can tell.'

Arabella had been content enough, at the beginning of the evening. But now she was tired, and his continual quizzing over something she could not change made her head ache. 'What does it matter to you?' she said, and stared back in challenge. 'In any case, I could not very well sit in London, waiting for a future that would never come. It is better, is it not, to go forth and seize the day, rather than hide in one's room expecting life to come to one?'

The last of her statement seemed to take him aback, and she saw anger blaze in his eyes. Then he smiled slowly and said, 'Perhaps. But they say that sometimes, discretion is the better part of valour. We will discuss your future again in the morning, when our circumstances are not so unusual.'

'I doubt that will be necessary,' she said.

And he smiled again, and said, 'You will find that I can be quite persuasive when I put my mind to it.'

She could feel a blush rising on her cheeks, and tried to force it back, thinking calm, sensible thoughts about her future in St Ives. Perhaps her life was not very exciting, but it was orderly, and free from worry. She would be on her way in the morning, and no amount of flattery from a dangerous stranger would change that.

But he had looked into her heart and seen that she was discontented. And he must know how he affected her, or he would not be tormenting her with it. If she let him, he would worm his way into her soul like the Devil himself, with sly words and dark looks, and promises of things she had no right to wish for. She must be on guard against temptation, for it was barely midnight and a long way from dawn.

They fell into silence, which she found uneasy, but which seemed to content him. Lightning flashed at the window, and she could hear the rain beating against the glass. But the great stone house stood firm against the wind, as immovable as its master. He yawned, and leaned his back to the wall beside the fire, stretching his legs out in front of him. She would have to step over him if she meant to try for the door.

She watched in trepidation as he opened a pouch at his waist, removed oil and rags, and set to cleaning the pistol that had been tucked in his belt, staring down the empty barrel, checking the flint, wiping the wood and oiling the metal. Then he removed a smaller pouch, of gunpowder, and poured it in the priming hole.

'If this is meant as a threat,' she said, 'you are not succeeding. You cannot be much of a man if you need firearms to subdue a single woman.'

He looked up at her without speaking. His gaze was steady and penetrating. And before he spoke, he gave her ample time to remember that he was man enough for anything he might set out to do. Then he said, 'It would make little sense to shoot you, after expending the energy necessary to save your life. Whatever nefarious plans you think I am hatching against your person, you must realise that they would not be nearly so satisfying to me if I had to put a ball in you to accomplish them.' His gaze lingered too long on her, as though he were considering whether she was worth the bother, even whole and unwounded.

And then he held out the gun to her, handle first. 'If I need to use this tonight, my adversary will not be dissuaded by lead. Go ahead,' he urged. 'Take it and examine it. If you think you can steal it and use it against me, it will do you no good. There is powder and flint at the ready, but no bullet. To pull the trigger will result in fire and noise, and little else.'

She refused to take it. 'Why bother, then?'

'Sometimes a flash of light and a loud bang are all that is necessary. It breaks the mood.' He glanced around him again, searching the corners of the room, and finished by staring at the closed bedroom door. And she saw in him a touch of the irrational fear he had shown to her in the hall. When he looked back at her, the madness had passed, and his tone and expression were quite ordinary. 'Lord knows, the mood in my home frequently needs disruption. Now, try and rest, if you will.' He gestured towards the bed, then tucked the pistol back into his belt, within easy reach. He leaned his head against the wall, eyes half closed, obviously on guard against something.

Did he honestly expect her to sleep while he sat on the floor, staring at her and thinking the Lord only knew what? She shook her head.

'Suit yourself. It matters not to me if you prefer to stay by the fire and keep me company.' His smile was smug.

Her eyes narrowed. That was not what she wished at all, and he knew it. But now he was looking at her as if expecting conversation. And his intense scrutiny while awake was every bit as bad as the fear that he would watch her sleeping. At last she decided anything would be better than the silence, and said, 'So, you were a cavalryman?'

He looked at her as though she were an idiot, and said, 'Yes.' He offered no further information, and made no attempt to set her at her ease.

'It must have been an exciting life?'

He continued to watch her. 'Some might say so.'

'But not you?' she pressed.

'I bought a commission and hoped to make my fortune. I failed.' He looked vague for a moment, as though examining his life objectively, from a great distance. 'Perhaps the navy would have been a better choice. There are rich prizes for the officers who take French ships. But at sea promotion is slow in coming, and the best money goes to those who make a career of it. I sought quick advancement, not a life spent in service and away from home.'

She looked around the room at the darkened and undecorated walls. 'I can see how you would find it hard to leave, if all this belongs to you,' she said dryly.

He laughed, long and hard, wiping the tears from his eyes. 'Yes, Miss Scott, it was with great remorse that I was willing to forgo the occupation of such a magnificent home to take up arms for king and country.'

She looked at the room again, with a critical eye. 'It would not be so bad if you were willing to put effort into it.'

'A fresh coat of paint, some new draperies, and a good dusting will make a world of difference. How could I have been so remiss?' He shook his head. 'How very like a woman.'

'I should hope I *am* very like a woman,' she answered back.

'I do not doubt it.' And the hungry look he gave her made her more than aware that he had not forgotten the fact.

Arabella turned the conversation carefully, hoping to distract his mind from the topic of her gender. 'But was it necessary to buy a commission to survive? Surely there are attached lands with the property that would earn you a living, if your tastes were simple?'

'A very small living, I assure you. I could afford a house in the village with what tenants I have left. But I would be unable to reside at Penlowen.' He stared towards the window, into the darkness. 'At one time my family owned all the land in the area. There were farms. Rich fishing. Even a small mine. The people were happy and prosperous. But then, everything changed.'

'How?' she murmured, thinking of the wild country they had ridden through, unable to contain her curiosity.

'An ancestor squandered it all. Let it fall to ruin. The tenants left, and bandits took the land for themselves. Since his time, one hundred years ago, the house has been uninhabited, and things have gone from bad to worse. I was raised in the village, not far from here, in a house little better than the rest.'

His face hardened. 'And when I looked out of my window, I could see this house, on the hill overlooking the town. I would stare at it, my belly empty and my mind full, and know that it should by rights come to me. That were it not for fate, and my family's weakness, I would be in a grand room, with coal in the fireplace, and not just food on my plate, but servants behind my chair. Living like a mouse in the town may have been good enough for my father, but it is not enough for me.'

He leaned towards her, staring at her as though willing her to understand. Perhaps he should have considered going to sea, for he looked very much like a ruthless privateer, with the pistol in his belt and the mad glint in his eye.

'I went to war, hoping to return a rich man. I got more than my fill of blood and death. Enough for any two men. But there was scant little reward to be found after the battles I fought. I hear the road from Vitoria was littered with treasure, but it all went to the dragoons.'

'Treasure?' she asked. 'Surely you did not mean to loot the battlefield.'

'To take the spoils of war is hardly looting,' he argued. 'Where the dead are going, they do not need a purse.'

'But those things do not belong to you,' she said.

'Nor do they belong to the enemy. I understand the Hussars drink champagne from the silver chamber pot they took from King Joseph's luggage. Rather common of them, in my opinion. But you cannot tell me that they should have returned the pot to its owner.'

'By that logic, you should have taken the strong box from the highwaymen. After you had finished with them, they had no further use for it.' Remembering, she shivered.

'Do you take me for a common thief, then? We are on British soil, not at war. And I am not sunk so low as to rob the coaches that cross my property. The men at the inn who run the mail coach know what is to be done with it, and I will see, God willing, that it is returned to them in the morning.' His chin rose, and in the firelight she saw nobility of character behind the ruthlessness he had shown. Then he looked at her, and his voice changed. 'But when I see something beautiful, abandoned in a place of violence, with no one to claim it, and I know that it will go to waste or to ruin, tell me why on God's earth I should wish to leave it behind?'

He took her hand and looked into her eyes. His gaze was deeper and more compelling than ever before. And she felt her will begin to fail. She pulled her hand from his and turned away. 'If you mean to compare me with an inanimate object that can be carted from place to place, without a thought to my feelings, then you are sorely mistaken, Lieutenant.'

'I meant to compare you to a treasure,' he snapped. 'But Miss Scott, if you wish to exercise your free will in the matter of tonight's rescue, then I will be only too happy to return you to the highwaymen's camp.'

The gall of the man—acting as though she needed to apologise for her response to his rudeness. Did he mean—if she did not succumb to his advances—to return her to the wilderness to take her chances with the thieves? The thought was beyond frightening, and for the first time she felt the suppressed panic overtaking her. 'You know I do not wish that, Lieutenant. I merely resent the fact that you view me as some cast-off or waste, for making this trip. I object to the idea that you know better than I what is a fit use of my talents. And I resent being held prisoner in this room.'

He leaned over her again, and she felt a definite air of menace. 'I spoke the truth as I saw it, Miss Scott. No matter what your opinion of the matter, the thought of you, with your fine eyes and your soft brown hair, still very much in the bloom of youth and beauty, spending the rest of your life bent over a sick bed is an abomination to me.' He moved closer still. 'Reading sermons to some dour old woman, with that sweet mouth of yours, when there are so many better uses for it.' His voice slowed, and she could feel his breath on her face. She knew he meant to kiss her.

And once he had done that there was no telling what might happen. For if *she* could not manage it, there would be no one else to stop him from going further. It was clear that in this house all propriety had been abandoned.

And a part of her cried out in silence. *Oh, yes. Please. Do with me what you will, for I want it. All that you can give. I want to feel alive…be alive, and not shut myself in a tomb.* And the shudder that went through her was just as much fear as it was arousal.

He saw it, and knew it for what it was. His lips came down upon hers and his hands touched her face.

And she wanted more.

It was madness. She was overwrought from the stress of the evening. She should be fighting to defend her virtue, not considering submission. She pushed him away from her and leapt from her seat, running for the door.

'Arabella, wait. You mustn't—'

But she was across the room before he could rise, and had drawn the bolt, put her hand to the knob and twisted. She threw her shoulder against the panel, and when the heavy oak door was open she rushed through it, out into the hall.

Chapter Four

$\sim\!\!\sim\!\!\sim\!\!\sim$

Arabella felt the door pulled out of her hand, as though he had yanked it away, and slammed it shut behind her. And for a moment she was plunged into a blackness deeper than any she had ever experienced. She wanted to believe that it was the result of the change from bright to dark, that her eyes would adjust, given time.

But the idea was snatched from her head just as the door had been pulled from her hand. It *was* dark, compared to the brightly lit room. But it was an unnatural darkness—a darkness of the soul and not the atmosphere. Even as she began to distinguish the shapes of things around her she became convinced that it would never be light again. There was no hope, no future, and she would not see another sunrise, for this was the dark of the grave.

Each breath held the chill of death, as well. The warmth of the bedroom leached from her, and left her cold to the bone. The air was heavy, too thick to think of moving through it. And even if she wished to, where would she go? She turned, sure that the door must be behind her, for she had not taken a step. But when she reached for it, it seemed a million miles away. She struggled, flailing her arms about her, though they felt as heavy as lead. And in every direction she reached she met no resistance but the heavy air. There were walls, she was sure of it, and furniture, for she could see shapes in the darkness. But why could she not touch them?

The stairs must be on her other side, only inches away, and she froze, afraid that a misstep would send her tumbling to the landing. But, worse yet, what if she turned to look for them and they were no longer there? She should feel carpet underfoot, but the ground felt soft and muddy, sucking at her shoes and dragging them down.

Where was she?

She could not move. She did not dare. And suddenly she could not breathe. It felt as though someone had pressed a wet cloth over her face, and each breath was a struggle. She opened her mouth to scream and tasted salt—of the sea or of her own tears, it was impossible to tell. She clamped her lips shut against the invisible water, which seemed to press in upon her from all sides, trying to force the last air from her body.

The darkness around her changed, and the hall was lit with a faint green glow. Whatever was happening to her, it was profoundly wrong. The lieutenant had been right. She should not have left the bedroom. But when she reached again for the door, to return to him, the knob seemed to swim away before she could grasp it.

If not the bedroom, then she must make for the stairs, and the front door at the foot of them. She would trust herself to the bandits and the storm. Anything but this. To remain in the house was certain death.

But once she was decided, she did not have the strength to make the descent. Her lungs burned from lack of oxygen. Her dress clung to her body, cold and wet, as tight as any shroud.

And her rational mind seemed to leave her as the warmth had left her body. This was how it would end for her. Alone in the dark waters. There was no hope of rescue. She had made her choice, and it had been a mistake. A huge mistake to leave him.

And now she would suffer the consequences and could never tell him that she had been wrong. One last gasp to let the sea inside and it would be over. She would scream to him with her final breath, but he would never know.

'Robert!'

A hand seized her and pulled her back into the bedroom. She felt the slam of the door as the dark water was gone and heat and light surrounded her, as did his arms. She took great gasping breaths, shuddering against him. He pulled her close, letting his body warm hers. She could help herself no longer and she wept, shivering with cold and terror.

And as she cried he whispered into her hair that he had her now. That it would be all right. She had nothing to fear. She was safe. He held her until her tears stopped and she no longer trembled. And then he held her still longer, crooning into her hair and stroking her back, pulling her down to sit beside him on the bed, wrapping the comforter around her shoulders.

She knew that she should get hold of herself and tell him to let her go. It was all highly improper. But it felt so good to be close to someone who was warm and alive, after the terrible emptiness in the hall, that she could not break from him.

As if he could read her thoughts, he said, 'Forgive me, Miss Scott. For everything. For bringing you here, and for my rough manners. For frightening you away. And for being so free with your person now. But I know how it feels. I have wandered alone through the halls of Penlowen, and I would have welcomed a human touch—if only to assure myself that I still lived.'

She nodded slightly, and relaxed against him. He continued to hold her. When she had mastered her voice, she whispered, close into his ear, 'What is it?'

She felt him shake his head. 'I am not sure. My ancestors, perhaps? Or the house itself? Whatever it is, it wants something that I do not know how to give.' His arms tightened about her in apology. 'I tried to prevent you from leaving. I did not want it to touch you so. But how could I explain? If I'd told you all, you would have thought me mad.'

She had thought him mad enough without any explanation. 'It would not have mattered. I would not have believed the truth had I not felt it myself.'

He pressed his lips against her hair and murmured, 'It was barely seconds, I swear. As soon as I could open the door I had you and brought you to safety.'

'How strange. It seemed much longer.' She shivered at the memory, and for a moment his arms held her even tighter.

'As it has to me. I have spent nights lost in my own house, praying for death, all because of an improperly trimmed wick or a candle left in a draught. As long as we are in this room, with the candles lit, we are safe enough. It will not trouble us if we stay in the light. It seems the house and I have a truce as regards this chamber and the stairs leading to it. I can stay here untroubled.' He laughed bitterly. 'If one can consider being confined to a single room as a life without strife. But in all other rooms of the house no flame will stay lit for long. And when the darkness comes…' He could not help a shudder of revulsion. 'You will think me a coward, but I do not venture out until dawn, once I have closed the door.'

She laughed weakly against him. 'You are no coward, Lieutenant Acherton, if you do not wish to face the horror that I experienced just now. Back in the forest—when you saved me…' She dropped her eyes. 'You were quite the bravest man I had ever seen. You still are, for I know of no one who would behave so fearlessly as to stay here.'

'Please.' He looked down at her and smiled in embarrassment. 'Now that we are comrades in arms, need we be so formal? Will you call me Richard?' He frowned. 'Although when you cried out for help it was to Robert.' His hands fell and he pulled away from her. 'Is there someone dear to you that might punish me for my impertinence?'

She frowned, as well. 'I know no one by that name. And, much to my disappointment, there is no one to care one way or another if you wish to call me Arabella.'

'Arabella.' His smile was almost shy, and he shook his head. 'Arabella.' He said it again, as though he liked the sound. 'I found it more than a little strange to hear you call for Robert when seeking rescue. For I rather thought that he was with you in the hall. I swear, he has walked with me on such nights as I've had the misfortune to venture beyond that door. Sir Robert Acherton was my great grandfather, and the last true inhabitant of Penlowen.' He was staring at her, seeming to savour every detail, and she began to feel even more ill at ease. At last, he said, 'He murdered his wife. And she was very like you in appearance. Perhaps it was more unwise than I first thought to bring you to this house.'

Chapter Five

Arabella closed her eyes as another chill went through her, as cold as the air in the hall. She was relieved that she was still seated, for she could feel her body swaying, as though ready to collapse. Had she been standing, she might have embarrassed herself by fainting. She hated women who succumbed to such displays. If she had been dealing with another, more impressionable female, she would have given the woman a shake and told her that it would do nothing to solve the problem at hand.

But to succumb herself might have been most gratifying.

She took a deep breath and reminded herself that she was not the type to run shrieking from phantoms. In any case, she had nowhere to run, for the door was blocked and there would be no exit until the sun rose. So she collected herself, opened her eyes to Richard, and did her best to appear unmoved.

'Tell me all—from the beginning.' When he hesitated, she continued, 'It is far too late to protect my delicate feelings. If there is something come to get me, I would prefer not to be taken unawares. What has been going on in this house, and why do you remain here?'

He stood up then, and paced the room, trying to collect his

thoughts. At last, he said, 'I told you my family met with misfortune? Well, Sir Robert was the source of it all.'

'What happened to him?' But, remembering the feeling of water on her face, the feeling of sinking beneath waves, she suspected she knew the truth.

'No one is sure. I think he was a suicide, since he is no more at peace in death than he was at the end of his life. He escaped the house before the magistrate arrived, and was never seen again. Family legend says that Sir Robert Acherton last inhabited this house in 1729, with the Lady Anne at his side. He was hot blooded—as was his wife.' Richard rubbed his temples. 'As are all the Achertons. If we have a curse, perhaps it is that, for even the best of us are prone to act boldly and love deeply. And we often pay the price for it.' He looked at her again, as though regretting afresh that she was there with him. Then he continued. 'As far as any could tell, they were a most happy couple, and she bore him two sons. In the autumn of that final year something happened. The oldest son remembered them arguing, but did not know what it was about. One night, after a particularly loud row, Anne disappeared, and no one saw her again. The boy could not believe that his mother would willingly leave him, or his brother. But his father would tell him nothing other then that she was gone and would not return.'

Arabella nodded.

'After that, things went from bad to worse. Robert was overcome by grief at the loss of his wife. He neglected the property, drank heavily, and did not sleep at all, wandering the halls of the house at night. At the urging of the family the boys were sent away to school, for their own safety.'

'The poor things lost both parents,' Arabella murmured.

'I fear so,' Richard said. 'For with the last check on his behaviour gone, the last link to his beloved, Sir Robert lost all sense. It got so that the servants were afraid to be in his presence. He shouted, he threw things, and when he spoke at all, he swore

that life without his Anne was no life at all. He would give anything if only he could have her back. Towards the end, the servants said he spent wildly—but not for himself. He bought gifts
for the wife he no longer had, as though material offerings could
bring her back from where he had sent her. He purchased silk
and velvet by the bolt, and jewels. He set the table with the
finest delicacies—always for two. But the food remained un-
eaten, for he could take nothing but bread and wine without her
there to share the meal.'

Richard was near to spitting in disgust. 'Have you no sym-
pathy for him, then?' Arabella asked. 'The man was distressed
in mind and spirit.'

'He was a murderer who brought his troubles upon himself,'
Richard replied. 'And he mortgaged the property on nothings for
no one. When his behaviour became too extreme for the rest of
the family to bear, they sent the magistrate to him, hoping to bring
a halt to it. But he had disappeared, just as surely as his wife had.'
He fell silent.

'And that is the end of his story. But what is yours? Why are
you here?' Arabella asked. 'The house is impossible to live in if
Sir Robert does not wish you here.'

'I came for the same reason all the heirs come back to
Penlowen, at least once.' Richard stopped his pacing and stared
down at her. 'We seek the treasure that is hidden here. Anne had
jewels before she died, but we've found no trace of them in one
hundred years. And not all the things Sir Robert bought would have
decayed with time. Where is the plate, the silver, the gold? He
could not have spent it all. My father tried and failed to claim the
house and its contents, as did my grandfather and my uncles, and
their uncles. Every male in the Acherton family has tried to take
the house from the spirit that inhabits it. They either died in the
attempt, went mad from it, or were forced to live with the knowledge of their defeat. Those who survived could not seem to settle.
They wandered, never staying in any place for long. My own

father lasted barely a night here, and refused to return. But neither could he leave it, living close by and allowing the shadow of the house to fall over his life and his soul. None of them could escape it. If they could not be here, they were unsure where they belonged.'

He sank back down beside her on the bed. 'I thought I could outrun it. That if I left the country, I could forget. So I bought my commission and saw Napoleon's army from the back of a horse. I have had enough travelling for three men. I want a wife and children, and a place to keep them.' He shook his head. 'And now here I am. Just like the rest. But I have no desire to be the head of a family that has lived in cowardice and failure for three generations. It is time to make a stand.'

'A stand?' He spoke as though he had dragged her to the front line of a battle.

'Yes. The house is mine. And somewhere in it is hidden the majority of my family's wealth, untouched since Sir Robert's time. The bastard hid the money and then disappeared, leaving his descendants to manage as best they could.' His eyes had a strange light in them. 'My predecessors took care to marry before they made their attempts, that there would be an heir remaining should they fail. And they left a trail of widows and orphans: foolish boys who would grow up to repeat their mistakes. But I am alone in the world, just as you are. If I have to take this house apart, stone by stone, I will learn its secrets. And if I fail, the curse ends with me.'

Madness was clear in him now. Greed and desperation were written on his face. He had been locked up too long alone in this house, arming himself against invisible adversaries, rambling about wealth that had been spent long ago. She touched his arm. 'You do not need to let it destroy you. If you must search, do it in the morning. But stay in the village at night, as your servants do.'

He shook his head. 'I tried. We have all tried. And we have found nothing. Whatever the secret, it will not show itself in daylight.'

'Perhaps because in the day you can see there is nothing to find.' She said it softly, not wishing to hurt him.

He shook his head, again. 'I refuse to believe it. We had everything once. And then it was all gone. He hid it, I am sure, for what else could have happened? The man was a recluse, not some London high flyer. And because of his folly, three generations of the family have lived in poverty. I ask you, Miss Scott, is it sensible to choose a life of sacrifice when you know you are born to be more? Is it not better to risk all if the reward is great enough?'

She imagined her own life, and the reasons for her trip. 'Sometimes it is important to recognise one's limitations, Richard, and accept them.'

'You do not understand,' he responded bitterly. 'I thought you, of all people, would know.'

And she felt his obsession fan the flames of her own dissatisfaction. If she had a choice to be other than she was, would she take it? There had been no choice. None. She was sure.

But what if…?

He stared into the fire, as though embarrassed to have revealed so much. When he spoke again, his voice was softer, more reasonable. There was no trace of madness in it. 'Perhaps you are right, Arabella. Perhaps there is nothing to find and I am just a fool. But I know this house is my birthright. I would rather live in misery here than in comfortable exile. I want a home.'

This she could understand, for she had often imagined just such a happy condition. She thought of him, holding her close, and wondered if there was someone he wished were at his side tonight. 'And you think Sir Robert will give you this one?'

Richard smiled grimly. 'I think it is well past time for him to do so. Perhaps if I can discover what it is he wants, and give it to him, he will leave me in peace.'

Arabella answered. 'He wants his wife. Can you give him that? For I do not think, after all this time, that the sea will give her up.'

Richard looked back to her, startled. 'Why do you say that?'

'What else could he want? Is it so hard to believe that the passion you described would survive death?'

'No,' he whispered. 'Why do you think the sea has her?'

'Because she drowned,' Arabella responded.

'But why do you say that?' he said, and took her by the shoulders, searching her face for an answer.

She thought back to her moments in the hall, when the sea had touched her face and the current had dragged her down. 'You must have felt it yourself.' She leaned her head towards the hall. 'Did you not understand what was happening to you?'

He was too close to her now, and his grip on her was so firm that she could not escape. 'Feel what? What exactly happened to you when you were alone in the hall?'

She did not like to think on it further, but muttered, 'Much what you described. It was very dark, and I was very frightened. Cold and beyond hope. I saw the door, inches away. But I could not reach it.' She averted her eyes, hoping that he would understand the horror of it and not force her to remember.

'You saw the door?' He was staring at her in amazement. 'Then it was not at all the same for you as it was for me. I am not just stumbling in the dark, my dear. I am blind. Beyond hope. For despair comes on me with the darkness, and I know I am utterly alone. But I do not remember the cold.'

'How could you not?' She stared at him in disbelief. 'That was the worst of it. Being cold and wet, and unable to breathe. I was sure that at any moment I would die, and I could not risk another breath for I knew I would take the sea into my lungs. And then it would be over.'

'You feared death?' He almost laughed. 'It is the fear that I must live for ever, as I am, that unmans me. And that it does not matter, living or dead, what becomes of me. The danger lies not in my next breath, but in the surety that death is welcome. For it would be a release. That is how my family meets its end if they stay too long at Penlowen. Suicide. Falls that are not accidents. Hanging. It is why I dare not risk putting a ball in my pistol. When the darkness takes me, I know I will use it on myself.'

'When *I* was in the hall, I wanted very much to live,' she argued. 'And knew that I would not.'

'But that is different.' The look in his eyes was wild again, and his grip on her shoulders grew so tight that she fought against him until he released her.

'It was no different. I was lost. Haunted. Sure I would die. I have never been so frightened in all of my life. And it did no good to tell myself that I was in the hall of a great house and in no real danger. I *knew*. It did not matter that it was not real, that I could see with my own eyes that it was false.' She wrapped her arms around herself, trying to hug the warmth back into her body.

He closed the distance between them again and gently took her hands in his, taking care not to frighten her. 'But you could see the door?'

'Dimly,' she insisted. 'Until the water seemed to close in. I could not move to open it. I thought I should faint. I could not breathe. It was horrible.'

'Of course. But you could see where it was.' The light in his eyes seemed to grow with the flickering of the candles. 'When I am in the hall, I am totally blind. It is not just darkness, Arabella. It is as if I have no eyes at all. I am afraid to touch my face, lest I find that they are gone. I am terrified to reach a hand out for fear that I will touch something wrong, something evil—or, worse yet, nothing. Nothing but void for ever. I am *lost*. I am alone, Bella. So very alone.'

The smile on his face grew subtle. 'But if we go together neither of us will be alone. You can help me. You will lead.'

'I will do no such thing. Only one thing is certain, Richard,' she argued. 'What lies outside this door is not natural. And I want no more part in it.' She took care not to look into his eyes.

He squeezed her hands in encouragement. But when she tried to pull away, he would not release them. And when he bent his head close to hers, his voice was low and insistent. 'It does not matter what you wish in this. I saved your life tonight, Arabella. And now, whether you wish to or not, you owe me a debt. I know what you thought when I brought you here. What you expected me to take in exchange. I saw the fear in your eyes. Well, no matter what you might think of me, I had no designs on your innocence. But, by God, if you hold the answer to this, then you will give me what I ask. Before the sun rises you will lead me to the treasure.'

She shook her head, feeling fear close over her like the imaginary waters of the hall. 'Where do you expect me to lead? Do you even know? I learned nothing when I went beyond that door.'

He released her, and reached to snuff the candles at the bedside until one corner of the room dimmed. 'We will know when it is time.'

She could feel panic rising like a tide in her as the room grew darker. 'You can't be sure. It is madness to think such.'

'You thought my behaviour mad before. How can this be any different? There is nothing to be afraid of in the dark, after all.' He threw her own words back at her and snuffed another candle.

She drew closer to the light of the fire and said in a rush, 'I was wrong. I admit it freely. You had good reason to be frightened and have proved it to me. Do not touch the candles.'

He wiped a line of them off the desk with the back of his arm and they rolled to the floor, the flames guttering and disappearing. 'The candles, and your fate, all belong to me, and I will do as I wish with them.'

And she could feel it as a presence crowded into the room, like an animal creeping along the baseboards in the gloom gathering there.

He felt it, as well, and stared into the empty corners in challenge. 'And the house is mine, as well. No one will take it from me.'

'At least leave the room lit,' she pleaded. 'I will take you into the hall. I will do my best for you. Then we can return to it if we must.'

'No looking back, Arabella.' He stared at her and smiled. 'You have nothing to go back to, after all. And neither do I. From now on we go forward.' He opened his arms, as if to welcome the darkness. 'Sir Robert Acherton—we will meet tonight, for the last time, and bring an end to this.'

'With our deaths?' she argued.

'I think not.' He paused, and reason returned as he looked at her. 'Whatever is in this house wants something. Has wanted it for a very long time. And it has punished my family in the same way for generations. Snuffing us out, one by one.' He pinched another wick between his fingers and the flame died.

'But tonight, for the first time in many years, something is different. You.' He pointed. 'Not of the family. And a woman. The first such to cross the threshold after dark for as long as any of us can remember.'

'And you mean to sacrifice me to whatever dark spirit rules here?' She rose and started towards the door again, only to realise that there could be no escape there.

He caught her wrist. 'Not sacrifice,' he murmured. 'While I live, it shall not have you.' He pulled her closer than was necessary, and smiled.

'And neither will you.' She pulled her arm out of his grasp.

'Do not think I will give you up so easily as all that.'

She felt a prickle at the back of her neck, and a tingling in her skin from the heat of his body and the strangeness of his words. Then he reached out and caught her again, wrapping his other arm around her, holding her close, as he had on the horse, until she stopped struggling.

Her mind told her that she was in grave peril. That she should fight, or scream, or flee. But her body insisted that she was safer here with him than she'd ever been. She felt the heat in her blood, and the desire to give in to whatever dark sin this man was offering.

His fingers trailed from her wrist up her bare arm, caressing her shoulder, stroking her neck, twining in the hair that fell there, moving it out of her face. And when he spoke, his voice was low and seductive. 'Tomorrow, if you still wish it, you can continue west to your bitter little job, fetching and carrying for some spiteful old woman. You can live for ever in the shadow of a pinch-faced hag, with no life to call your own. Go and be glad of it. For it will be peaceful and quiet and altogether safe. No one will hurt you there, Arabella. No one will care enough to bother.'

The words stung. He made a life of safety and good sense sound like a living death. She did not want to hear any more.

But when she turned her face away, he cupped the back of her neck with his hand and put his lips to her ear, whispering, 'Tomorrow you may leave, if you find my company so unbearable. But tonight you will stay with me and do what I need. If it pushes you to the edge of madness, if you be more frightened than you have ever been, tonight you will stay with me.'

She pulled away. 'And what have I ever done to you that you would wish such a fate upon me? Do you hate me, to wish such a thing? Why did you bring me here, knowing that this could happen?'

He drew her back and held fast. 'I do not hate you. Quite the contrary. But I would rather see you destroyed in a blaze of glory than live your life as you plan it, wasted in safety and security. It is a half-life, nothing more. You will die unspent. Help me tonight and I swear to you that you will have equal share in what we find. And Miss Witherstone be damned. For you will be able to do as you wish tomorrow.'

Arabella wanted to argue with him that he had no cause to question the course she had chosen for her life, and certainly no cause to damn some harmless old lady that he had never met. She did not need any more than she had, nor had she wished to risk all for a freedom she had never desired, until he'd begun pouring foolishness into her ears tonight.

But traitorous thoughts rose in her mind, telling her it was all true. She hated her life, hated fate for forcing her hand. What he was suggesting was no more mad than the way she felt when he held her. She shook her head and tried to pull away from him again, even as she longed to feel the heat of his lips against her ear.

'Think on it, Arabella.'

The movement of his lips as he spoke was like a kiss against her temple, and she could feel the darkness gathering in the room, creeping into his voice to seduce her.

'You will survive it. I know in my bones. For you are strong. And tomorrow you will have your wildest dreams.' Then he put out the candles at his side and the room grew darker still.

Money. Treasure. She could have servants instead of being one. She would have the freedom to choose. He was swaying with her, rocking her body in time to her thoughts. If she kept her eyes closed, she would not see the shadows, coiling on the floor like snakes, ready to strike. But when she opened them, she was looking into his eyes, which were as dark and frightening. To look into them was like standing on a cliff and waiting to fall. The terrors of the house retreated until her mind saw only Richard Acherton.

His smile was bright and warm, as the candles had been. And he seemed to be seeing things in her that she could not find herself. His words seemed so real, and the future he painted was as bright as the darkness was not.

'Great reward is not gained without hardship,' he whispered. 'Treasure is not got without risk. Be brave, Arabella. And you can take all. You will not do it alone. We will be together.'

He gripped her hand and squeezed again, and he felt solid and real in the unreality gathering around them. She must remember that. She would not be alone. And it was loneliness that the house had used against them.

She squeezed his hand in return. 'You will not let go?'

'I would be just as lost without you as you would without me. Together we are safe. I think.'

She did not like the tone of doubt at the end of his statement. But suppose he was right? What had she been afraid of really? An illusion. It was not possible to drown in a corridor, safe and dry and far from the ocean. Even the storm could not breach the walls of Penlowen. Her mind had played tricks, just as his had as he'd wandered the house. If they did not succumb to the nonsense, then there was no reason to doubt success.

He held up an unlit candle and pushed it into her hand. 'I will make it dark. But you can keep this in your free hand, and I will keep the flint handy in mine. If our plan seems doomed, we will light the candle and be safe.'

She nodded. 'All right, then.'

'You will help me?'

'If we do it soon. I do not know how long my nerve will hold.'

He grinned. 'Long enough, I'll wager. We'll do it now, as soon as I can douse the last of the light.'

'But what is it, exactly, that you mean to do?' For she doubted that she would have any more luck than he, even with sight, if he meant her to lead him like an ape down the corridors of a strange house.

His brow furrowed. 'I am afraid we must trust the house to show us what to do.'

'For it has been trustworthy and helpful before?'

His face quirked in an ironic smile. 'True enough. I thought I could trust it only to try and kill me if I ventured forth in search of secrets. But in truth, it is our own folly that destroys us. It is not the spirits in the house, but the way we react to them. Tonight it will be different. When we have made the room dark, we will see if it is at all bearable. If you are able, then lead me to the door and open it. Take me out into the hall. Go no farther than you feel you can, without becoming lost or disorientated. And if your spirit falters, then tell me. We will light the candle and return to the bedroom.'

'Very well.' She nodded.

He moved quickly around the room now, snuffing candle flames, and she felt her apprehension growing along with the darkness.

And then he was back at her side, standing so close that she'd have deemed it most improper only a short time ago. 'I still have to deal with the fire,' he muttered, looking down into the flames. He smiled again, and looked back at her. 'Ready, then?'

She nodded, watching him.

'Here we go.' He seized the basin on the stand beside the wall and tossed the contents onto the flames.

Chapter Six

The fire disappeared in a cloud of smoke. It went dark, without trace of ember, as though something had swallowed the light from it. She coughed the foul air out of her lungs and closed her eyes against the sting.

She felt his hand shoot out from nowhere, to seize her wrist in a grip as tight as iron and pull her body close to him. 'Arabella, are you there? I cannot see you.' There was a plaintiveness to his words, as though he'd already begun to doubt the wisdom of his plan.

She opened her mouth to speak, but closed it again in panic. Now that the fire was gone, the room was icy cold. The smoke looked and felt like fog. The house was taking hold of her again, playing tricks with her. She must not let it.

His hand had slipped down to twine with hers, and she could feel him give an encouraging squeeze. 'Arabella?' His voice was near to normal again, but she could sense the edge of panic disguised beneath it. 'Speak to me. I know you must be there. I can feel you.'

She could not. She did not dare open her mouth, for she knew that to do so would be certain death. The water would rush in to fill her lungs. She felt the darkness take her again, the terror and the loneliness. It was as though she was sinking deeper and deeper as the water pressed upon her and the air was forced from her lungs.

From somewhere far away she could feel the grip of Richard's hand and she focused on it, knowing that he was there and would not let her go. She struggled against the feelings around her to squeeze it, and felt a weak squeeze in response. He was still beside her. They were still in the bedroom, together. If they could hang on to each other, this would pass and they would be all right.

There was a feeling in the darkness that was almost like a pause. As though something had startled it, or a voice had been heard through the dark, salty water. She was not moving, but she felt struggle and panic. A desperation, to find the source of the change and go to it.

She concentrated on her own body, making it move. If she tried, she could feel the grip on her hand, and she moved closer to Richard, fighting the tide which was trying to carry her out to some imaginary sea.

Lies. Her brain was lying to her. She forced her eyes open and felt them adjusting to the dark, blinded by the occasional flash of lightning and the fitful appearance of moonlight through the racing clouds. She could see it all, although the room seemed to waver before her, as though seen through currents.

And the man beside her was staring into the gloom, eyes wide and sightless, tears streaming down his face. The darkness swirled around, him, lapping like waves, slapping at his face and plucking at his clothing, trying to force itself between their interlocked fingers. The despair was so real that she could see it trying to take him away. His free hand stretched before him, groping for anything that might give him comfort, and his body trembled like a sick animal.

She squeezed his fingers again, and he caught at her arm with his other hand, patting, as though to reassure himself that she was real. And she could feel the darkness retreat for a moment, although she found it no easier to breathe.

It was some comfort to see him there, and to know that when she died, it would not be alone. For she was sure that she must die if she did not take a breath. She could feel the water on her face, even though she could not see it. Feel it pulling her down, away from him. It covered her face, and she could not spare a hand to fight it. She was growing light-headed, and her lungs burned to take the breath that would end the torture. But when she did, she would lose all sense, would slip from his grasp, and they would both be lost, inches from each other and yet horribly alone.

She could not be expected to do as he had asked. The situation was hopeless if they could not manage to move even a few feet. She needed air. At last she could stand it no more, and she gasped and took in nothing—dark, void. This was the end, then. She gave herself up to it.

Suddenly his groping hand reached up and caught her, wrapping around her throat to hold her at the back of the neck, and he dragged her face forward to meet his. And as he sealed his lips to hers she felt air forced back into her lungs, and her mind cleared. He held her there, feeding her with his own breath, and the salt on her lips was not the sea but his tears. She felt life returning to her, and reason. They were beset on all sides. But he would keep her safe, just as he had promised. To the last breath, he had said. And that might very well be what she took from him.

Arabella brought a hand to his face and parted from him, touching him lightly on the lips with her fingertips, a gesture of thanks that brought a sad smile to his pained face.

She stayed in the circle of his arms and turned away from him, to assess the situation with a clear head. It was dark in the bedroom, but not as black as pitch. She could see the outline of the windows, and the shapes of the furniture, reforming as her eyes adjusted to the murk. The fireplace was before them, just as it had been when he had thrown the basin at the fire. It was close enough for her to reach out and touch. On impulse, she did—and heard her partner moan as she stepped away from him.

She reached back to catch his hand and lead him forward. He clutched at her convulsively, then calmed and took a step after her without hesitation, letting her lead.

Very well. He trusted her. She would trust him, as well. She turned back and lifted her lips to his again, stealing another breath. Then she led him closer to the wall with the fireplace. He would recognise the feel of it, the strange stonework and the heat it held. It would give him some comfort to know the landmark.

She pressed his hand to it, along with her own, and froze. It was ice-cold, as was the air around it, with no trace of residual heat from the fire. She could feel the realisation in his hand, as well. Panic stilled as he recognised it, and a shock of awareness that all was not as it should be.

And then she felt the draught.

To feel wind whistling down the chimney would be no surprise. It was open to the outside, and the storm would make the fire draw in strange ways.

But the air was coming from beside them, where there should be nothing but blank stone wall. She turned her head to look. In the shadows, cracks in the stone that had been invisible in the firelight stood out in sharp relief.

'Arabella, what is happening?' It was strange to hear the weakness in his voice, and she thought it must pain him that he could not be strong for her. So she turned back and kissed him again, letting him breathe for her and take her comfort in the exchange.

Then she led him back a few feet, so that she could see more of the wall.

The other side was different. More even. The room was unbalanced, and shadows angled strangely in the light from the full moon. She was sure of it. If there was nothing to hide, then wouldn't the builders have striven for symmetry in making the room?

Too strange, if the solution to the problem were under their very noses. But it made sense, did it not, to keep one's treasures close?

And then the lightning flashed again—a sustained brightness, throwing everything in the room into stark relief. And the disturbing carvings on the fireplace combined with the shadows from the window, making…

She paused. It could not be. She waited for the next flash. There it was again. A hand. Pointing along the floor.

She tugged Richard back to the fireplace, following the pointing finger up the wall.

She took his hand in hers and guided it until it rested on the stone beside the fireplace. Then she put her lips to his and murmured, 'Priest's hole.'

She saw him smile in understanding. He reached up, running his hand along the seam, and she could feel the breeze—not some dire omen, but wind from the hiding place behind the fire. She searched, as well, until she found a loose stone, and she placed his hands upon it, helping him to push.

It swung inward with a grinding noise, until they could reach behind it to feel a handle.

He tugged, and tugged again, until a section of the wall pulled away. Even without breathing, she knew that the air would smell of death.

It was dark. She could not imagine what might lie in front of them, but knew that it must be terrible, and that she could not bring herself to walk forward in blindness any more than he had. The fear began to take her again, stronger than before.

And then she remembered the candle. She had tucked it into the ribbon at her waist as they searched the wall.

She freed it, and held it out to him.

He reached out, groping with his hand. It took but a moment for him to recognise it and understand what she meant him to do. He fumbled for the flint in his pocket.

And then she felt the wind increase, and the darkness was

coming for them, rising out of the hole in front of them like a spirit rising from an open grave.

He felt it, too, as cold as ice upon their skin. The shock of it made his hands shake, and the flint slipped from his grasp and clattered to the floor, lost in the darkness swirling at their feet.

Whatever it was, it was coming closer, angry that they had dared to disturb its rest. She could not move to pull them away, for the man who was her only hope was frozen to the spot, as well. Without a light to forestall it, it would take them. It would drag them down into whatever hell it inhabited, and they would be unable to stop it. She felt a final scream rising past the lump of fear in her throat.

And then he seized the pistol out of the belt at his waist, pointed it at the candle in her hand and pulled the trigger.

The concussion was deafening in the close space—louder than the crash of thunder that accompanied it. But the gunpowder flashed, bright fire in the darkness, and the wick in front of it blazed to life.

She felt the darkness rush back from them, as though burned by the light. And she gasped, sucking in air, as the candle in her hand settled into a protective glow that drove away the illusion.

Richard cupped a hand around it, and she felt him straighten as he shook off the effects of the miasma. But he did not move from her side.

The scene before them was almost more horrible than the darkness had been. The room behind the fire was barely large enough for one, perhaps two—the supplicant and the priest. A heavy chair took much of the space, and she could see the mildewing velvet of the cushion through the gaping ribs of its occupant.

It was a skeleton. Bare of flesh, but with remnants of what must have been a rich wardrobe. A heavy ring set with stones decorated his finger.

'Madam, may I introduce my ancestor, Sir Robert Acherton? He who has been causing us much trouble.' Richard's voice was unsteady, but she could hear the strength returning to it as the light of the candle burned brighter.

She looked behind them at the door. 'Do you think he knew, when he shut the door, that he would meet his end here?'

Richard looked grimly at his ancestor, and then turned the candle to shine on the door behind them. 'There is the handle, plain on the inside. If he was alive when he entered, he could have opened the door at any time.' He shuddered. 'But when he comes on me, when it is dark, I feel what he felt. The loneliness is unbearable. I doubt he cared that rescue never came.'

'No wonder he was restless.'

Richard's voice was almost sympathetic. 'He could not bear the sorrow, and the guilt. So he shut himself up here with no food or water and waited for death. I know they searched the house for him when he disappeared. How difficult must it have been to ignore the people calling to him and sit in silence, waiting for the end?'

Then he reached down to the hand of the corpse and pulled the ring from its finger, setting it on his own hand.

'Dear God, no, Richard. You mustn't.' She pulled at his sleeve.

'Why ever not?' There was a rebellious hint to his voice. 'It is mine by rights.' He addressed the corpse in front of him. 'Sir Robert, I stand before you, the only living heir to this house. If you want your line to continue at all, then leave me in peace. In return, you shall have the decent Christian burial you must crave.'

Arabella waited, listening, half expecting that there should be some answer made, but none came. 'How shall we know if he accepts?'

'I suspect he will have little choice. I played his game and won.' He smiled. 'Or rather, you did. How did you find the answer so quickly?'

'In moonlight it is plain enough that there is a secret to the fireplace.'

'But it was impossible to leave this room unlit long enough for me to tell.' He smiled at the corpse in the chair. 'Well played, sir. I am proud to claim you as family. But it was foolish of you to do away with the woman you loved. You deserved to suffer for it.'

Tell him.

The words rang clear in Arabella's head—a woman's voice, so close that she might have been speaking in her ear.

Tell who? Tell him what?

And then she remembered the feelings in the hall. 'He did not kill her.'

'Eh?' Richard looked back at her absently.

'It was an accident. She left him. She must have slipped and fallen. When I was in the hall…' She shrugged in confusion. 'She was so sorry. She wanted to come home, but it was too late.' She looked at Richard in confusion. 'It was never his fault that she died. He was innocent all along.'

'Well, it was most unfair of him to take it out on me, who never did him harm.' Her companion was changed now that the secrets of the room had been discovered. He stood taller, and there was more of the rakish confidence she had seen when he was on horseback and far from the house. He smiled down at her. 'But he forced you to steal kisses from me when we were in the dark, so I cannot be too cross with him. Crafty devil.'

'That is not at all what I was attempting,' she muttered, embarrassed. 'I could not take a breath for myself.'

'I will not tease you on your immodesty, for it was a most sensible solution to the problem at hand.' He smiled more softly. 'But I am sure we did not enjoy it quite so much as we should have, had the circumstances been better.'

'Oh.' She had to stop herself, for on the tip of her tongue there was an offer to try again now that they had more time. How audacious would he find that?

If he noticed the change in her, he did not remark on it. Instead, he held the candle up to illuminate the room. 'But I promised you a reward, did I not? It will be a damn shame—pardon my language—if all we gain after that ordeal is the good name of the pale Sir Robert.'

There was a rough table beside the chair, but its surface was empty. Underneath lay a chest of considerable size, built into the wall. Richard smiled. 'To hold the instruments of mass, when the room served its proper purpose. But there is no telling what it might hold now.' He smiled at her again. 'Are you eager to see?'

She could not help but nod.

'Let us look, then.' He offered the candle to her, and pulled the table aside so that they could open the chest.

It was hard to see the contents by the glow from a single candle, but even that dim light picked up the glitter of jewels within, and the dull shine of worked gold.

'The Lady Anne's jewel case,' he said in awe. He closed his eyes and his shoulders sagged for a moment, as though a great weight had been removed from them. A grin spread slowly across his face, and when he opened them, his eyes shone, as though they reflected the light from the treasure. 'I knew it must exist. I never doubted it.'

He had been right all along. Obsessed, perhaps. But who would not be, with wealth so close and yet unattainable? She shook her head in amazement. 'It is so large.'

'He could deny her nothing when she was alive. Family legend says that she was a proud beauty, and vain.'

She felt a twinge of annoyance that all that was known of the woman was so unflattering. 'Perhaps you misjudge her.'

He ignored her words and dipped his hand into the coffer. When he drew it out, he held the end of a string of pearls, each bead large and perfectly matched to its mates. He drew and drew, until the strand was long before her, almost as tall as she was herself. They glowed like moonlight in the flame of the candle.

'Do you like this?' he asked, feigning uninterest. 'Payment enough for one night's work? Or would you like more?'

She watched in fascination as he rolled the orbs between his fingers, noticing for the first time how graceful his hands were, although there was nothing fine or gentle about them.

'What do you think they are worth, Arabella? How many months of your time? You could sell them one by one and still have a rope of them to wear around your pretty neck.'

She stood perfectly still, hypnotised by the idea of it. He reached out to her, touching the strand to her face, trailing it along the skin. Then he looped it several times about her throat, letting one of the strands slip inside the high neck of her gown so that the cool beads rested against her bare skin.

The touch of them was erotic, and she allowed herself the pleasure of it, thinking absently that she should refuse. It was far too generous a gift. An honourable woman would never take such a thing from a man who was little better than a stranger to her. Everyone would wonder what meek little Arabella Scott had done to earn such a prize.

And while she could sell them, as he suggested, they felt so good against her skin. So right. It would be even better if her gown were silk, and not this horrid rag. Cut low, so that he might admire the flesh beneath the pearls. She closed her eyes and licked her lips, and heard the intake of breath from the man next to her.

Yes. That was much better. He was noticing her.

And it occurred to her, through a haze of pleasure, that these were not her thoughts. She had no need of pearls, or low-cut gowns, or flirting. She had never thought anything so outrageous in all her life.

Suddenly she realised that the pearls carried with them a bit of their owner, and that it had been a mistake to think she could wear them without feeling the effects. She reached up a hand to pull off the necklace, but her fingers paused.

Thoughts came softly to her head, gentle and quiet. The feeling of pearls on bare skin was better than icy water, was it not?

What right had she to complain? There was nothing to be afraid of, for there would be no more terror in Penlowen, only joy. If she liked the feel of the pearls, then she must know that there were sensations even better than that. She could have them, and the necklace, as well. Anything she wanted. They were a gift from the Lady Anne. All she had to do was let go.

Just for tonight….

Chapter Seven

Her hand dropped away from the pearls in surrender. Then she set the candle she had been holding down on the edge of the table and turned to face Richard, smoothing her hand down over her body and up over the bare skin of her arm. She sighed at the growing warmth inside that was so much better than the cold had been. Then she opened her eyes and looked at Richard, watched him watching her. Hungry.

She fingered the beads idly, touching them to her lips. Then she took a strand from around her throat and stepped close to him, looping it over his head.

'Darling… You have returned to me.'

Had Richard said the words, or had she heard them in her mind? It did not matter. He reached for her and kissed her, and she opened her mouth to let him in.

It was different from the kisses in the dark, when he had given but taken nothing in return. Now he explored her mouth with his tongue, bit at her lips until they felt hot and full. How strange that she felt the sensations elsewhere in her body, and that her knees felt weak, even as her mind filled with strange energy.

When he broke from her, Richard's expression was shocked, confused, as he pushed away the pearls that bound him to her.

She saw the desire, still bright in his eyes, even as he shook his head. 'Arabella, I am sorry. I never meant to… It was not me.' He looked down at his hand as though he did not recognize it, and then struggled to pull the ring from it, to cast it away.

His expression amused rather than frightened her. Apparently the ring came with a price, as well. It would do little good to fight, for he would never be free of his ancestor until Sir Robert had what he wanted.

She caught his hand and held it, then drew it to her lips, kissing the palm and sucking at the fingers. She led it to her breasts, rubbing her body against it until she felt her nipples harden, knowing it would be oh, so much better when he touched skin, and not the fabric of her gown. She leaned forward until her lips touched his throat, kissing the broad shoulder under the collar of his shirt.

It was wonderful. She might be trapped by the will of another, as she had been in the hall, but at least it was better than being trapped in her own life. All fear was gone, replaced with exhilaration and raw sexual excitement. Her body was heavy with something other than the weight of water—still wet, but empty and free. There was only one thing that could help.

And it came to her that this was what she had wanted all along. When they had ridden through the storm she had wanted to turn her head and taste his body, feel his response. But she had been too afraid.

No more.

So she gave in to her desire and licked, pushing his shirt aside so that she could settle her mouth on his nipple to bite and suck.

His hand had stilled on her breast, as though he feared to touch. So she grew more bold in her caresses, placing her palms flat on his chest and running them down his stomach, digging her fingers into his waist and slipping them beneath the top of his breeches.

He groaned, and she felt his hand tighten on her, squeezing, rubbing his thumb hard over the place where he knew her nipple must lie. And through the haze of desire she heard Richard murmur, 'Oh, my God, Arabella. You are an innocent. But so sweet. You do not know what you are doing to me. I cannot help myself. Nor do I wish to. Forgive me.' And she felt it as he stopped resisting and reached beneath her chin with his other hand to force her lips to his.

This time the lips on hers were not gentle, but held the commanding presence of her husband, taking what he had taken so many times. He pulled her body to his, so that she could feel how much he needed her. And then his hands were struggling with the fastenings of her dress.

He pressed her ear to his lips and whispered, 'How could you leave me? Do you have any idea what I suffered?'

She whispered back, in a voice that was not her own, 'Robert, you fool. If you'd loved me as you promised, I would never have left.'

'But I did,' he whispered. 'I swear it. I loved you more than life. Can you not see? I waited. I bargained with God, and then I bargained with the devil, and neither answered me. I died waiting for a sign from you.'

She held him tight, stroking his face, touching his hair. 'I could not give it. I fell, Robert. I ran from you because I was angry. I could not see for the tears in my eyes, and I strayed too near the cliffs. I fell. And once it had me the sea would not let me go.' She was crying salty tears again. Salt like the sea that had been in her lungs.

He kissed the tears away. 'You did not want to go? I found your dress. A piece of it had torn and was hanging from a bramble. I prayed that you had only left me. That you were safe somewhere. But I feared the cliffs, and that in your anger you'd injured yourself to punish me.'

'I never meant to hurt you so. If I could have, I'd have returned.' She laid her head against his chest again, and it was good to feel the heart beating there. 'But I am home now. I am with you.'

'For ever,' he murmured, and kissed her again.

Arabella warmed herself with the love they had felt for each other, for it was like spring sunshine upon her face. It was beautiful to know that the two sad souls would no longer suffer, and she felt the rising tide of desire again, letting it take her, as well.

Richard was tugging at her clothing, undoing hooks and laces, pushing cloth aside. Anticipation made her skin tingle. But he seemed confused, and was taking too long. She brought a leg up to ride his hip, rubbing against him as though she done it a hundred times, but she never had. And then she pushed his hands aside and fought her way out of the strange clothing, eager to lie skin to skin, as Robert and Anne did, every night.

When she stood bare before him, wearing only the pearls, she knew that she should feel embarrassed. But she did not. For the voice in her mind told her that there would be no shame in what happened if it were done for love.

He stared at her for a moment, as though he had never seen anything so beautiful. And then he reached for her, pulling her close and touching—breasts, belly, thighs, anywhere and everywhere he could. Then his lips followed his hands, tasting her. He knelt at her feet and held her body to his mouth. Arabella had never felt anything like the feelings growing within her. And yet she knew that this was just the beginning. He could hold her there, on the brink, or send her falling over the edge with a flick of his tongue. And Arabella was afraid, for the first time, that Anne might have lied to her. It was all too much. She would die if he did not stop. Her spirit would soar from her body.

But she felt Anne give a shaky, contented sigh, and heard her words: *Not yet.*

She pushed him away, looking down at his eager face, and he smiled up at her, as though it were all a game. So she smiled back to tease him, and stepped out of his reach, walking across the cold stone floor in her bare feet to get the candle. She walked past him again, and felt his eyes following her as she set it on the table beside the great, soft bed. And then she beckoned to him to follow her.

He was at her side in an instant, and stood very still as she undressed him, stripping off the open shirt, kneeling to help with his heavy boots, undoing his breeches, touching and kissing him, exploring his body until he groaned with need.

At last he pulled her to her feet and pushed her back onto the mattress. Then he climbed up beside her, spreading her legs and moving between them. Arabella knew if there was ever a time to stop, it was now. But she saw her life through the veil of Anne's passion for her husband, and for the first time in her life she had no desire to be calm and sensible. She knew what it meant to be lonely and without hope, even if she'd never known the remedy for the feeling.

But Anne knew. And she would never be lonely again.

Arabella felt a wave of desire that was all her own as Richard came into her, taking away the emptiness with his body. The pain of it was a surprise, for though it was her first time, it was something that Anne had done many times before. But it felt so good to be with him at last that she ignored it. She pulled her knees up to squeeze his body with her thighs, and he pushed her down into the bed, his hands on her breasts and his mouth on hers.

Then she could feel Richard retreat. He was trying to be gentle, struggling not to hurt her, but was unable to give her up and let her go. His movements slowed into a gentle rocking, giving her time to adjust. When she tried to match his pace, she gasped in shock at the sensation that washed over her body. It was stronger than before, and wonderful. Why had she resisted this? What had she been afraid of? She did not understand what was happening to her body—if it was natural, or some trick of the spirits. But she knew that it was something she did not wish to stop. Nothing mattered to her any more but the next few moments and the pleasure she knew they would bring. So she gave herself over to the longing she felt from the past, and heard her own voice whispering encouragement to Richard, begging for more.

He kissed her gently in response and shook his head, still trying to protect her. So she raked her fingers down his back, clutching his hips to hers, writhing beneath him, rubbing her breasts against his chest, loving the way it felt and the response it evoked. She could feel his will break as need overcame him. He thrust his tongue into her mouth, hard and deep, and was not gentle when he moved in her, but demanding, his body as hungry as his kiss.

And suddenly she was no longer cold, would never be cold again, for she had her love. The feeling in her burned like a fire, and she let it consume her, gasping as the rush of trembling heat flashed though her. Anne cried out in triumph and left her.

But the tension in Arabella was not spent. And she was afraid that now that it had awakened, it would never leave her. She would be forever hungry, a slave to feelings she didn't understand. She moaned in frustration, struggling to free herself from Richard's arms.

He broke the kiss, and whispered, 'Look into my eyes.'

And when she did, she knew that it was truly him, staring into her soul as he had before. He knew what she needed. When he looked at her, she wanted nothing more than to give herself to him, to surrender all. And so she did.

She felt the trembling in her begin again, coursing through her, pounding like waves in the sea. When she could stand it no more she let it break her, shuddering against him. And he was shuddering, as well, his body moving to the beat of her heart. He came into her one last time, and then he sighed and collapsed against her.

When she returned back to herself she was naked beside him on the bed, tucked tightly to his body under his arm. It was strange to feel him so close: the muscles of his arms and legs against her own limbs, making her feel soft and small, the hair on his body under her hand, where she could stroke it if she wished.

Which she should not wish, she reminded herself. She should

panic. Leap from the bed and proclaim herself shocked at the liberties he had taken. Demand that he take her to the nearest inn immediately and give her no more excuses about storms or highwaymen, no more nonsense about malignant spirits.

But it seemed beyond foolish to pretend, at this point, that he had taken advantage of her. He could hardly be blamed for what had happened. Neither of them could. He had not had to drag her to bed. She had gone more than willingly. Or her body had, at least. She had even been the aggressor, had ignored his attempts at restraint.

Lady Anne had been most insistent.

Richard rolled away from her so she could see his face, and he smiled.

It was very annoying of him.

She lay very still, wondering what he was thinking. Her mind ran back over the events of the last few minutes and she feared she could see them reflected in his eyes. She could feel herself blushing, and it was even more annoying that his smile broadened in response.

He sighed and dipped his head to kiss her. It was the same as she had felt before, and yet it was different. But then, everything was different now.

'Are you all right?' he asked, his arm tightening on her waist.

She was not sure. But at last she said, 'Yes.'

If he knew she lied, he chose to ignore it. 'That is good. I was worried.'

That was something, at least. He was concerned for her feelings. But what was she to say to him now? How could she even meet his gaze in daylight? Anne had been most helpful in some things. But where was she now that Arabella needed her advice? She had been a fount of information before and during, but she had left no hint as to what normally happened between lovers *after*.

Arabella reached out with her mind, and it was as if she were feeling around her, groping in the darkness for something she could not see. But where there had been a sense of foreboding and unease there was now nothing but an empty house, settling back to normal after a violent storm.

'They are gone, aren't they?'

She felt Richard tense against her, as if he, too, was searching. 'I think so. And at peace, now that they have found each other.' Then he seemed to relax, and stretched against her, yawning. His hand reached out and captured hers, twining her fingers with his own as though nothing had changed between them.

And as his body rubbed against hers, desire reawakened in her, and along with it the need to touch him, arouse him and postpone the awkwardness of the next few hours.

She felt a pang of irritation that people who had been dead a hundred years should find their lives so easily sorted out at the expense of hers. She had to admit it—she envied them. They had given her a taste of something she had no right to know and then gone on their way, knowing that they would be together for eternity.

And while she had been quite content when she'd been ignorant of it, now she would know what was missing from her future and be less happy because of it. She would go back on her way tomorrow. Even if Richard kept to his promise and gave her a reward for the night's work, she could not very well tell people how she had come to have it without risk of revealing the more interesting details of this night. She might not have to seek a position, but she could not hope for marriage. How would she keep what she had done a secret? For the joy of it filled her, so that she was sure the truth must shine from her like a beacon. Even if no man would have her, she did not wish to hide the truth.

But now that she knew what it meant to be with Richard, how could she survive without it?

'You are sure you are all right?' Richard asked again. 'For you are very quiet.'

'Fine,' she said, in a voice that was too firm. 'Why should I be otherwise?'

He ignored the strangeness in her tone and said, 'I was worried that you might be regretting what happened now it is done.'

She was not sure of the right answer to this, either. For if she regretted doing it once, it made no sense that she should be worrying that she might never do it again. And if this was to be the only time she was to love, she could not have asked for better. Nor would she have wished for a different partner. At last, she shook her head.

'Good. Because, try as I might, I cannot bring myself to apologise for it.' He stretched against her and yawned again. He was completely relaxed, as though to be lying with her was the most natural thing in the world. Then he looked at her, and smiled again. 'And, if you have no regrets, it makes what I have to say much easier.'

'Really?' She failed to see how it was likely to make any portion of her life 'easier', but it was unfair of her to say so since what had happened was hardly his fault. So she held her tongue.

'I am not as glib as I should be when dealing with the fairer sex. I am too blunt, by far. And I fear, earlier, that I made you angry when I said you were not fit to be a lady's companion. I had been racking my brain, wondering what I could possibly say in the morning that might convince you to cancel your plans and remain here.'

'Here?'

'With me. Yes.' He was smiling again. 'It is rare to find a woman of such uncommon good sense, and even more so to find one who would stand at my side to fight as stalwart as any of the soldiers in the Peninsula. One does not know how deep trust is until one's back is to the wall and one must depend on another. And I dare say we have faced trouble together that was a more than adequate test. But to find one so lovely, as well… The combination must be unique in all the world.'

Lovely. No one had ever called her that before. Men, in her experience, had been quite content to overlook her. But Richard had said the word with a reverent insistence.

She looked at him in surprise and watched him go ever so slightly pink in the cheeks—for he had not been looking at her face, but had been admiring her naked body, stretched close to his.

He dragged his gaze back to her face. 'It is not your…I mean, *our* present condition that moves me to speak. I held this opinion almost from the first, I assure you. I was amazed at my good fortune in finding you, unattached, practically abandoned on my doorstep. But to point out to you your many fine qualities, and suggest you tarry in the area so that we might come to know each other better, after so limited an acquaintance? I feared you would laugh in my face and take the next coach to St Ives.'

She thought about it for a moment, and smiled. 'You were probably right.'

He moved against her again, and she could not deny to herself that the friction of their naked bodies was delightful. Since the worst damage had already been done to her reputation, it hardly seemed important to pretend outrage over his touch.

When she did not flinch from him, his hand at her waist dipped lower, to cup her hip and pull her body against his in a much more intimate way. His voice was almost a growl. 'And now I have gone and done that which I've thought of doing since the first moment I saw you.'

'Really?' She felt her heart flutter at the thought that he had wished to lie with her, but it was no longer with fear. 'You thought that we should…?'

'From the first. It made my blood boil to see highwaymen threatening such an angel, but it heated me in quite a different way to feel you huddled against me on the horse, totally dependent on my aid. I could see that you feared me, but I swear, I meant you no harm. But to be forced to play gentleman to you when you were in my room in candle-light, with the bed so near…' He groaned. 'Agony. If I thought myself a man of honour,

I could not take advantage of the situation—although it was rife with possibilities for seduction. I meant to resist. And would have succeeded under other circumstances. I would have kept you safe and taken you to the inn in the morning.'

'I do not doubt it,' she replied, even though she knew she had.

'But I feared that you would want nothing to do with me once you were able to continue on your way. To visit you in St Ives would have been to remind you of a most traumatic incident. And I could not mention the time we'd spent together alone in this house without doing harm to your reputation. What could I say that would not hurt or offend you? I doubt I would have been able to manage more than a few words of conversation before losing my nerve. And I would have lost you, as well. Thank God for the timely intervention of my ancestors.' He smiled down at her and kissed the top of her head. 'You are utterly ruined, are you not?'

'I fear so.' But as she thought on it she decided that, after what they had shared, she did not fear anything. She could not resist a smile of wicked pleasure.

He grinned back. 'And fit for nothing except to stay here and provide companionship to me.'

Stay here with him? For a moment she was overwhelmed with joy at the idea, imagining herself as his bride, growing old beside him, watching the land prosper and their children grow.

Then her mind cleared. Her life was changing so rapidly that she had trouble keeping up. She was becoming foolish. He could not mean what she hoped. He must think that since she had been willing tonight she would be willing again, and that with a woman so brazen, he needn't be bothered with formality. Tempting though it might be, she would be a fool to throw her honour aside so quickly. She fought down her sadness and readied a polite refusal.

He had noticed her hesitation, and now muttered, 'Hell and damnation.' And then he coloured in embarrassment again and pulled away from her, becoming strangely formal.

He sat up on the bed, wrapped the sheet about his waist, and took one more admiring glance at her before covering her with the counterpane.

Then he said, 'Pardon my language, Miss Scott. This is not going at all the way I'd hoped, and now I've compounded my offence by swearing. I meant to offer honourably, of course.' The words rushed out of him, giving her no time to respond. 'There is nothing havey-cavey about it, I assure you. We will find a vicar in the morning, and see if there is a way to get a ring from that jewel box fixed permanently in its proper place on your hand. If you wish, I will make you Mrs Richard Acherton. Not so grand as some names, or as fine a husband as you deserve. But marriage to me must surely be better than a life of forced companionship to some old lady? My name is yours.' He hesitated. 'If you will agree to take it, that is.'

After so many years of believing that no one could want her, it was as heady as wine. She leaned her head back into the pillow and closed her eyes, convinced that it must be some strange dream, and when she opened them she would be in the carriage, still on the road to St Ives.

'It is all so sudden.'

She felt him stretch out on the bed beside her. His lips grazed her ear, and he whispered, 'If it helps to hear it, you will have servants to live in, now the spirits are laid to rest. And tomorrow I will show you the house. It is mine now.'

She opened her eyes to see his smile, so close that she could have kissed it if she chose.

Then he said, 'Actually, the house will be yours, as well. No matter what your answer, after tonight you have earned your half of it. I owe you that.' His voice was tight with emotion. 'If you wish to go, I will not breathe a word of what has occurred between us. I swear to you. But I will sell some of the jewellery, and you may take the proceeds to use as a dowry…' The thought seemed to upset him, and he hurried on to say, 'Or for anything else you might wish.'

Then he looked away from her face and down at her body. 'But I will never sell the pearls. For I rather fancy the way they look, lying upon your skin.' He sighed. 'They should stay just where they are. As should you, in this room in Penlowen, with a husband who adores you.'

She followed his gaze with her own, and let the cover fall away. She felt her body respond as he reached out to touch the necklace and the pearls slid against her bare breasts. And she looked at him again, and his eyes darkened with lust. His fingers followed the beads as they trailed over her nipples and lay against her belly. 'Please,' he whispered. 'Say yes.'

'Yes,' she whispered back. And she felt wanted, for the first time in her life. In love, at peace, and at home in his arms and his bed.

His lips came down upon hers, and his hand reached to cup her breast. 'Then let us celebrate what I hope will be a very brief betrothal.'

And he leaned across her to the snuff the candle on the night table, and plunged the room into warm and friendly darkness.

* * * * *

Here's a sneak peek at
THE CEO'S CHRISTMAS PROPOSITION,
the first in USA TODAY *bestselling author*
Merline Lovelace's HOLIDAYS ABROAD *trilogy*
coming in November 2008.

American Devon McShay is about to get the Christmas surprise of a lifetime when she meets her new client, sexy billionaire Caleb Logan, for the very first time.

Silhouette®

Desire

Available November 2008.

Her breath whistled out in a sigh of relief when he exited Customs. Devon recognized him right away from the newspaper and magazine articles her friend and partner Sabrina had looked up during her frantic prep work.

Caleb John Logan, Jr. Thirty-one. Six-two. With jet-black hair, laser-blue eyes and a linebacker's shoulders under his charcoal-gray cashmere overcoat. His jaw-dropping good looks didn't score him any points with Devon. She'd learned the hard way not to trust handsome heartbreakers like Cal Logan.

But he was a client. An important one. And she was willing to give someone who'd served a hitch in the marines before earning a B.S. from the University of Oregon, an MBA from Stanford and his first million at the ripe old age of twenty-six the benefit of the doubt.

Right up until he spotted the hot-pink pashmina, that is.

Devon knew the flash of color was more visible than the sign she held up with his name on it. So she wasn't surprised when

Logan picked her out of the crowd and cut in her direction. She'd just plastered on her best businesswoman smile when he whipped an arm around her waist. The next moment she was sprawled against his cashmere-covered chest.

"Hello, brown eyes."

Swooping down, he covered her mouth with his.

Sheer astonishment kept Devon rooted to the spot for a few seconds while her mind whirled chaotically. Her first thought was that her client had downed a few too many drinks during the long flight. Her second, that he'd mistaken the kind of escort and consulting services her company provided. Her third shoved everything else out of her head.

The man could kiss!

His mouth moved over hers with a skill that ignited sparks at a half-dozen flash points throughout her body. Devon hadn't experienced that kind of spontaneous combustion in a while. A *long* while.

The sparks were still popping when she pushed off his chest, only now they fueled a flush of anger.

"Do you always greet women you don't know with a lip-lock, Mr. Logan?"

A smile crinkled the skin at the corners of his eyes. "As a matter of fact, I don't. That was from Don."

"Huh?"

"He said he owed you one from New Year's Eve two years ago and made me promise to deliver it."

She stared up at him in total incomprehension. Logan hooked a brow and attempted to prompt a nonexistent memory.

"He abandoned you at the Waldorf. Five minutes before midnight. To deliver twins."

"I don't have a clue who or what you're…"

Understanding burst like a water balloon.

"Wait a sec. Are you talking about Sabrina's old boyfriend? Your buddy, who's now an ob-gyn doc?"

It was Logan's turn to look startled. He recovered faster than Devon had, though. His smile widened into a rueful grin.

"I take it you're not Sabrina Russo."

"No, Mr. Logan, I am *not*."

* * * * *

Be sure to look for
THE CEO'S CHRISTMAS PROPOSITION
by Merline Lovelace.
Available in November 2008 wherever books are sold,
including most bookstores, supermarkets,
drugstores and discount stores.

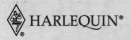

REQUEST YOUR FREE BOOKS!

Harlequin® Historical
Historical Romantic Adventure!

2 FREE NOVELS PLUS 2 FREE GIFTS!

YES! Please send me 2 FREE Harlequin® Historical novels and my 2 FREE gifts (gifts are worth about $10). After receiving them, if I don't wish to receive any more books, I can return the shipping statement marked "cancel". If I don't cancel, I will receive 6 brand-new novels every month and be billed just $4.94 per book in the U.S. or $5.49 per book in Canada, plus 25¢ shipping and handling per book and applicable taxes, if any*. That's a savings of 20% off the cover price! I understand that accepting the 2 free books and gifts places me under no obligation to buy anything. I can always return a shipment and cancel at any time. Even if I never buy another book, the two free books and gifts are mine to keep forever.

246 HDN ERUM 349 HDN ERUA

Name _____ (PLEASE PRINT) _____

Address _____ Apt. # _____

City _____ State/Prov. _____ Zip/Postal Code _____

Signature (if under 18, a parent or guardian must sign)

Mail to the **Harlequin Reader Service:**
IN U.S.A.: P.O. Box 1867, Buffalo, NY 14240-1867
IN CANADA: P.O. Box 609, Fort Erie, Ontario L2A 5X3

Not valid to current subscribers of Harlequin Historical books.

Want to try two free books from another line?
Call 1-800-873-8635 or visit www.morefreebooks.com.

* Terms and prices subject to change without notice. N.Y. residents add applicable sales tax. Canadian residents will be charged applicable provincial taxes and GST. Offer not valid in Quebec. This offer is limited to one order per household. All orders subject to approval. Credit or debit balances in a customer's account(s) may be offset by any other outstanding balance owed by or to the customer. Please allow 4 to 6 weeks for delivery. Offer available while quantities last.

Your Privacy: Harlequin Books is committed to protecting your privacy. Our Privacy Policy is available online at www.eHarlequin.com or upon request from the Reader Service. From time to time we make our lists of customers available to reputable third parties who may have a product or service of interest to you. If you would prefer we not share your name and address, please check here. ☐

nocturne™

ESCAPE THE CHILL OF WINTER WITH TWO SPECIAL STORIES FROM BESTSELLING AUTHORS

MICHELE HAUF

AND

VIVI ANNA

WINTER KISSED

In "A Kiss of Frost," photographer Kate Wilson experiences the icy kisses of Jal Frosti, but soon learns that this icy god has a deadly ulterior motive. Can Kate's love melt his heart?

In "Ice Bound," Dr. Darien Calder travels to the north island of Japan, where he discovers an icy goddess who is rumored to freeze doomed travelers. Darien is determined to melt her beautiful but frosty exterior and break her of the curse she carries...before it's too late.

Available November wherever books are sold.